SUMMER FEVER

PAMELA BETZ

Summer Fever

Meadows House Publishing
Saint Louis, Missouri

Printed by CreateSpace, An Amazon.com Company

ISBN   978-1530480906

For

My late parents, Walter & Katherine Kruzich

And

James R. Sodon, for his encouragement

Chapter One

"Are the rumors true?"

"When's the wedding?"

"Why isn't he with you?"

"Is he coming later?"

While a camera zoomed in for a close up of Brandy Cole's face, she smiled coyly and responded, "No comment," to the questions reporters fired at her.

Matt Zeller muttered an obscenity as he slouched further down on his sofa. He knew he should change channels immediately but, like someone coming upon a car wreck, he couldn't tear his eyes away from the disaster.

A switch to a different camera allowed Brandy's lush body to fill Matt's big screen television. That body had heated his blood but could never warm his heart. Sunlight caught the shimmering material of her dress. No, he corrected, that was no dress. That was just a few scraps of expensive cloth preventing her from getting arrested for indecent exposure.

"Matt Zeller has publicly stated several times he has no intention of marrying anyone. Is the reason for his change of heart because you provided him with an alibi the night of the murder?" a female reporter asked.

"No comment," Brandy repeated. When she winked at the camera, Matt closed his eyes and took a deep breath to control his anger.

God, he wished he'd never met her.

She knew damn well their brief fling had been purely physical because he'd never given any woman the impression marriage was ever a possibility. Unfortunately, he now realized that when Brandy set her sights on something, she barged ahead with ruthless determination without always considering the odds of failure. She apparently didn't let truth stand in her way, either.

The camera remained focused on her beautiful face while she toyed with a lock of her professionally tousled, long blonde hair.

Matt shook his head, wondering why he'd ever touched her. The cloying scent of her expensive perfume, her dresses that flirted with tacky obscenity and those calculated emotions only disgusted him.

Though he hadn't talked to her in weeks, she hadn't yet realized he was as through with her as a doctor is with a dead man. Ever since she deliberately dodged the police instead of verifying his alibi.

It always tore at his insides every time he thought of the night several weeks ago when he'd hosted a birthday party for Rick, his band's drummer. His biggest mistake had been the way he'd handled things when Rick's friends started passing around drugs and refused to leave. He hadn't called the police, fearing a distorted version of events would reach the tabloids.

Instead, he'd left with Brandy to spend the night at her place. When morning arrived with the news a young woman had been found dead in his apartment, he felt sick with guilt.

How could he not feel responsible?

According to the coroner's preliminary report, the cause of death was a drug overdose, possibly forced. Evidence of rope burns on the woman's wrists and ankles indicated restraints had been used. The report also stated she had been raped.

Brandy had deliberately evaded police for over two days when they wanted to check out Matt's alibi. He later learned she had feared her reputation would be tainted, especially since the media had erroneously reported he was going to be charged with murder.

If the situation hadn't been so serious, he would have howled with laughter. Brandy Cole had bared every inch of herself repeatedly for every men's magazine worldwide. She flashed her private parts as readily as other women flashed smiles but when he needed her to back up his alibi, she suddenly worried about her reputation.

When detectives finally caught up with her, she did verify his whereabouts on the night in question but he would never forget her delaying tactics had caused him to spend several tense hours with the NYPD.

Although results of his semen and hair samples didn't match those found on the victim, the press continued to hint he somehow may have been involved in the girl's death. Reporters remained camped outside his apartment building and chased him everywhere he went, causing him to become a recluse, venturing outside only when necessary.

Police had yet to turn up any real suspects that would lure the news hounds off his tail, which was the main reason he was planted on his couch instead of attending the Academy Awards across the country in Tinseltown. Not that he minded skipping the event but if he'd shown up with one of the sexy starlets who'd invited him, the ridiculous rumors he knew Brandy had started about their alleged engagement would no longer have any legs.

"As you heard, Brandy Cole will neither confirm nor deny if she and rock star Matthew Zeller will soon wed. I guess we'll have to wait and see if marriage will be her reward for providing the handsome bachelor with an alibi the night the murder occurred in his apartment last month.

"For more on this story's continuing developments, stay tuned for the Sara Kell Report coming up next. Sara has an interview with Matt's mother you won't want to miss.

"Live from Hollywood, this is Tom Stephens."

Matt felt like throwing the coffee table at the commentator's perfect smile. Or maybe he should just jump off the balcony now and save himself a lot of time and misery.

Matt stared out the window of his apartment, ignoring the low ring of the telephone as he watched the heavy traffic several stories below. He wished he could trade lives with someone in one of those cars traveling at a snail's pace on Park Avenue. Wished he could shed his skin and become someone entirely different. Then he could walk right by the reporters without having microphones shoved in his face while flashbulbs blinded him.

He'd foolishly thought money and fame would chase away the dark cloud hanging over his head since birth. He should have known it would remain just as firmly in place as ever.

Whenever his thoughts turned dark and morose, he usually sat at the piano and played, sometimes to create, other times to soothe. He felt too edgy lately to do anything but mourn the life he never had.

He seldom allowed himself to wallow in self-pity but, sometimes, he couldn't help it. Why couldn't he have been a kid who had played on a baseball team coached by his dad? Or someone who'd had a mother who could chase a nightmare away with a gentle touch of her hand? If he'd been raised by loving parents, he wouldn't feel so damn alone right now. But he hadn't been so lucky and all the wishful thinking in the world wouldn't change the past.

He definitely should not have watched the interview with his mother. Although he'd known what to expect, seeing her lie on national television still turned his stomach. He wondered how much the Sara Kell Show had spent getting Dawn clean and sober before stuffing her into pricey clothes. She sure hadn't looked like the blowzy hooker he'd been unfortunate enough to live with the first seven years of his life. If the reporter was worth anything, she would have taken a trip to Joliet and nosed around for the truth.

Doesn't anyone do their job right anymore?

Now, it was just a matter of time before someone from the old neighborhood sold the story of the Zeller family. It had been something he dreaded since becoming famous -- having the public spotlight on the dirty little corners of his childhood. Not that abuse or neglect was anything new but those old feelings of shame were already starting to tug at him.

He knew it wasn't his fault Dawn, a foul-mouthed drunk who had used him as a punching bag, was his mother. It wasn't his fault she'd been a prostitute who'd regularly brought men home.

She had never really been a mother to him, nor had she ever made an attempt to create the illusion of a decent home life. Why would she? She certainly hadn't cared about his emotional or physical well-being.

At too young an age, he had learned more about the baser side of man than a child ever should. He had learned to lower his expectations, until he finally had no illusions that anyone loved him. That he was lovable.

It wasn't his fault his father, equally enamored with alcohol and other women, had been absent more than he'd been present until the day he'd walked out for good.

He hadn't chosen those people for his parents. Who in their right mind would? A pack of wolves could have done a much better job of raising him. Nevertheless, a mantle of shame had settled on his small shoulders when he was too young to realize it wasn't his burden to bear.

He knew a child wasn't responsible for the actions of the parents, thanks to the court-ordered counseling he'd received years ago when he was in foster care. He'd learned you don't always have to be a product of your environment.

He'd thought he could leave all the emotional debris of his past behind by focusing his energy and channeling his emotions into music. It had been his salvation. The stardom he'd achieved had been an unexpected bonus to the personal fulfillment his talent brought. He felt he had a lot to be grateful for.

Why, then, was he moping around, still wishing June Cleaver would walk through the door and make the bogeyman disappear?

Turning from the window, he wandered into the study to retrieve the bottle of water he'd left on the desk. He sat in the soft leather chair and stared at the screensaver on the computer.

God, he felt ancient. Old before his time. Twenty-nine going on eighty.

As he watched animated fish swim across the screen, he ignored the frantic blinking of the answering machine's red light. Thanks to Brandy's performance in Hollywood a few days ago, not to mention his mother's ridiculous interview, the media circus had intensified.

He hated feeling helpless but that's exactly what he was because everything was beyond his control.

The press was trying to link him to the murder but his only crime had been poor judgment, and the guilt he suffered every day seemed too light a penance.

If only he hadn't been such a fool, fearing bad publicity and not calling the police, a young girl would still be alive.

If only he'd never given Brandy the time of day, he wouldn't have to deal with her and the rest of the world thinking he was stupid enough to marry her.

If only Dawn hadn't surfaced after twenty-two years of absence, the sad story of his childhood may have remained buried in the past. He'd mistakenly thought if he ever had to take a publicized walk down memory lane, it wouldn't hurt so much now that he was an adult.

Maybe he was stupid, after all.

He wanted to run away from everyone and everything but knew the famous Matt Zeller couldn't. Still, he fantasized about having the freedom to go wherever he wanted. To take a walk and breathe fresh air. To be ignored by the public, even if for a short while.

Slowly, an idea emerged from his troubled thoughts. Why couldn't he become someone else? At least temporarily. Maybe his desire to change places with someone wasn't just desperate fantasizing. The more he considered the possibility, the more hopeful he became. If he could pull this off, it would be better than all the Valium in the world.

He had a few free months before the start of his tour to promote the new CD. He'd love to cancel it but didn't want to disappoint the guys in the band or his fans. Not to mention the legal ramifications, which would end up costing him a huge amount of money. But if he could grab some peace and quiet before rehearsals began, his idea was worth a shot.

He picked up the phone.

Chapter Two

"Hello?"

Hearing his best friend's voice brought a smile to Matt's face. "Vinny, what's up?"

"Hey, Zeller! I've been calling you for days! Especially after Dawn's interview. Damn, she's got a lot of nerve trying to act like the poor neglected mom! I guess reporters don't care if their story is based on facts or not. How do you keep from decking those bastards?"

"Beats the hell out of me," he grumbled.

"I guess the time to worry's when they start ignoring you, though they are carrying this latest b.s. too far," Vinny sympathized.

"Listen, buddy, I need you to help me out. Those bastards still ambush me constantly. I can't even leave my apartment without it becoming a media event. I expected all this to die down by now but there's no sign of that happening, especially since the media are giving Brandy and now Dawn all this attention. I have to get away before I go nuts. At least until the media has someone else to torment."

"You know you're always welcome here," Vinny reminded.

"It'd be great to see you and Gina but as soon as the reporters start camping on your sidewalk, I'm afraid that Italian temper of yours would explode. You'd start picking them off with your deer rifle." He could easily picture Vinny upsetting his quiet neighborhood with a few shotgun blasts.

"I could say I was cleaning it and it accidentally went off."

Matt let out a bark of laughter. "I'm serious! I was thinking...if I change my looks, you know, cut off my hair and use a different name, I could travel around until this mess gets cleared up. Everyone will expect me to hop a jet and party in some foreign country, which is exactly what I won't do. I want to disappear right here in America. Drive along the highways and blend in with a few million other people.

"Can you get me a fake driver's license? A different car and registration?" He hated hearing the desperation in his own voice.

"As much as you hounded me to stay legit, now you want me to start breakin' the law again?" Vinny laughed. "You know you can count on me. I'll get you what you need. When do you want everything?"

"Soon as possible." He felt the tension in his neck and shoulders ease. "Gina's been dying to chop off my long hair, so now's her chance. I need to look completely different if this is going to work. I need you to call and reserve a suite in your name at one of the hotels outside Chicago. That way nobody will be tipped off and you'll only have a short drive to meet up with me. I'll make it there somehow even if I have to wear a dress and a wig."

"I'd pay anything to see that!" Vinny chuckled. "Okay. I'll call you..."

"No," he interrupted. "I'm not taking any calls. I'll give you a ring tomorrow night around eight, okay?"

"Anything you say. Hey, don't worry. We'll work this out."

By the time the conversation ended, Matt wished he really could hide out at Vinny's house but knew that was impossible. Vinny and Gina lived in a quiet, stately area but the neighbors were friendly, frequently breezing in and out of each other's homes. His visits always caused quite a commotion under normal circumstances. Going there now would ruin his plans.

The memory of when he and Vinny first met years ago popped into his head, causing him to smile. They weren't brothers by blood but were the only family each cared to have. Except for Gina. He'd been so relieved when he'd first met her and discovered she was perfect for Vinny.

It would have been hell if he'd disliked the woman his best

friend had married but thankfully everything had worked out and now he loved them both.

They were the only people in the world he trusted.

"William Tyler Reese?" Matt questioned a few days later. No matter how many times he spoke the name, it still sounded odd.

"The Third," Vinny emphasized.

"Bill isn't a bad name. I kind of like it." Gina continued snipping off Matt's long tresses.

"Well, I think it sounds like somebody who went to Harvard or Yale to me," Vinny defended.

"Sounds like a good old boy from the south," Matt said, using a Southern drawl. "I hope I get used to it."

"It's fine," Gina assured. "But lose the lame accent."

"You worry too much." Vinny examined the label on the beer bottle he held. "So, what's up with Brandy Cole? Why does she keep hinting you and her are the real deal? Is she a stalker or what?"

"I think a stalker'd be easier to get rid of. There was nothing between us but sex. Period. I'd hardly call that a relationship. When she took her time to talk to the police after the murder, that did it. No more slap-and-tickle with her for me.

"This so-called relationship she's been blabbing to the press about exists only in her scheming little mind. I've only been spending time with her for a short while. Her IQ must not be much higher than her bust size if she thinks she can get a ring through my nose." He made a rude noise. "I haven't met any woman I'm willing to sign my name on a dotted line for."

"You know, Matthew, someday you're going to meet a gal who'll have you eating those words," Gina predicted.

"Honey, you know since you broke my heart and married that loser over there, I'm a confirmed bachelor." He let out a

14

long sigh.

"Screw you, whatever your name is." Vinny drank the last of his beer with exaggerated coolness. "So, tell me, what was Brandy like in bed?"

Gina leaned back and rapped her husband on the head. Ignoring his yelp, she turned her attention back to Matt's hair.

"You know, if it were Vinny, instead of complaining about her IQ, he'd brag about her bust size. Next time you want your usual five minutes of sex, dear, go call Brandy."

The men laughed.

"Ain't she a sweetheart?" Vinny got up and gave his wife a quick peck on her cheek before getting another beer.

She brushed the hair from Matt's neck and shoulders. Touching him on the arm, she said, "Okay, Matt. I mean, Bill. Go look in the mirror."

After walking into the bathroom, he was startled by the stranger staring back at him. Gone was the long, wild mane of dark golden hair and in its place was the very short style currently preferred by young businessmen.

He returned to the sitting room. "Gina, you're fantastic! No wonder your hair salon does a great business."

"I keep telling you I won't feel like it's mine until you let me pay you back the money it took to get it going. You putting up the money for the car dealership for Vinny was too much to spend on us as it is. You're a silent partner, but it's your money that does all the talking," she scolded from her relaxed position on the couch.

He shrugged. "You know if I don't spend my money, the government is more than happy to grab it. I need the tax breaks. Besides, I'd rather have Vinny selling pricey cars than stealing them."

"Ha ha." Vinny gave him a rude gesture then asked, "Does your manager know about your plan to disappear?"

"Not exactly. I told him to call you if an emergency came

up. I told him it better be an emergency, too, or I'll be looking for a new agent. I didn't want to take the chance of someone leaking my whereabouts. I got a new cell phone and number so only you guys will have it."

"If this plan of yours doesn't work, maybe you should go public with the truth about the past. Then Dawn can't keep lying about how she's starving and can't pay the gas bill while her selfish son is lighting cigars with thousand dollar-bills. I mean, you perform in front of record-breaking crowds. Go on television. Give one of those reporters an interview to clear the air," Vinny suggested.

Seeing the dark look on Matt's face, he added, "Or not."

Dressed in khaki trousers and a burgundy polo shirt, Matt stood still, patiently waiting for Gina's assessment. She took her time circling him, eyeing his appearance carefully.

"Well, you should be happy. If I passed you on the street, I wouldn't even know you. People are used to seeing you dressed like you're part of the Grunge crowd. The press will never catch on. You haven't been recognized anywhere here in Chicago the past few days despite you and Vinny acting like lunatics, so you'll be okay everywhere else. I think those wire-rimmed glasses were a stroke of genius on my part."

"Yeah. You look like one of those young, anal retentive executives," Vinny quipped.

"Music to my ears." A satisfied grin spread across Matt's face.

"Keep in touch, okay? Let us know if you need anything." Gina said.

"Of course I'll keep in touch. Don't I always?"

"I don't like the idea of you being on the road all by yourself." She brushed a speck of lint from his sleeve. "You call us whenever you stop somewhere."

Although he was amused, he was also deeply touched. He

hugged her tightly. "I'll be fine, don't worry. I just hope this works. Otherwise, I'll be in a psych ward."

Chapter Three

Matt cursed and pumped furiously on the accelerator but the engine continued to lose power. He steered the car onto the shoulder of the road just before the motor completely died.

After several attempts to restart the engine failed, he hit the steering wheel with the heel of his hand and snarled. Not satisfied, he let loose a string of curse words, including some that questioned the car's parentage.

Sighing in defeat, he let his head roll back against the headrest. He should have known something was bound to go wrong. Things had been going too smoothly for the past several weeks.

He got out of the car and gave the surrounding countryside a cursory assessment. To the right were fields of soybeans. Only an occasional grove of trees or a fallow field broke up the monotony. On the left, countless rows of tall cornstalks almost ready for harvesting rustled in the wind.

He muttered a few curse words, thoroughly aggravated with himself as he looked straight ahead at the HAVERSFIELD 2 MILES sign. Why had he been careless enough to stray from the main highway? Just because he had a sudden, irrational urge to head this way?

He snorted, hoping the next time he got an impulse to do something stupid, he'd be smart enough to ignore it.

Maybe if the circumstances were different, he could appreciate the peacefulness of the area. Today, he could only focus on the fact it was eerily uninterrupted by other motorists. Which meant he would have to walk until he found help.

He grabbed his sunglasses from the visor before locking the car. As he started walking toward the Haversfield exit, he was thankful his shoes were comfortable.

At least the weather was cooperating. He couldn't recall ever seeing such a vividly blue sky. The sunshine felt warm on his face, the breeze cool.

He breathed in the fresh country air, noting it lacked the stench of city life. The wind then served up a strong aroma of cow manure, a reminder that everything has its purpose. He watched a pair of crows circle high before floating down for a graceful landing on the ragged scarecrow slumped in the middle of a cornfield.

By the time he reached a sign indicating a right turn would take him to Haversfield, he had walked off much of his aggravation. After rounding a bend in the road, he spotted a service station on the edge of a small cluster of buildings. He could tell someone was working because the large bay doors were open.

Gravel made crunching noises under his feet as he left the road and crossed the front yard, where two weathered gas pumps stood. HARVEY'S GARAGE was boldly lettered in red across the front window of the cinder block building. Looking into the bay area, he saw a pair of legs sticking out from under a fairly new Cadillac.

"Excuse me. I need some help. I'm having a problem with my car."

"You wouldn't be here if you wasn't, now, would you? Go have a seat, if you like," a gruff voice drawled.

"Smartass," Matt grumbled under his breath as he retraced his steps to the front of the building.

He stepped around the gallon of antifreeze serving as a doorstop. Once inside, he noticed the blue and gray tile floor was long overdue for replacement. The humming of a shiny red soda machine to his right attracted his attention.

He dug into his pocket for change. He hadn't realized how thirsty he was until now. After making his selection, he downed half of it in practically one swallow. He grabbed a tattered fishing magazine and sat on a scarred wooden chair.

Several minutes later, he glanced up as the mechanic from under the Cadillac finally appeared. Grease and oil splatters stained the man's blue overalls, causing him to wonder if they'd ever been laundered. His gray hair looked surprisingly clean.

Reaching into a back pocket for a handkerchief, the mechanic attempted to erase the oil smears from his face before asking, "Now, what's the problem with your car?"

"It died a few miles away from here. I left it on the side of the road. The engine started missing, then it just quit."

"Let's go take a look." The man headed out the door, not bothering to lock up.

"Name's Harvey," he said, after they were seated in his tow truck.

"Mine's Bill Reese."

Matt had been on the road for more than a month and still felt uneasy using his alias. Even when he was young and in trouble, he never had felt comfortable lying. Now, his entire life was a lie.

Only temporarily, he reminded himself. After all, the whole point of this cross country drive had been to get away from malicious gossips, the nosey public and the lying herd of jackals commonly known as the press. And how else could he do that but by lying?

"You're not from around here," Harvey stated with certainty.

"No, I'm not. I'm from Illinois." At least that was true. "Chicago." That was not.

Harvey raised an eyebrow and glanced over at him. "What brings you to this neck of the woods?"

"Just passing through. I'm headed up to St. Louis."

"Well, let's see if we can get you back on the road."

It took Harvey little time to discover the fuel pump was shot. He hooked up the car and towed it to the garage. After making a few calls, he informed, "I'll likely have a rough time gettin' that pump. Probably take a day or two but I'll hunt up what I need from someplace. Should'a bought American."

Matt pursed his lips, mentally using the string of curse words that was starting to sound like a mantra. "What about a delivery service? UPS?"

Harvey looked at him as though he'd just said something vulgar. "Let me explain something. First, I gotta get the pump, then check out the fuel line. Now, unless you're Batman and saw the universal sign for help in the sky, do you need to leave right this minute?"

A comedian. Just what he needed. Matt took a deep, steadying breath. "Is there a car rental agency around here?"

Scratching his chin, Harvey considered the question before responding, "Nope."

He let out a slow hiss of air. "Well, in that case, is there a hotel around? Or a motel?"

"Summer Taylor has one of them bed and breakfast places downtown. About two blocks away. You can't miss it. Just walk straight that way until you get to the stop sign, then hang a right."

Matt retrieved his suitcase from the car and started walking. He soon discovered "downtown" Haversfield consisted of about two square blocks.

He would have laughed had he not been so angry at himself. In such a small place, he wouldn't be able to blend in with the anonymous crowds because there *weren't* any. He'd have to be on his best behavior because his every move would be noticed just because he was a stranger.

After turning at the stop sign and continuing on just as Harvey had instructed, he saw a white, two-story house with blue shutters. It sat back quite a distance from the street, in the middle of what looked like a quarter-acre of well-tended land. Hanging from a post was a tastefully painted sign with the words TAYLOR HOUSE.

He stepped onto the brick walkway leading to the house. Flowers bordered the base of the wide porch and more overflowed from hanging baskets swaying in the breeze. As he trudged up the steps, he noted the exterior of the house was well maintained. The porch's white wooden railings were in perfect condition. The gray planked floor looked so freshly painted, he checked to see if he'd left a trail of footprints.

When he knocked on the screen door, there was no response. He rang the bell, wondering if he could be heard over the rock music blaring from the backyard.

A large, black and tan dog came running from the side of the house, charged up the steps and stopped within three feet of him, barking menacingly the entire time.

"Hey there, pup. It's okay." His attempt to make friends with the animal wasn't working.

"Gyp! Quiet!" a female ordered as she followed the dog's path. "Sit!"

The animal sat but still seemed to hold Matt in contempt, for he growled softly.

When Matt moved his wary gaze from the dog to the person on the stairs, it surprised him to see a young woman. A young woman who happened to be one of the most gorgeous females he'd ever seen.

He wondered if her dark auburn hair was naturally curly since it fell almost to her waist in ringlets. Her faded red t-shirt bearing the St. Louis Cardinals insignia and baggy carpenter jeans couldn't camouflage the shapely figure underneath. He looked down, noting the paint splatters on her clunky old hiking boots.

He removed his sunglasses and looked into eyes so incredibly dark blue, he assumed she wore tinted contacts. She looked barely out of high school, causing him to worry if she was familiar with his music.

"Can I help you?" she asked, giving no sign she knew his identity.

"Yeah, sweetheart. Could you go get your mom for me?"

Folding her arms across her chest, the young woman bent one leg at the knee. "That'd be kind of hard since she's six feet deep."

"Oh. Sorry." He felt his face flush. Was everyone in this town a smartass? "My car's over at Harvey's and I need a place to stay for the night. Is the person who runs this place around?"

"You're looking at her. Follow me." She walked past him and opened the screen door. "Gyp, you stay outside," she commanded over her shoulder.

Matt followed her into the house while the dog obediently remained on the porch. His shoes squeaked on the polished wooden floor of the entrance hall. When he glanced at the wide staircase across from the front door, he guessed the bedrooms were all upstairs.

He continued trailing after her as she turned left into a spacious living room so tastefully decorated, he wondered if it had been done by a professional.

He had learned a lot about different pieces of furniture and styles when his penthouse apartment had been redecorated after the murder while he took up residence at a hotel. The interior designer had driven him crazy with discussions regarding everything down to the smallest detail. Matt had made some decisions but left others to her discretion.

After all those careful consultations, he'd been disappointed to discover his redecorated apartment still didn't feel like a home. Despite its new look, he couldn't forget a murder had taken place in his bedroom, which was why he'd moved into the guest room. He planned to sell it when the media feeding frenzy ended.

Redoing his apartment had cost a bundle but he thought this house looked much more appealing. Antique crystal lamps rested on tables probably handed down from one generation to the next. He wanted to flop on the overstuffed dark green sofa and take a nap. He thought the two matching chairs by the fireplace encouraged intimate conversations on a dark, wintry night. Things that normal people do. Glancing at the clutter of figurines and photographs resting on the marble mantel, he knew those must have taken years to accumulate.

In front of a large bay window overlooking the driveway, the shine of a beautifully kept baby grand winked at him. He longed to run his fingers over the keys. It had been weeks since he'd played.

"Have a seat," the young woman directed, while she went over to the antique desk. As she sat down, she withdrew what looked to be a ledger from the top drawer.

He remained standing.

"How long will you be staying?" she asked.

"Until my car is fixed." Watching her make a note in the ledger, he thought it absurd someone so young was in charge of a place like this.

"I'll need to see some form of identification."

"Sure." He calmly took his wallet from his back pocket and handed over an Illinois license bearing his new name.

She completed his registration. "Breakfast will be the only meal provided. If you don't show up by ten o'clock, you're on your own."

"Okay." He wondered if she maintained such a snippy attitude with all her guests.

"Smoking is not allowed anywhere inside the house. And, of course, no drugs."

"I don't do drugs," he countered, wondering why people expected the worst from him regardless of his appearance.

"Fine. And just so you know, I won't put up with rude or obnoxious behavior. Or drunks."

Her remarks sparked his anger but he bit back a crude retort. After all, he was the one needing a place to stay, not her.

"You have your choice of three bedrooms. Each has a private bath. I'll show you the way."

As he followed her up the stairs, he couldn't help but appreciate her slender form. He caught a whiff of the pleasant scent of her perfume. Light and subtle, unlike the offensive, heavy fragrances favored by the women in his social circles. But the women in his circles would be fawning all over him right now. He couldn't imagine this one doing any such thing even if she knew his identity.

He was given a quick tour of the bedrooms. The last one she showed him had a pleasing view of the backyard. The queen size bed and antique dresser were more than adequate for one night. He looked around the room once again, thinking it was much more welcoming than one at an expensive hotel.

"This'll be fine."

"Good. I'll leave you here to settle in. If you need anything, let me know." She turned to go but he quickly grabbed her arm.

"Wait! You didn't tell me your name." He thought he saw a flash of alarm cross her face but it passed so quickly he wasn't sure.

He suddenly released her arm, as though the contact had singed his hand.

"Summer Taylor."

He looked once again into those incredible eyes. Too bad her personality sucked. Plus, she had that annoying Southern drawl. Forcing himself to be polite, he extended his hand. "Glad to meet you, Summer."

She hesitated before briefly shaking his hand and hurrying

from the room.

Summer's first impression of Bill Reese had been that he was so attractive, he was probably used to women throwing themselves at him. She had to admit her own pulse had fluttered a bit when she saw him standing on the porch. But when he opened his mouth, his attitude made her want to smack him.

Maybe other women didn't mind strangers calling them "sweetheart" but she did. She hated the way he had looked her up and down, as if they were about to negotiate her price for a lap dance. Well, that might be stretching it a bit, considering the way she was dressed.

For some reason, he looked familiar but try as she might, she couldn't place him.

"Excuse me, where can I get some decent food around here?"

Why did everything he said sound like an insult? Summer wondered. She set her glass of sweet tea on the kitchen table and rose from the chair.

Looking at him standing in the doorway, she guessed he stood six feet tall or more. He had the body of a professional swimmer, lean but toned. The Cubs baseball cap he now wore covered his extremely short, dark blonde hair and sunglasses hid those smoky green eyes, but he was still too damn good looking.

Why did God put such an attractive face on a jackass like him?

"Maisie's Bar and Grill is about a block away. The food's good. Just head right once you leave here. You can't miss it."

"Thanks." He started off toward the front of the house. A few seconds later, she heard him yell, "Could you please come here?"

She muttered a mild oath. Was Bill Reese going to be a

continual pain in the rear end? She walked to the front door and saw Gypsy firmly planted on the steps, growling menacingly.

"Your dog evidently doesn't like me coming or going." He had a wry grin on his face.

"Gyp, come here." She spoke sternly and the dog meekly walked through the front door she held open. "He's usually friendly."

"I *usually* have no trouble making friends with animals."

She remained silent, although she wanted to say, Gyp's *usually* a pretty good judge of character.

"Thanks for the help." He sounded overly polite before descending the stairs.

As she watched him walk away, she wished Bill Reese's car had broken down a couple of states away from Missouri. Oh, well, there had been other customers she had disliked. She'd survive this one too.

Besides, she didn't have time to stand around and think about Bill Reese. She had to finish painting the trim on the garage.

Chapter Four

Matt headed down the street, muttering insults he wished he could have spit at Ms. Summer Taylor. She had nerve insinuating her dog sensed he was some psycho out to perform a number of sinister acts if given the chance. Her attitude really ticked him off. If he didn't need a place to stay, he would have really blasted her.

Apparently, life as Bill Reese wasn't going to be a total breeze. Why was it no matter what his name was, trouble came his way?

As he approached Maisie's, he made a conscious effort to lighten his thoughts. When he opened the door and stepped inside, he feared things were going to get worse.

The few patrons stared at him as though they were trying to recall if he'd been featured on *America's Most Wanted*. After a few moments of deliberation, they apparently decided he was no more threatening than the fish mounted on the walls. They turned their attention back to their food.

They had no idea who he was.

He let out the breath he was holding as he walked across the yellowed linoleum to sit on a stool at the counter. Although the place must have been built decades ago, he noticed the tables and booths were well maintained. The same could be said of the clean walls, despite the fish.

The only waitress stopped chatting with a customer further down the counter and headed his way. The look in her eyes made him feel like a swimmer who'd just caught the eye of a shark.

Superstar Matt Zeller was used to women looking at him like that. Average guy Bill Reese didn't want the attention.

"You're new. What's your name, sugar?" Smiling, she handed him a menu.

"Bill." He sneezed, assaulted by the gallon of heavy perfume she wore.

"Bless you. You staying awhile?"

"No." He saw the hope fade from her face.

"Maybe I can change your mind," she suggested in a low voice.

He stifled a bark of laughter. He felt as though he were in a scene from a bad movie. "Sorry, but as soon as my car's fixed, I'm gone. Got a schedule to keep."

"That's a shame. Well, you want anything to drink?"

"Iced tea."

"Okay. I'll give you a minute to look at the menu."

While he ate, the people in the restaurant left him alone and that pleased him immensely. So did the liver and onions. He wasn't as fortunate when it came to Lisa, who used her free time between customers to hang around him. He ignored the suggestive remarks she tossed his way but doubted she even noticed his lack of interest.

As he wiped the napkin across his mouth, she once again sauntered over. "Need anything else, honey?"

"I don't think so. Just the check."

"Anything you say." She winked and lightly touched his arm. "Hope to see you again. Don't forget, my name's Lisa."

He supposed other men would find her sexy in an obvious, cheap sort of way but nothing about her appealed to him. She wore too much makeup. Her hair looked stiff and he'd bet his next royalty check that blonde color came from a bottle.

She reminded him of someone. He tried hard to think of who it was but couldn't come up with an answer.

After he paid the bill, he walked over to the door leading to the other side of Maisie's, which was a Saloon, according to the sign over the doorway.

He didn't really feel like sitting around drinking but the only alternative was to head back to Summer's, where he felt about as welcome as a case of leprosy.

It would be safer to hang out and observe the natives.

He strolled inside, at first thinking the place was a dump but soon reconsidered. Just because it wasn't a Hard Rock Cafe was no reason to condemn it.

He gazed at the large pictures of movie stars from the 40's adorning the walls and wondered if anything had been changed since that decade. The poster of a young Frank Sinatra hanging above the jukebox was a larger version of the one in his apartment back in New York.

He listened to the trio of men seated at the middle of the bar debate the odds of the Cardinals making it to the World Series. The men stopped briefly to acknowledge him and then resumed their discussion.

Choosing a stool a little distance away, he ordered a beer from an elderly man who was more interested in watching a *Matlock* rerun than waiting on customers.

After a short time, the oldest member of the small group looked over and asked, "You just get into town?"

Matt nodded, guessing the man was forty-something. His brown hair was slightly graying at the temples. Laugh lines were permanently etched at the corners of his green eyes, his pleasant face deeply tanned. He looked harmless enough.

"Where you from?"

"Chicago."

"Oh. You visiting someone?"

Not wanting to appear unfriendly but also not anxious to volunteer any information, he responded, "Just passing through. I was headed for St. Louis when I started having car trouble. It's over at Harvey's now."

"Well, don't you worry none. Harvey's a whiz with cars. He knows what he's doing even though he moves kind of slow. I'm Bob McDuff. This here is Ernie Hughes and he's Howard Erikson." He gestured toward each man as he spoke his name.

30

The men Bob introduced looked younger, maybe around Matt's age. Ernie had blue eyes, blonde hair, an unshaven face and a thin, long-limbed body. Howard was a striking man. The look in his brown eyes gave the impression his mind was diligently working to create some mischief to liven things up.

"You staying at Summer's?" Howard asked.

"Yeah."

"I'm related to her," he added.

Matt had to bite his bottom lip to refrain from blurting out his condolences.

"Now, ain't she a looker?" Bob drawled.

"She's a nice girl, even if she's a little smart-mouthed now and then," Ernie added.

Matt forced a smile. He wasn't about to piss them off and voice his opinion.

"Guess you already know things are kind of dull around here. Not much to do except watch liver spots form on Bob." Howard took a handful of peanuts from the plastic container on the bar and popped them into his mouth.

Ernie snickered but Bob tilted his head in Howard's direction. "This here's the village idiot. But don't worry, he's harmless. At least that's what all the women say."

Matt laughed.

Summer wandered out to the back porch with Gyp at her heels. The back of the house faced west, giving her a spectacular view of the sunset.

Settling on the swing, she ran her fingers through her hair, still damp from her shower, hoping the warm evening breeze would dry it quickly. She watched Gyp as he spotted a nervy squirrel leisurely trespassing across the yard and suddenly bounded off the porch.

She wished she hadn't called Julie, her best friend, because their discussion still bothered her. The main topic had been relationships. Or, more accurately, the absence of such in Summer's life.

Just because Julie had recently met someone, she'd been argumentative about Summer's situation. She had pointed out, as she usually did, as long as Summer lived in the sparsely populated Haversfield, she would never find anyone to fall in love with and get married. Especially since the town's few eligible men were interested in Summer but she never gave them any encouragement.

Julie lived over an hour and a half away in Poplar Bluff but the two got together as often as they could. They had become friends while attending Southeast Missouri State College in Cape Girardeau. Since graduation, Julie often asked Summer to move to Poplar Bluff. Although it wasn't a major metropolis, compared to Haversfield, it certainly had more to offer.

Julie frequently claimed Summer was wasting her life away, isolated in "that little hick town." She didn't have any family left, other than Howard and his parents, so what was the point of staying? Summer always insisted her house was the only sense of security she had, the only link with her heritage. Besides, she was in no hurry to get married.

The basic meat of the conversation had been chewed over numerous times before. Although she wouldn't admit it to Julie, she was often lonely and still missed her grandmother. She wondered if she'd ever get used to being the sole occupant of this big house. This latest bout of loneliness had lasted longer than usual but she was confident it would pass. It always did.

She watched as Gyp climbed the steps. The gentle wind toyed with her hair and felt comforting as it softly caressed her skin. Inhaling deeply, she let out her breath in a long sigh, causing the dog to rest his head on her leg. She reached out to scratch behind his ear.

"At least I've got you."

By the time Matt left Maisie's, he had consumed too many beers but he'd had a great time. Those three guys had invited him to come back later in the week for a fund raiser Maisie's was hosting. Some poor guy named Neil Kittle had died of a heart attack, leaving a widow with two kids still in high school.

Though the reason for the event was sad, Bob mentioned a band had been hired and everyone in town would show up to support the Kittle family. Matt appreciated the invitation but said he'd probably be long gone by then.

He strolled back to Summer's, wondering why the sarcastic witch who was temporarily his landlady wasn't as friendly as the other people in town.

How did she expect to stay in business if she treated her customers like escaped felons?

But why did he care, anyway? That was her problem. He was just thankful things were running smoothly for him. Getting stranded here wasn't so bad, after all. Assuming a new identity had turned out to be one of his best ideas. It was providing him the opportunity to repair his frazzled nerves. He wasn't much of a drinker but he'd enjoyed hanging out with those guys in Maisie's and having a bit more beer than he was used to.

As he opened the front door, he expected Gyp to lunge at him, hoping to rip open his throat. Instead, he heard music softly playing as he stood in the entrance hall.

He couldn't remember the rules about which parts of the house were off limits but didn't want to go upstairs to sit in his bedroom with nothing to do. He wasn't even sleepy.

Besides, in one hand he held a carryout bag from Maisie's, containing a hamburger bought for bribery purposes only. His other arm cradled a six pack of beer.

He headed toward the kitchen.

He hadn't paid much attention to the layout of this end of

the house when he first arrived but remembered directly across the hall from the front room was a formal dining room. Farther down the hall on the left, he noticed what looked like a family room. Taking a further look in there, he paused briefly when he saw Summer asleep on a sofa, her protective animal sprawled out on the floor nearby.

Matt, ignoring the dog's soft growl, admired the large, bleached pine entertainment unit across from the couch. The doors stood open, displaying a television and stereo system on the shelves inside. An Adele song was softly playing.

He looked at Gyp, waved the bag in the air and then continued the short distance into the oversized kitchen. After putting the beer in the refrigerator, he searched the cabinets for a plate. It didn't occur to him to use the dog's dish.

Unwrapping the peace offering, he cut up the hamburger, noticing Gyp stood in the doorway and watched.

Warily, the animal entered the kitchen as the scent of meat overpowered his need to show dominance. When Matt set the plate on the floor, Gyp walked over and politely sniffed the food. He began eating but continued to glance occasionally at his benefactor.

When the dog finished, he looked up and belched out his thanks. Encouraged, Matt crouched down and held out his hand. Gyp appeared to think the situation over before cautiously stepping closer and allowing this new source of food to pet him.

Having accomplished his goal, Matt turned his attention back to the refrigerator and wrested a beer from the plastic encircling the six pack. He popped the top while absently listening to the disk jockey's chatter coming from the stereo in the other room.

"It's time for the national debut of one of the songs from Matt Zeller's soon-to-be-released new CD. As usual, we're talking Grammy material. Here it is, folks! For the first time ever! *When We Gonna Meet!*"

That got Matt's attention. He started to move in time to the Reggae style music he had written, swinging his hips and dancing around the kitchen. He lifted his arms as though he held a partner and began to sing.

> *"I met you in a dream once,*
> *and I've never been the same.*
> *You gave me a glimpse of heaven*
> *but you never said your name.*
> *Our hearts will love, our souls will join,*
> *I swear you told me this!*
> *Right before our moonlit meeting*
> *ended with a kiss.*
> *Come back to me, baby! When we gonna meet?*
> *Come back to me, baby! When we gonna meet?*
> *Well, I been waitin' and searchin',*
> *were the words you spoke true?*
> *I don't know what my next move is,*
> *or is that up to you?*
> *I been lookin' everywhere,*
> *will you be 'round tonight?*
> *When will you materialize,*
> *so I can hold you tight?*
> *Come back to me, ba..."*

"What are you doing?" Summer interrupted, startling him so much, he almost dropped his beer.

Quickly recovering, he lifted the can to his lips and took a slow swallow with deliberate calmness.

After setting the can on the table, he grinned. "Trying to steal your silverware, sweetheart. I thought I'd liven up the town a bit with some grand larceny."

"Do not call me sweetheart." She shot him a reproving

glare before moving across the room to close the back door. She again passed in front of him, heading for the hallway but he quickly looped an arm around her waist, halting her departure.

"C'mere, baby," he coaxed, pulling her roughly against him and nuzzling her ear. "Are you old enough to drink? Wanna have a beer with me?"

"You're drunk." She shoved him away. "I suggest you go to bed."

"Only if you tuck me in."

She continued on her way, throwing over her shoulder, "Breakfast tomorrow is at eight sharp, *Mr. Zeller.*"

"Eight? Why so early?"

She didn't answer as she went into the family room to shut off the stereo before continuing down the hall to the stairs.

"She sure can bring a good time to a screeching halt," he told Gyp. The dog gave him a sympathetic glance before leaving to follow his mistress.

Since Matt had no one to play with and felt tired anyway, he went up to his bedroom a short time later. He'd almost drifted off to sleep when he finally realized she'd called him Mr. Zeller.

He sat up, mumbling a vile word.

Summer got ready for bed, trying to calm herself but her hands still shook. One of the top rock stars in the world happened to be in her house! No wonder she thought he looked familiar! The short hair and glasses had thrown her.

She had to admit he was one hell of a piano player, singer and songwriter. His talent had earned him a few gold and platinum records, plus a few Grammys.

He also had a chip on his shoulder the size of Alaska and a reputation for being fast and wild. And liking his women that way too.

She knew he had been trying to dodge the fallout from a murder committed in his apartment. It should have been only a ten second spot on *Entertainment Tonight* instead of the media event orchestrated by the press. She had dispassionately followed the story in the papers and on television, thinking the reporters had gone way overboard classifying any move Matt made as "news."

Every scrap of information regarding his sex life, whether truth or rumor, she guessed, had been encapsulated into luring headlines across front pages of allegedly credible publications as well as the sleazy tabloids.

She remembered he had somehow managed to disappear a month or so ago. As much as the press speculated on the star's whereabouts, they hadn't found him yet. She'd read somewhere he had an upcoming tour scheduled soon. With all the negative publicity, she wondered if it had been postponed.

She shook her head in amazement. Her life had suddenly taken on a surrealistic air. She had met Mr. Rock and Roll himself.

She hated to sympathize with him now that she knew he was a horse's ass.

Chapter Five

Matt put his face against the pillow and prayed for death. The pounding headache, a result of his fun at Maisie's, competed with music blasting loud enough to rearrange his rib cage. Each note of *When Love Comes to Town* drove the intensity of his hangover up a notch. He normally liked the old song by U2 and B.B. King but, right now, he wanted the entire world to shut the hell up.

He clumsily groped the nightstand for his watch, blinking several times until his hazy vision cleared enough for him to see it wasn't quite eight o'clock. He looked around the room, recalled where he was and groaned.

He was stuck in the middle of nowhere.

Slowly rising to a sitting position, he tried to clear the fog from his head. Yawning, he scratched his chest and wished he could have slept another few hours. Maybe then his head wouldn't feel like a nuclear testing site.

When he remembered his cover was blown – thanks to his own stupidity, queasiness rolled through his stomach.

And who did he have to blame for that? Good God, he was an idiot. He dimly recalled making a pass at the unfriendly Ms. Taylor and decided idiot seemed too kind a name to call himself.

Would she throw him out this morning? Had she already alerted the press? Could she be so heartless?

The only consoling thought entering his head was if she wanted to notify the media, she'd had all night to do so. Since there didn't seem to be a circus of reporters outside, he assumed she hadn't yet revealed his identity.

He should have known better than to cloud his judgment with alcohol. He'd never been much of a drinker. Last night had been a rare exception because he'd been having fun and, before he knew it, he'd drank more than his modest limit.

He quickly got up, pausing briefly when it felt as if his head would explode. After a few minutes in the adjoining bathroom, he pulled on a tee shirt and jeans. He spotted the glasses Gina had been so proud of, deciding it was pointless to wear them since his landlady knew his identity. As much as he dreaded it, he headed downstairs to face the consequences of last night's foolishness.

He assessed the odds of sweet talking his landlady into keeping his identity a secret. He quickly decided he had as much chance of accomplishing that as fans had of resurrecting Elvis.

Maybe if he didn't mention anything about last night, she wouldn't either. Yeah, and maybe June Cleaver was his mother after all.

He headed straight to the family room to turn down the deafening music before shuffling into the kitchen, where his squeamish stomach was assaulted by the aroma of bacon and eggs.

He slid onto a chair, leaned back and stretched his long legs out under the table. His eyes fastened on Summer's back as she stood at the stove and cooked.

She certainly didn't dress to impress anyone. The sleeves of her gray sweatshirt were cut off a few inches above the elbows and her jeans looked older than she did. But, he had to admit, she still looked gorgeous enough to make a part of his body sit up and pay attention.

"You're late. There's a plate." She waved a fork toward the counter next to the sink. "Throw whatever food you want on it. This ain't Denny's."

A snort of laughter escaped him despite his assessment that her attitude, for a businesswoman, sucked.

He slowly rose, hoping food would chase away his hangover. Taking a plate, he asked, "Anybody ever tell you

you're rude? You're supposed to pamper your guests."

"I'm not a den mother."

He couldn't stop himself from walking up too closely behind her and murmuring against her ear, "Well, that's good because I ain't no boy scout."

"Ouch!" he yelped, after she rammed her elbow backwards into his ribs. "What'd you do that for?"

"I warned you I don't put up with obnoxious behavior. Keep your distance." She turned and gave him a wide, phony smile.

Eyeing the tiny gold hoop in his left earlobe, she added, "Or I might decide to pierce your other ear with one of my dull knives. And, by the way, guests usually eat in the dining room."

"Well, I guess that don't apply to me 'cause you sure haven't been treating me like a guest," he complained.

Rubbing his midsection, he cast a wary look at her before proceeding to put food on his plate. As he sat back down, he asked, "You got any coffee around here?"

He caught the look of exasperation on her face. She started to say something, but, instead, took a cup from the mug rack plainly visible above the counter and poured coffee from the equally visible coffeemaker. After placing the cup in front of him, she turned back to the stove. She turned off the burners, put food on a plate and sat across from him at the table.

He studied her for a minute. "You haven't been doing this very long, have you?"

"Doing what?"

"This bed and breakfast thing."

"Long enough," she replied.

"This is probably your first year. How old are you, anyway?"

"Over twenty-one. Not that it's any of your business." She focused her attention on the dog. "Why is Gyp sitting by your side? He didn't like you yesterday. What did you do to change

40

his mind?"

A look of innocence appeared on his face. "I didn't do anything. Maybe he had a change of heart. First impressions aren't always accurate, you know."

She raised an eyebrow and turned her attention to her plate.

He took slow bites, hoping his stomach would straighten itself out. At least the jackhammer in his head seemed to be easing.

"So, you know who I am," he suddenly blurted, breaking the silence of the last several minutes.

She lifted her eyes to meet his and nodded. "I thought you looked familiar. And when you sang along with the stereo and knew the words to that new song, it wasn't exactly hard to figure out."

She started laughing and his annoyed glare failed to quiet her. If he wasn't so worried about losing his anonymity, he probably would have chuckled along with her but, at the moment, he couldn't appreciate the humor of the situation.

His ego took another hit when he realized she wasn't the least bit impressed that he, one of the biggest rock stars in the world, was sitting at her kitchen table.

After she could control herself enough to talk, she stated the obvious. "That wasn't the brightest thing to do."

He chewed on his bottom lip until he could politely speak instead of yelling. "Would you do me just this one favor? Don't tell anyone. Please."

He hoped she felt enough sympathy for his circumstances to help him keep his secret.

"I really need a break from the media," he added, wondering if offering her money would guarantee her silence if begging didn't work.

Putting down her fork, she studied him for a few minutes. "Okay," she finally said, surprising him. "But you'll probably be able to remain anonymous since you look entirely different. Besides, most people around here are into country music."

"Except you. Judging from your choice of radio stations."

"You have to admit, it gets your heart pumping."

"I can think of a better way to get my heart pumping." He didn't know what kept prodding him to act like a Hugh Hefner wannabe but he gave her a suggestive leer.

She compressed her lips in a tight line and stood up. Snatching the plates, she announced, "Breakfast is over."

"But I'm not done!" He unsuccessfully grabbed for his plate.

"Oh, yes you are! Now, get lost. Don't you have to go see about your car?"

Matt grabbed his baseball cap and sunglasses before heading out the front door. The air felt a little cooler than yesterday, although the sun shone from a cloudless blue sky.

When he reached Harvey's, a handwritten sign taped to the door fluttered slightly in the breeze. *Closed due to death in family.* Cursing under his breath, he turned and walked in the direction of Maisie's.

He strolled into the restaurant, annoyed to see the same waitress as yesterday. She was speaking with the only other patron, an elderly man seated at one of the tables. Her eyes lit up like a Broadway marquee when she saw him. That irritated him even more.

He slid onto a stool at the counter.

"Well, hi there, honey!" She handed him a menu. "Want some coffee?"

"Sure." He'd forgotten her name. Briefly glancing at the tag on her chest, he read *Lisa* before quickly looking away. The last thing he needed was her thinking he was interested in her ample breasts.

He studied the menu, still brooding over Summer chasing

him out of the house. Especially since he hadn't finished eating.

"What's cooking that smells so good?" he asked as Lisa placed his coffee on the counter.

"Me, ever since you come in," she purred.

He glanced at her over the rim of his cup as he took a sip. "I'm only interested in one thing. Pancakes. Throw in some sausage and hash browns too."

She gave his order to the cook. When she returned to keep him company, he wished other customers would suddenly walk in and demand her attention.

Even after she placed his food in front of him, she hovered around, chattering incessantly. He concentrated on eating and showed little interest in her conversation, grateful when people began ambling in.

"The lunch specials are really popular. The room fills up fast soon as the clock hits eleven." She reluctantly left his side. In just minutes, all the tables and counter stools were occupied.

Matt continued eating, savoring every bite. He'd been to the best restaurants throughout the world and decided Maisie's could compete with any of them. Which could explain the marked increase in his appetite since landing in Haversfield.

When he finished his meal, he felt as stuffed as a Thanksgiving turkey. Until he looked at the pies sitting in the plastic display case.

"Are those pies fresh?" he asked Lisa, who was clearing away his empty dishes.

"Everything in here is." She batted her eyelashes.

"Is that a banana cream one that keeps winking at me? Give me a piece of that."

"Is that all you want a piece of, sugar?"

"I'm afraid so. I'm just passing through." He feigned a

sudden interest in the other customers.

She waited on other tables but as soon as she had a few minutes to spare, she returned to talk to him. Occasionally, he nodded his head or offered an "Oh," or, "Is that so?" when necessary.

She placed her elbows on the counter and leaned forward as she talked, adjusting her low neckline so it slid even lower.

He ignored the bait she offered.

"You coming to the fund raiser Maisie's having for the Kittle family?" she asked. "Maybe we can sit together."

"I'll be gone by then." Even if he wasn't, he had no desire to spend an evening with her.

He had always disliked cheap, obvious women, which made him wonder for the hundredth time why he had ever given Brandy Cole a second glance.

"Well, if you make it, I'll save you a dance." She grinned coyly.

He forced a slight smile, although it felt more like a grimace.

"Lisa, you got other customers," warned a burly man through the open portion of the wall separating the restaurant and the kitchen.

"He's such a pain in the ass!" she groused but left to wait on the other patrons.

Matt dug out his wallet and placed enough money to cover the bill on the counter. He was normally an overly generous tipper but he didn't want her to misinterpret anything as encouragement. He decided to leave just an average tip.

Once outside, he looked up and down the street, trying to come up with a plan to kill a few hours despite the lack of things to do. He didn't think the town even had a movie theater. And he certainly didn't want to park his butt on a barstool in the tavern and sip beer all afternoon. The only hope of diversion appeared to be the string of stores lining the downtown area.

It did occur to him that, despite Lisa annoying him to death with her suggestive remarks and Summer treating him like he was an escaped convict, he wasn't having such a bad time in Haversfield.

Chapter Six

Summer glanced up at the beautiful cloudless sky, glad the perfect weather was continuing again today. Especially when there were outside chores she needed to get done, like fertilizing the rose bushes in the back yard.

She'd rather flop on the hammock strung between the two dogwood trees near the garage because, thanks to her boarder, she hadn't slept well last night.

Since learning Bill Reese's true identity, she feared reporters would somehow discover his location and come snooping around. They would turn the nasty details of her life into humiliating headlines just to sell papers.

They could easily find a few residents all too eager to start up the gossip once again about her childhood. Not everyone in Haversfield had a kind heart. Then she'd get caught up in the edges of Matt's ongoing saga and she could just imagine what the press would insinuate. It wasn't just her reputation she was concerned about. She had a business to run.

She contemplated all this as she tended the rose bushes. When she finished, she knelt by the foundation of the back porch to pull weeds from the cluster of petunias. Like the front, the back also had a large porch spanning the width of the house.

"Well, boy, I don't know why you changed your opinion of him but I still think you-know-who's a jerk. If I'd known he was going to be this much trouble, I would have told him I didn't have any vacancies."

Gyp cocked his head to one side, listening intently to her dialogue.

"Let's hope Harvey will have his car fixed soon. Mr. Reese is probably already bored with our little town. He's used to the wild life of the big city and women hanging all over him. I don't think he'll be satisfied with just a beer at Maisie's."

She stopped her tug-of-war with a stubborn weed, sat back on her heels and sighed. "I really shouldn't be so quick to criticize him, Gyp. I guess that's not fair. I know how it hurts when people misjudge you. It's just hard not to consider him a horse's ass. You know, because of his behavior and all."

A sudden stab of guilt pierced her conscience because she knew she had been rude from the moment he had arrived. But, she justified, it was only in response to his insulting attitude. Every time he opened his mouth, he managed to fire up her temper.

Something about his presence bothered her. Maybe it was because of his lifestyle. Or his arrogance.

Maybe all that bad press wasn't wrong.

"The only good thing I can say about him is he's a great musician or I wouldn't have bought any of his CD's. But after this, I doubt I'll buy any more," she told the dog.

Attacking the weed with a hand spade finally enabled her to extract the deep roots from the ground. Surveying the yard, she didn't see anything else needing attention.

"C'mon, let's go in. It's time for lunch."

By late afternoon, Matt grew tired of carrying the bags crammed with his purchases. He'd found a couple of great gifts for Vinny and Gina. And himself. Who would have thought an electronic game could be so much fun? So what if he was having his childhood a little late. Better late than not at all.

When he went into Summer's house, he took the bags up to his room. Right after he told himself to avoid her, he headed downstairs and poked his head into every room but the house was empty.

He finally found her sleeping on the back porch swing. The dog lay on a rug in the corner, only opening his eyes briefly before stretching and dozing off again.

Considering the situation, he didn't know whether he should leave her to her privacy or sprawl in the vacant, well-padded chaise longue that beckoned to him.

He had a right to enjoy the outdoors, didn't he?

He chose to stay and ignore her presence rather than die of boredom in his bedroom. Laying back with his arms up and bent, his head resting on his hands, he studied her.

She looked so young and innocent, but he knew looks could be deceiving. From the way she handled herself around him, she was no shy, retiring country girl. She sure didn't seem intimidated by his presence. And she appeared sufficiently able to take care of herself.

His fame and fortune obviously didn't impress her. Nor did his *devilishly handsome good looks* -- not his words but those used to describe him in the countless news items spewed out by the press since the murder.

More importantly, why did her indifference bother him?

He wished she'd wake up. Fighting with her was at least something to do but he'd bet if he woke her, she'd take a swing at him and his ribs were still a little sore from this morning. He decided he wasn't that brave.

He watched as the wind gently ruffled her hair. Even without makeup, she looked flawless despite the faint sprinkle of freckles across her nose and cheeks. That cute nose she loved to stick up in the air was in the middle of an oval face. Her perfectly arched eyebrows and long lashes sure didn't appear to need any artificial help.

When her lips slightly parted, he suddenly wanted more than anything to kiss her. Irritated by his growing arousal, he warned himself about entertaining any lustful thoughts regarding her. He was supposed to be ignoring her presence, anyway.

Pulling the bill of his cap down over his eyes, he decided it was in his best interests to take a nap. It'd certainly be safer.

Summer stirred and positioned herself more comfortably. She felt so tired, she didn't want to open her eyes.

She wished she'd slept peacefully last night but it was stressful having a guest like Matt Zeller, who didn't know how to be polite and keep his distance.

Surely Harvey would have his car fixed by now so he could drive off to Sodom and Gomorrah or wherever he was headed.

Not fully awake, she sat up and stretched, her movements instantly freezing when she heard snoring not more than four feet away.

He had a lot of nerve coming out here and sleeping with her. Well, near her. How rude. The thought he might be intruding probably hadn't entered his thick skull.

He was acting more like an invited guest rather than a paying customer. She felt like turning over the chaise longue and dumping his butt on the porch floor.

She shouldn't have let him eat breakfast with her. Give him an inch and he'd take the whole highway.

She looked at the white lettering on his black tee shirt. *I'M THE GUY YOUR MOTHER WARNED YOU ABOUT.*

Not *my* mother, she silently sneered. Disgusted, she rose and went inside.

It only took a few seconds for Matt to figure out where he was when he slowly opened his eyes. One good thing about this town was it made him sleep like the dead, which was exactly what his overwrought nerves needed.

Looking over at the swing, he was disappointed to see it was empty. He checked his watch, then rubbed his eyes while wondering what to do next.

It was almost time for dinner but, although the food was great at Maisie's, Lisa's constant double entendres were growing tiresome.

He reluctantly pushed himself off the chaise and stretched, noticing the back yard appeared as meticulously tended as the front. Suddenly, a preferable alternative to dinner at Maisie's popped into his head.

"Hey, Summer!" he yelled, jerking open the screen door.

"Quit your bellowing! I'm right here." Seated at the kitchen table, an account book open before her, she shot him an annoyed look.

Grinning sheepishly, he pulled the chair out next to her and sat down. "I'm sorry. I didn't mean to interrupt you." He knew his voice sounded overly solicitous. Like a used car salesman trying to unload the biggest lemon on the lot.

"Yeah, right."

"I was wondering, would you make dinner? I'd pay you, of course."

She stared at him, lowering her chin while raising her eyebrows.

"Well, you know, since dinner doesn't come with the room. Maisie's is okay, but I'm kind of tired of being over there. And couldn't you use the money?"

She continued to study him.

"I'll pay you. You could eat too," he magnanimously offered. "We could have a nice dinner together and get to know each other."

"Now, there's an idea." Her voice was soft.

Encouraged, he placed a hand over hers and looked into her eyes. "It could be fun. You never know what could develop."

"I'm sorry I have to decline your offer. Perhaps another time." She smiled sweetly. "Like when the people of Mars and Earth unite and become one nation."

She flung his hand off and stood up. "Unless Gyp requests your company when he eats, you won't be having any dinner here."

50

She closed the account book with a snap and left the room.

He was tempted to yell out, *"Does that mean you're not interested?"* just so she'd return and continue arguing with him. But he reconsidered.

She hadn't thrown him out yet and he didn't want to push his luck.

He breathed a sigh of relief when he saw Lisa was not working. A young girl maybe all of fifteen years old came to stand by his booth, patiently chewing her gum while he scanned the menu.

"How's the catfish?"

"I never eat it, but people order it a lot. Nobody died from it yet."

"Well, that's recommendation enough for me. Could you bring me an iced tea while I'm waiting?"

"Sure."

He'd just taken a sip of his beverage when Howard and Bob strolled in. Spotting him, they headed his way.

"What's up, Bill?" Howard asked.

"Nothing."

The two men slid into the vacant side of the booth.

"You mind company?" Bob asked.

"Not at all. What are you guys doing?"

"Bob's wife done run off and left him," Howard cheerfully stated, selecting a dinner roll from the basket in the center of the table.

"Don't listen to him. She's up in St. Louis. Our daughter just had a baby this past weekend. Ruthie went up there to help out."

"Harvey didn't get you back on the road yet?" asked Howard.

"Nope. He's closed today because of a death in the family."

"Oh, that's right. His mother-in-law had a heart attack. He

and the wife had to go all the way to Joplin."

"Chrissie, honey, can you bring us some menus?" Bob called out.

The young girl stopped wiping off the counter and put her hands on her hips. "Jeez, you mean you don't know it by heart? It ain't changed since I been in third grade!"

She let out a noise of exasperation as she grabbed two menus and headed their way.

"I'd complain about her, but she's Maisie's granddaughter," Bob muttered, after she'd slapped the menus down and went back to resume her cleaning.

Summer knew her bad mood could be directly attributed to her obnoxious paying guest. She still couldn't believe he had actually thought she would consider making him dinner if he paid her.

"He thinks he can buy anything," she fumed. He actually had the gall to suggest they see what would develop.

She should have decked him.

If only he hadn't shown up now, at the time of year when business slowed down. Why couldn't it be spring or earlier in the summer when different county fairs and festivals attracted a steady stream of customers to this neck of the woods?

If he continued to act like an idiot, she could always throw him out. That thought comforted her.

Still, she sincerely prayed someone else would arrive so she didn't have to be alone with the visiting superstar who probably thought of Hugh Hefner as a role model.

She walked into the family room and turned on the stereo, only to be further annoyed when *What I Should Have Said*, one of Matt's songs, filled the silence.

"Ha!" she snorted. "He should be singing what I shouldn't have said."

She flopped on the couch and picked up the trashy

romance novel a guest had left behind. She had been trying to get interested in the lame plot, which was apparently thrown in as an afterthought to break up all the scenes involving milky white thighs and passionate hip thrusts. By the time she had gotten to page twelve, the main characters had already had a five page steamy sexual encounter.

She made a mental note to purchase a good murder mystery the next time she went shopping. She tossed the book onto the coffee table.

It occurred to her maybe Matt couldn't be blamed entirely for her bad mood, although she didn't like being fair to him. Maybe the lingering frustration over her conversation with Julie needled her more than she cared to admit.

Well, so what if she never met anyone and got married. There were worse things in life than being single.

"Enough of this moping around." She sat up. "C'mon, Gyp. Let's go for a walk. We need the exercise."

The dog paced impatiently while she tied the laces of her shoes.

Chapter Seven

After they finished eating, Matt, Howard and Bob walked into the bar and found Ernie perched on a stool, his eyes glued to the television mounted high on the wall.

"Ask for an M, you idiot!" Ernie yelled.

"In his opinion, *Wheel of Fortune* is the only thing on television worth watching. Other than baseball, of course," Howard explained, before ordering a round of beer.

"As usual, you're picking the wrong letters, Mr. Potato Head." Bob removed the toothpick from his mouth.

"You guys come here every night?" Matt asked.

"Well, Bob is usually home, trying to talk Ruthie out of filing for divorce. And Ernie, well, hell, where else is he gonna go?"

"Screw you, Howard," Ernie and Bob responded simultaneously.

Matt laughed, becoming more thankful his car broke down exactly where it did. Damned if he wasn't having a great time with these guys. He felt almost normal.

"Say, how about a friendly game of poker?" Howard suggested.

Bob and Ernie liked the idea.

"Where at?" Matt took a sip of beer from the longneck bottle.

"Summer's," Ernie casually informed.

He almost choked on his beer. "A friendly game at Summer's? I once saw an alligator friendlier than her."

"Don't worry. We'll protect you." Howard gave his shoulder a quick pat. "Let's walk over there."

Matt didn't think it was a good idea. He had been rather rude. Oh, okay, he'd been obnoxious and he honestly couldn't explain why.

"Hey, cuz! Wanna play cards?" Howard yelled through the back door screen of Summer's house a short while later.

Summer made her way from the family room to the kitchen. "Sure. The three of you feel like losing?"

"There's four of us," Howard corrected.

"I thought you guys had better sense," Matt heard her mutter as he followed the others inside.

He watched Ernie get the cards from a kitchen drawer while she took a coffee can from the pantry. Bob ripped open one of the packs of beer he'd carried in, placed five cans on the table and put the rest in the refrigerator. Howard fiddled with the old boombox on top of the refrigerator until Trace Atkins' voice could be heard.

He stood still, feeling uncomfortable. Or, more precisely, out of place.

When they all were seated, Bob started shuffling the cards. "See, we got a system. Everybody starts out with the same amount. Even if you're the big winner of the evening, you don't keep the money. It all goes back into the can. Since we just play for pennies, you don't forfeit much. Dealer's call."

Matt glanced at Summer while Bob dealt the cards. She had drawn her hair back into a ponytail, which, along with her squeaky clean face, caused her to look like she should be doing homework instead of playing poker. But she was still a knockout. When her eyes met his, she stuck her nose up a notch and looked away.

Once they started playing, he noticed she remained fairly reserved and wondered if his presence was the reason. The guys must normally have a good time with her or she wouldn't be included in their games.

He then became aggravated with himself for thinking so much about her. He forced himself to concentrate on his cards while the men exchanged insults, feeling honored when they started taking shots at him. It made him feel like he belonged.

As the evening progressed, he couldn't help noticing she was making just as much of an effort as he to avoid making eye contact.

They had played a few hours when Ernie said, "This is my last hand. I got too much to do tomorrow to be draggin' my tail. Two big orders of sod are going out, plus I'm supposed to pick up my new van."

"All right. Don't get your bloomers in a twist," Bob commented around the big cigar stuck between his teeth. Because Summer didn't allow smoking in the house, he had gone outside occasionally to light up for a few quick puffs.

"What did you say you do, Bill?" asked Ernie.

"I, uh, travel around for a pharmaceutical company. I'm in sales." Matt told himself it was a necessary lie. "It's just a job."

"That don't sound bad unless it's the traveling you don't like," commented Bob.

"Yeah, well, some people have to do real work instead of sitting their fat asses down all day at their John Deere dealership, pretending to know something about farm machinery." Ernie studied his cards and asked, "You ever figured out yet which one of them machines is a tractor?"

"I wouldn't be so cocky. You know what they say...if you ain't smart enough to do anything else, you grow sod. Hard to believe my Ruthie's your sister," Bob lazily remarked. "But Howard's the one that's got the life. Running his daddy's hardware store, counting nails out to customers while he wears that macho leather apron to impress the ladies. I hear he's always wanting to take them in the back room and show them his *tool*. Hey, Howard, ever think to hand them a magnifying glass when you do that?"

"Now, ya'll be nice," Summer laughed.

"You should talk! You've been so mean to me since I got here, Gyp showed me his hiding place under the porch!" complained Matt. He then exchanged high-fives with the other

56

men.

"Well, I wish you'd start using it," she replied, laughing.

The men hooted but his warm gaze settled on her, causing her to blush.

When the game finally broke up, Ernie and Bob left together but Howard lingered over one more beer before leaving. He hugged Summer, then slapped Matt on the back. "See you tomorrow."

"That was a lot of fun." Matt turned to face her once they were alone.

"It always is," she smiled. "You couldn't ask for better guys to hang around with."

He remained in the kitchen, not ready to turn in for the night. Besides, she hadn't been as hostile toward him this evening and he didn't want to part company just yet.

Could her more tolerant attitude be attributed to the beer or was she changing her opinion of him? He hoped it was the latter.

"So, Bob's wife is Ernie's sister?"

"Yeah. They're really funny when they start razzing each other about family issues." She reached up to change the station on the boombox before straightening up the kitchen, although the men had cleared off the table before they left.

When Van Morrison's *Into the Mystic* came on, she started to slightly sway to the music. "I love this old song."

His blood heated as he watched her. He didn't want to analyze why he was so attracted to her, especially since he'd told himself numerous times he didn't like her.

"Wanna dance?" He stepped closer to her.

She hesitated just for a second before sliding into his arms.

She has to be drunk if she's letting you touch her, his conscience warned.

With any other woman, his thoughts and actions would center on getting her into the bedroom for a night of sex. It was out of character for him but he felt content just holding her in his arms, feeling her softness pressed against him.

That didn't mean if she started taking off her clothes, he wouldn't thank God. But dancing with her like this was so damn seductive, he wouldn't mind if they just danced for hours.

When the song ended, a cut from his new CD immediately began. It surprised him when she remained in his arms. He kept dancing her around the kitchen, thankful the disk jockey had chosen this slow blues number. It had a strong beat but reeked of sensuality. At least he thought so.

He started to softly croon in her ear.

"The road is lonely, the way is long,
with no one at my side.
I should be used to this, it's all I know,
but it's still an empty ride.
Cold hearted ladies call to me,
and beckon with their smiles.
They don't know I'm hip to them,
although it took a while.
I'm missin' what I never had,
and, brother, that's no lie.
I'm missin' what I never had,
sometimes it makes me cry."

A soft guitar solo followed. He tilted his head back so he could look into her eyes. He felt something he couldn't define and, for a split second, sensed such a powerful connection between them, it almost brought him to his knees.

They were no longer dancing but she didn't move away. He placed his finger under her chin and gently exerted enough pressure to lift her head slightly. Mesmerized, he lowered his lips until they met hers for a kiss that was soft, needy and slow.

Achingly slow.

Tightening his arms around her, he deepened the kiss. His pulse began racing, his body hardened because she was kissing him back. It became hard to tell when one kiss ended and another began. A passionate fire had ignited between them and neither one showed any sign of wanting to douse the flames.

He cursed himself when he ruined it all by putting his hand on her rump, pressing her against his arousal. If the impact of the mood breaking could be measured on the Richter Scale, he guessed it probably would have registered an 8.5.

She stiffened and shoved him away. Although redness crept into her face, he couldn't tell if she was as affected by their contact as he or if she was just pissed.

She threw him a terse "Good night," before rushing out of the kitchen.

He stood there, frustrated and confused, wanting to go after her but sensing it would be unwise.

He would be willing to bet there were fifth graders who handled similar situations with more finesse.

Chapter Eight

The trill of birds roused him from a troubled sleep. He heard no other sounds of life, just the quietness of living in a small town. Checking his watch, he noted it was not yet seven o'clock. Hours before his usual rising time.

Guilt and confusion had made him toss and turn much of the night. Questions nipped at the edges of his conscience, robbing him of a peaceful slumber.

Had he imagined Summer's responsiveness to his kisses? Hadn't she fully cooperated until he'd put his hand on her rear end?

What would have happened if he hadn't put his hand where she obviously didn't want it? Had the beer interfered with her judgment or his?

Why did it matter? The old Matt Zeller would never have cared.

Did Haversfield put some kind of drug in the drinking water that altered personalities?

He was a loner. He knew it and so did everyone else. So, why would he let a rude, obviously unstable woman bother him so much? Unless the stress of the past few months had affected him more than he'd imagined.

Swinging his legs over the side of the bed, he wondered what her attitude toward him would be like this morning. If anyone had a right to be mad, he did. After all, she was just a tease, wasn't she?

Well, wasn't she?

As he pulled on his clothes, he still couldn't believe he was spending this much time worrying about an event that had no significance in his life. So what if she was still angry about last night. He still didn't understand why she'd gotten mad in the first place.

When he remembered what it had felt like to kiss her and to have her body pressed against his, he felt himself grow hard. Frowning, he knew he'd better get a grip on his libido and keep his hands to himself. He had to ignore her because he already had enough trouble to deal with.

He passed her bedroom on his way downstairs but didn't hear any movement. She wasn't in the kitchen and there sure wasn't any breakfast waiting for him. Or coffee.

Scratching his head, he considered his options. He was certain Maisie's and even the bakery he'd noticed the other day was open this early. But, damn it, he wasn't going anywhere. He was paying for a bed and breakfast. If the owner was lax in running her business, he couldn't be faulted for helping himself.

He poked around in the refrigerator, taking out the eggs and sausage links. The meat was nearly done when Summer and Gyp came in the back door. He looked over his shoulder, noticing her face was flushed.

"Morning."

She acknowledged his greeting with a cool nod and headed for the refrigerator.

"Where have you been so early?" He watched her pour a glass of orange juice. The bike shorts she wore showed off shapely, long legs. Her tank top was damp, sticking to her sweaty torso, causing all kinds of erotic images to torment him.

He felt himself once again become aroused against his will and better judgment. He should be getting used to it by now but it was still uncomfortable.

"Running."

Turning his attention back to cooking, he forced a casual attitude. He cracked open a few eggs. "There's the plates. Help yourself. This ain't Denny's."

From the corner of his eye, he saw her hesitate before taking a plate.

While they ate, he kept looking over at her and she kept avoiding eye contact. He tried drawing her into a conversation but she answered his questions with as few words as possible.

He'd never worked so hard to get a woman to talk to him. It surprised him sweat beads hadn't popped out on his forehead.

Once they were through eating, he watched her clear off the table and start to wash the dishes. His imagination once again took over, cruelly teasing him with arousing images of her and him. Together. On the table. Or the floor.

He tried to tell himself he had such a strong desire to have her under him, naked, only because he hadn't been laid in weeks. The trouble was he knew it wasn't true. He'd previously gone sexless for periods of time and hadn't ended up acting like he lived in a cave.

Maybe he really was on the verge of a nervous breakdown. He felt as though he'd become someone else and didn't have an instruction manual.

He couldn't stop himself from walking up behind her, moving close enough for their bodies to touch. Placing his hands on her waist, he rested his cheek against hers even though he felt her stiffen.

"I want to dance with you again," he murmured. He wanted to do much more than dance but then she could probably figure that out.

"You need to understand I'm not part of this town's entertainment," she sharply replied, stepping out of his grasp. "I realize you're probably bored being stuck in this backward town but you'll have to look elsewhere for a little diversion."

"Fine." He snapped. Turning, he left the room without saying anything further.

Damn her, anyway. She sure as hell had responded to him last night. He hadn't imagined anything.

Well, she didn't have to worry. He'd keep his distance and

hopefully tomorrow Harvey would get his ass back and fix the damn car.

He shoved open the screen door, letting it slam in his wake.

When he had said, "There's the plates. Help yourself. This ain't Denny's," Summer might have appreciated his style under different circumstances. Right now she was just too upset.

While she had been jogging earlier, she couldn't run away from remembering the way he held her last night or the way he sang in her ear as they danced. Most of all, she couldn't forget the way he made her feel when he kissed her. All her common sense had simply disappeared the moment he touched her.

It was a good thing he had placed his hand on her butt when he did, shocking her back into reality.

She tried convincing herself she had reacted to him only because she was lonely and he was the first guy to kiss her since...well, she couldn't remember.

She just couldn't be attracted to him! She refused to be. Otherwise, it would mean she was just a silly feather-brained groupie, for God's sake! How humiliating! Because she sure wasn't crazy enough to believe someone like Matt Zeller could be interested in her for anything other than sex. He was bored and needed a little diversion. And she had almost stupidly complied.

She couldn't relax and shrug off last night, which was why she had been abnormally quiet during breakfast. She felt foolish. And, to her horror, she wanted him to kiss her again.

As she finished cleaning up the kitchen, she couldn't stop thinking of the previous evening. He had been downright appealing. Even fun. He'd fit in with the guys easily enough and had even shown he had a good sense of humor.

But she couldn't forget he inhabited a totally different world from hers. A world where recreational sex came as easily to him as breathing. He was a major league player while she hadn't even made the minors.

Remembering the way she'd melted against him made her face grow warm and her breathing quicken. What had possessed her to dance with him? Worse, to kiss him? She couldn't put enough of a spin on the situation to make herself feel any better.

God, she had behaved like a starstruck fan, although she could console herself with the fact it wasn't his fame and fortune that had attracted her. It was him. The way he looked, smelled, smiled. A lifetime of careful control had crumbled the minute she'd stepped into his arms.

She hated that she had not been strong enough to resist him. Of course, he probably considered any attractive woman fair game. She was angrier with herself for going along with the program.

What if Harvey didn't return soon? She put her fingers to her temples and knew she had to make sure he kept his distance. It had been difficult enough to survive in this town. She still had the emotional scars to remind her, not that she'd ever been able to forget for any length of time.

Matt stomped over to Harvey's and, of course, the garage was still closed. Although he didn't know the direction of Howard's hardware store or Bob's dealership, the downtown area didn't exactly stretch out for miles. He knew he'd stumble across one of them within minutes. Common sense told him Ernie's sod farm would be too far to reach on foot.

As he walked by Maisie's, he wished Summer wanted him to look down *her* blouse like Lisa did. But she had teased him with a few kisses, then acted like she suddenly remembered she was a nun.

Maybe he just didn't belong in a small town. In larger cities, there were scores of women who would be agreeable to

64

spending a few hours with him, playing under the sheets. Just some great fun with no strings attached. That's all he'd ever wanted. The only reason he was fixated on Summer was because...because...okay, why *was* he fixated on Summer?

Continuing down on West Oak Avenue, he was too aggravated to appreciate the quaintness of the town. Many of the storefronts had been spruced up, big barrels of flowers adorned the sidewalk and every thirty feet or so a park bench encouraged socializing.

At the first intersection, he noticed Erikson's Hardware a short distance down the block. He nodded a hello to the old-timers congregated on the bench in front as he walked under the green and white striped canvas awning before pushing open the screen door.

Howard sat on a stool behind the counter, reading *Sports Illustrated*.

"Hey. That all you got to do?"

"No, but it's all I'm gonna do," he lazily drawled.

Leaning his elbows on the counter, Matt asked, "Why is your relative so hard to get along with?"

"I take it you mean Sum. Don't worry. That's just an act to keep people away. It keeps her from getting hurt. A lot of people are like that." He turned a page of the magazine.

"You have a girlfriend?"

"Nope." He shrugged. "Used to, until she decided she couldn't stand the thought of living in Haversfield all her life. She got a government job in Atlanta and took off a few years ago."

"Oh. Sorry."

"What are you sorry for? It wasn't your fault. Anyway, as you can see, I survived."

"You run this place by yourself?"

"Mostly. Especially during the winter when my parents go hang out at their condo in Florida."

"Do you get to take off when they get back?"

"Them being gone all winter's all the vacation I need." He added, "I take off every once in a while and go fishing or go on a trip with Ernie. My dad would be breathing down my neck right now if my mom hadn't dragged him off and threw him on a cruise ship. They're floatin' in the Caribbean right now."

Matt lifted his baseball cap to scratch his head. "What do you do for entertainment around here?"

"Entertainment? What's that?" An exaggerated look of puzzlement formed on his face.

Exasperated, Matt shook his head. "Doesn't anybody even have a pool table?"

"Bob's got one. I'm going over there tonight to keep him from slashing his wrists. He hates being alone. Why don't you come with me? He really misses Ruthie but don't mention I said anything or his bottom lip will be stuck out from here to Kansas. I'll pick you up around six. Don't worry about supper 'cause he's gonna barbecue."

When a steady stream of customers demanded Howard's attention, Matt left and wandered over to Adler's Drug Emporium. Inspiration struck while he browsed the stationery section.

He purchased two thick tablets of lined paper and a packet of pencils. Why not take the melody he'd been whistling, put it down on paper and see what he came up with? What better way to spend his time? Well, he could think of one but it was much more preferable with a female partner. If she was willing, that is.

When he stepped into Summer's house, the silence was broken only by the ticking of the grandfather clock in the hallway. He felt both regret and relief she wasn't around.

He settled at the piano, running his fingers lightly over the keys, pleased it was in tune. Soon his troubled thoughts drifted from his mind. The burden of being Matt Zeller and Bill Reese eased as he became just a man working on a song.

Summer used her foot to push the door of her Jeep until it closed. She hated making more than one trip from the car to the house, which was why she was determined to make it to the kitchen with all seven plastic bags. Before she reached the back steps, she heard someone playing the piano. The music stopped for a short time, then began again.

He had evidently taken over the front room. The jerk just assumed he had the run of the house. He sure didn't have the faintest idea how a guest was supposed to conduct himself. None of her other paying customers had ever been so pushy.

None of them ever kissed you and left you wanting more, either. Isn't that why you're upset?

She set a few bags on the porch while she opened the door. She had to fight the impulse to wander in and watch him, which made her question her sanity as she put the groceries away. She fully intended to avoid him as much as possible no matter what psychotic impulses flitted into her empty head.

She decided to leave the first floor to him. She went downstairs to clean the basement.

She worked like a woman possessed, sweeping the cobwebs from the rafters and vacuuming the dust from the floor while doing a few loads of laundry. After she straightened out the storage room, hunger spurred her upstairs for a quick snack.

She'd just finished eating when the doorbell rang. As Gyp barked and raced to the front door, she followed, discovering two older women standing on the porch.

"Do you have any vacancies?" one asked.

"Yes. Come in." She smiled, thinking that with chaperons in the house, it would be harder to make a fool of herself.

She led them into the front room for the registration

process while nervously glancing around. The last thing she needed was her famous, unpredictable guest making himself more at home than he should.

She said a silent prayer of thanks when she saw the piano bench was vacant.

Chapter Nine

"Well, sugar, you decided on what you want?" Lisa looked expectantly at Matt. Lowering her voice to a suggestive whisper, she added, "Or maybe it's somethin' that ain't on the menu."

Oh, God, why wasn't there a fast food restaurant on the corner? Then he wouldn't have to put up with Haversfield's version of Madonna.

"A bacon cheeseburger is what appeals to me right now." He gave her a bland smile, thinking she had to be dimmer than a burned out bulb not to realize he wasn't interested. "And an order of fries."

"You wanna beer?" She scribbled on her order pad.

"No, just water."

After she handed his ticket to the cook, she turned her attention back to him but was interrupted when a group of elderly ladies came in.

"Oh, hell! That damn church group!" she hissed. "Those old bitches can't see the damn menu and take about a day and a half to make up their minds! Now I'll have to shove two tables together."

He watched her walk away, thankful the women had chosen to show up at the right time. He opened the discarded issue of the *Haversfield Times* someone had left on the counter.

While enjoying a Lisa-free meal, he felt so grateful, he wished he could pick up the tab for the church group without drawing attention to himself.

There was a car in the driveway when he walked back to Summer's house, making him wonder if other paying guests had arrived. He hoped not. It was selfish on his part but he liked being the only guest.

On the other hand, it sure would make it easier to keep his hands to himself if other people were around.

As he walked through the doorway, he heard voices coming from upstairs. Stopping at the foot of the staircase to shamelessly eavesdrop, he figured out, from what he heard, Summer was showing two women to their rooms.

He sat down at the piano and began softly playing. He enjoyed warming up with a little classical music first. He was in a Chopin kind of mood today.

He next resumed working on the song he'd started earlier. Trying various chords, he wrote down a few notes on the musical staff he'd drawn on the tablet from Adler's. After a while, he erased a few notes and replaced them with others until he was satisfied.

Nothing soothed his jangled nerves more than his music. Except for sex. And, these days, frequent thoughts of having sex with a certain woman upstairs were working overtime jangling his nerves.

Summer left the ladies to settle in their rooms. When they mentioned they'd be driving over to a neighboring town for dinner, she began worrying about being alone with Matt.

She supposed it was just as well they wouldn't be serving as chaperons. He would probably embarrass her in front of them by swatting her on the butt and calling her *sugar britches* or something.

She took clean linens from the hall closet and forced herself to do what she'd been avoiding. Since he was once again planted at the piano, she felt safe enough to enter his room.

While she cleaned his bathroom, seeing his razor and other personal belongings on the shelf above the sink unnerved her. The lingering fragrance of his aftershave triggered the recently made memory of the feel and scent of him.

As if she had been able to forget for any length of time even the smallest detail of that encounter. It wasn't for lack of trying, either.

She changed the sheets on the bed, praying he would stay downstairs until she was done. She quickly dusted the furniture and vacuumed the floor, constantly worrying he would stroll through the doorway any minute. When she finished, she threw the soiled linens into the hall, gathered up her cleaning supplies and hurried from the room.

Damn him, damn his car and damn Harvey's mother-in-law for picking a most inconvenient time to die.

"Hey, cuz. What's up?" Howard wandered into the kitchen to say hello, noticing his new friend preferred to remain in the front room.

"Not much."

"I'm gonna take Bill over to Bob's. Want to go? We're just going to eat ribs and shoot pool." He watched while she made a salad.

"No, thanks. Some other guests showed up, so I have to get ready for the morning."

He knew better. He wasn't so dense he couldn't detect the tension in the air between her and Bill. Shoot, it was as obvious as a dinosaur sitting at the table playing solitaire.

Whatever the problem, she obviously didn't want to talk about it.

"Well, guess we'll get going. See ya later."

"Bye."

After she heard the front door close, she told herself she was glad he wouldn't be hanging around, making her feel tense. The two ladies had driven off earlier, so she was alone.

She sat at the table and ate while paging through the new J.C. Penney's Fall and Winter Catalog, wondering how she would look in the pencil slim skirt and jazzy top that bared the midriff.

She made a rude noise.

What would she need with clothes like that in Haversfield? Where would she wear them? To Maisie's? Most people in this town considered bib overalls a fashion statement. Besides, it wasn't like she had a real social life. Other than taking off occasionally to spend a weekend with Julie, she spent most of her time hanging with Howard, Bob and Ernie.

Her fork stopped midway to her mouth as her mind chose that moment to recall Julie's frequent warning about ending up alone if she remained in Haversfield. Maybe the reason she'd been so affected by Matt's kisses could be blamed on the lack of men in the area.

Yes, that had to be the logical explanation.

When she finished eating, she decided to take a long bubble bath since she'd have the house to herself for a few hours. She'd soak the tension out of her body while she started the new book she had picked up at the store.

She stretched out in the tub while Gyp settled on the tiled floor for a nap. She opened the paperback, anxious to be swept away from reality into a world of murder.

The men seldom spoke as they made a serious dent in the six slabs of ribs Bob had barbecued to perfection.

"Where's Ernie?" Matt looked at Bob.

"He got himself a date, believe it or not."

"With who? Or what?" quipped Howard.

Bob wiped his hands on a paper towel. "When he went to pick up his new van, there was a new gal working in the office. She handled the paperwork. According to Ernie, he and her yukked it up a bit and when he asked her out, she accepted."

"Well, ain't that a shock? Ernie on a date."

"Now, Howard, that's like the pot callin' the kettle black,

ain't it?"

Matt stopped gnawing on a rib bone long enough to laugh.

"Screw you, Bob." Howard took a long drink of beer before asking, "You ever been married, Bill?"

"Nope. Not me." He shook his head. "I'm not cut out for that sort of thing."

When Summer heard a car in the driveway late in the evening, she got up from the bed to look out the window. It was only Howard's truck. Going back to bed, she picked up her book and resumed reading.

She heard Matt climb the stairs and close the door to his bedroom. She had to keep going back to the beginning of the page because the mental image of him undressing interfered with her concentration.

God, please, she prayed, get him out of town.

She placed dishes of breakfast food on the dining room table while making polite conversation with the guests. Her voice faltered when he entered the room.

His eyes briefly scanned her face before he cordially greeted the ladies and took a seat. Within minutes, the women had drawn him into a conversation about traveling.

As she moved in and out of the room, she grudgingly noted he easily adapted to different people and situations. Telling herself he probably didn't have a sincere bone in his body, she fervently prayed Harvey would soon be busy hammering or welding or doing whatever was necessary to get his car in running condition.

After breakfast, the women drove off to Cairo, Illinois to visit a friend. The town wasn't a great distance away, so they expected to return by early evening.

Matt left a short time later, without saying one word to her. He returned shortly, taking over the piano once again as

73

though he owned the place.

Assuming he probably had no luck at Harvey's, she didn't know whether to laugh or cry.

He worked all day, except for occasional pauses. He had no desire to go to Maisie's for lunch and get a liberal serving of sexual suggestions from Lisa, so he skipped eating except for two blueberry muffins he surreptitiously swiped from the kitchen.

When his hunger pangs could no longer be ignored, he steeled himself for another onslaught of Lisa's sexual remarks and walked over to Maisie's. Seeing Chrissie made him smile with relief.

"The new school year's gonna start soon, isn't it? What grade are you in?" He slid onto a stool at the counter. "Or do you already know everything and don't have to go anymore?"

"I'm a junior." She grinned, continuing to pop her gum. "I guess you need a menu."

He looked up as Howard came in, walking as though he had the weight of the world on his shoulders.

"Hey." Howard sat down and beckoned to Chrissie.

"Hey, yourself. What's the matter with you? You look like somebody just told you there's no sex in heaven."

"Yeah, well there ain't none here, either." Howard nodded at Chrissie as she held up a coffee cup.

"My dad just called for his daily report. You have no idea what a source of migraine headaches he is when he wants to be informed of every little detail regarding the business while he's away.

"How much grass seed was sold? How many shovels? Did the order of topsoil come in? Did I remember to run a sale on lawn mowers? Do I remember to turn on the alarm when I leave at night? I do, even though I can't think of anybody around here ambitious enough to rob anyplace.

"When am I gonna paint the front of the store? Did I order more fishing lures like he told me to? Hell, we're already ass deep in fishing lures! Instead of playing tourist whenever the ship docks, he calls me and tries to create an ulcer long distance."

Matt bit back a grin, sensing there was more to this than met the ear. "It must be hard working with relatives."

"You don't even know the half of it," Howard morosely responded. "When they come home, that's when I really start daydreamin' about runnin' off and joinin' a circus. But when the dust settles, everything gets back on track, somehow."

"You ever think about going into another line of business?"

"Yeah. But around here, the chamber of commerce ain't exactly bulging with new memberships, if you get my drift."

"I guess not." He took a sip of coffee.

"Well, I take it Harvey ain't back yet from burying his mother-in-law. He must be digging the grave himself. You gettin' anxious to hit the road?"

"Not really. I'm enjoying my time here so far." He couldn't honestly say he was anxious to leave. Leave to what? Another town where he would have to remain anonymous? The old Matt Zeller wouldn't have minded but Bill Reese did.

Sure, people were friendly enough in other towns but he'd kept his distance, fearing someone would recognize him. But Haversfield was different. This was the only place he had made friends and felt connected to people. He fit in here. He had formed easy friendships with the guys. And Summer...

"What about your job?"

Matt blinked, looking much like a cartoon character who'd just been hit on the head with a hammer. Oh, that's right! He was supposed to be a salesman.

Thinking fast, he shrugged. "My boss is fairly laid back. Besides, I haven't had any time off in a long time."

He felt uncomfortable lying to Howard, but felt he had no

choice.

"Have you had the fried chicken yet? It's tonight's special. All you can eat." Howard didn't bother to glance at a menu.

"Sounds good to me."

Both men were subdued during dinner, each lost in his own thoughts. Over a final round of coffee, Howard asked, "You coming to Maisie's tonight?"

"I guess. Are you?"

"I don't know. I ain't exactly in the best of moods." He massaged the back of his neck.

"Might cheer you up."

Howard stuck a toothpick between his teeth. Finally, he nodded. "Sure. What the hell else I got to do? Besides, you'll need help keeping Bob and Ernie from gettin' out of hand."

Summer rummaged through her closet for something to wear with her jeans. Choosing a white tank top because she knew it would be hot in Maisie's, she tossed it onto the bed.

She removed the towel wrapped around her head and used a wide-toothed comb to rid her hair of tangles, thinking it was time to get a few inches chopped off.

She fished her seldom used cosmetics out of the top dresser drawer. The only time she fussed with her appearance was when she wanted to strut her stuff out in front of the other people in town who had shunned her at a time it had hurt most. But she was a big girl now. She could take care of herself.

Tonight, the men would come sniffing after her. She might dance with one or two but she would reject any of their attempts to get cozy because, in her opinion, they thought she was just like her mother. In reality, they considered her the sexiest thing they'd ever seen up close and live. And a few did wish she was just like her mom.

She knew most of the women would smile and wave a cool

76

hello before turning to their companions and sharing any detrimental remark about her they could recall or get by with creating in the hopes of elevating their own status with the men.

She did have a few friends around town but not many she really trusted enough to let into her life.

She checked herself in the mirror one last time. Though she was a grown woman, she always saw a lonely little girl staring back. She wished she didn't resemble her mother, although her grandmother had frequently stated she was much prettier than her parent had been.

Her usual attack of nerves threatened to get the best of her when she thought of mingling with the crowd but she forced herself to take deep breaths. She really didn't want to go but she would force herself to walk out the door and attend the fundraiser because Neil Kittle had been a nice guy.

Chapter Ten

Matt laughed at something Howard said. When he looked up and saw Summer standing in the doorway, he felt the air stop in his lungs. He couldn't catch his breath and thought his heart had actually stopped beating.

She had done something to her hair. It looked wilder. Fuller. Longer. And she wore makeup. No one could possibly mistake her for a teenager tonight. She looked like a movie star or a model and, damn it, he didn't like the way the other men were leering at her.

What the hell was the matter with her leaving the house dressed like that?

"Well, lookee there, Bill. Your landlady's here," goaded Ernie.

It took him a few seconds to find his voice. "I got eyes, Ernie." He tried to appear unaffected but the other men guffawed and poked each other like grade school boys.

He watched as she stood there, surveying the crowd until a female voice yelled, "Summer! Over here!" She waved, acknowledging the woman, and made her way to a table occupied by three females and two males.

He only half listened to the bantering between Bob and Ernie, who had his date from the previous night with him but that didn't stop him from the usual practice of trading insults with the guys.

Tipping his beer, he slowly swallowed. His eyes were riveted on Summer, who obviously preferred sitting with a table of strangers across the room. Okay, maybe she did know them but why couldn't she sit right here?

Still smarting from her rejection, he couldn't figure her out. He knew what he'd felt when they kissed and it sure as hell wasn't resistance on her part. So why had she been pushing him away ever since? Just because he put his hand on her ass?

Okay, maybe that wasn't the smartest thing he'd done but how long did she plan to stay steamed at him?

He turned his attention to his companions but kept a watch on her. "She sure is in the wrong business. She's about as friendly as an alligator."

"Now, you go easy on her. She's had a rough life. But she's a good person," informed Bob, causing Ernie and Howard to nod in agreement.

He kept any further remarks about her to himself, knowing he wouldn't get any sympathy from his companions.

The men exchanged idle, often laughable observations about the crowd and watched the people on the dance floor. They drew him into their harmless banter despite his preoccupation with Summer.

Fully aware he was setting himself up for good-natured harassment by the other men, he stood up when the band began playing a slow song. Despite warning himself to sit back down in his chair, he felt brave enough to cross the room.

He came to a stop clearly within Summer's line of vision but she ignored him. What else could he do but grab her arm and haul her onto the dance floor?

He pulled her into his arms. "Hey, sweetheart, you didn't say hello when you came in. That's not very polite."

"Pardon me, Mr. Neanderthal. I didn't intend to upset your delicate feelings."

He laughed and gave her a quick kiss before she could anticipate it coming. He pulled her indecently closer, subtly rubbing his hips against hers in time to the music, and rested his cheek against her temple.

"My, my," he murmured. "Don't you clean up nice?"

"Oh, what's the matter? Not used to women that bathe?" She struggled to put a little distance between them but he had no intention of letting her.

Chuckling, he whispered in her ear, "Smartass."

She didn't want to be attracted to him. She felt like a fish out of water in normal situations but now felt like a goldfish trying to swim with sharks. He was so out of her league, it was phenomenal. And, she reminded herself, he would be leaving soon.

"How old are you, anyway? You old enough to be drinking?"

"I'm twenty-six. Not that it's any of your business," she countered.

"Didn't we already have a discussion the other morning about how rude you are? Can't you be nice? I'll make a deal with you. If you behave yourself just for tonight, I'll give you breakfast in the morning."

She didn't know how he meant that remark but it came out sounding so suggestive, she blushed. She intentionally stomped a booted foot down on his Nike.

"Ouch!" he yelped, stepping away but still keeping her in his arms.

"Oh, was that your foot?" she asked with mock concern.

"If my car doesn't get fixed soon, I'll be in a body cast because of you by the time I leave," he complained.

"If I'm lucky."

He cautiously drew her closer.

She relaxed and foolishly told herself there wasn't any harm in just dancing with him. After all, they were out in public. What could happen?

When the song ended, the band went right into another one and he refused to let her go. He continued to hold her against him, dancing way too closely, although the song wasn't a slow one.

What was wrong with her? He was lewd, arrogant and probably doing more damage to her fragile reputation. She should walk away and ignore him for the rest of the evening.

80

"I like your short hair," she blurted, feeling just a heartbeat away from a psych ward.

He tilted his head back and looked into her eyes. "Did I just hear you give me a compliment?"

"Yeah, well, don't let it go to your head. It's big enough already."

They continued the dance without speaking. When the music stopped, he put his mouth to her ear. "Let's call a truce for tonight, okay?"

Frowning, she looked into his eyes. "I don't know."

She pulled away from him, turned and rejoined her friends.

He had no sooner sat down when Lisa appeared and claimed him for a slow dance. Although she pressed against him and whispered suggestive remarks, his arousal only wanted Summer.

He suddenly knew who Lisa reminded him of. His dear old mom. Just that thought alone made him dislike her even more.

When the song ended, he extricated himself from her grasp and went back to sit with the guys.

"Well, boys, our little Romeo come back. Lisa's been making cow eyes at you all evening while you been rubbin' bellies with Summer," Ernie teased. "I'm surprised once Lisa got hold of you, she let you loose."

He ignored him, nodding for the waitress to bring another round. He tried to focus his attention on his companions, instead of worrying about what Summer was doing.

"The band's pretty good. Where are they from?"

"I think I heard somebody say they're from around here. They just started working," Bob said.

Matt watched Summer dance with three other men. He glanced at her occasionally, hoping to appear indifferent.

"Looks like you got competition, Bill. One of her old boyfriends just got here," Ernie warned.

He swung his gaze to the door. It bothered him to see a

tall, attractive, blonde man standing there. He wanted to smash his fist in the guy's face but didn't recognize the motivation as jealousy because he had never been jealous before in his life.

"Now, wait a minute." Howard wagged a finger. "Daryl's never been her boyfriend, although he's sure been trying hard enough. Years ago, she went out with him once, but that was all.

"Anyway, instead of worryin' about Bill's love life, you better pay attention to your own. Have you noticed your date hasn't come back from the restroom yet? Could be because some guy standing by the bar is flirtin' up a storm with her."

Ernie looked across the room and shrugged. "Hey, if she wants to flirt with someone, who cares? Besides, I don't think she likes to fish."

Laughing, Matt found himself relaxing again.

The band took a break, giving Maisie, a small woman dressed in jeans and a Hawaiian shirt, the opportunity to address the crowd. "We all loved Neil Kittle. He was always the first one to offer his help when anybody needed it. We sure do miss him but we need to do all we can to help out Bonnie and their two boys.

"Dig deep in your pockets and fork over your money. Write a check but if it bounces, I don't need to tell ya'll I'm a hell of a shot with my rifle."

When the laughing subsided, Maisie continued. "Fill up those plastic buckets bein' passed around. Then we'll pass 'em around again. And have some more drinks. Ya'll tend to be even more generous when you're three sheets to the wind."

Maisie laughed along with everyone else before announcing other fundraisers scheduled for the Kittle family during the next few weeks. "Now it's time to get them boys back up here to play us some music!"

While the crowd showed their appreciation for Maisie as

she left the stage, Matt made a mental note to contact his accountant to arrange a sizable anonymous donation.

He looked over at Summer, not liking the way Daryl rested his arm along the back of her chair.

"Maybe I should rescue Summer." He tried to sound casual. Rising, he headed in her direction.

This time when he grabbed her hand, she came willingly. When she stepped into his arms, he briefly considered taking her to her quiet, empty house and seeing what would happen if they picked up where they left off the other night.

Then, for some reason, the "Romeo of Rock" -- not his words but, again, those of the press -- was suddenly stricken with a moral dilemma. Although he couldn't explain it, he didn't want alcohol to influence her decision to be intimate with him.

Damn it. Why did his conscience decide to take a stand now? It normally let him go about his business without interference.

"How many beers have you had?" He looked into her eyes, trying to gauge her soberness.

"I don't know. Maybe two or three. Why?"

Was that enough for her to get drunk? Staring at her intently, he demanded, "Are you drunk? Maybe you shouldn't have anymore."

"Gee, who put you in charge of liquor control? I am not drunk. I can still walk a straight line. Besides, what business is it of yours?"

She had him there. Ignoring her sarcasm, he demanded, "You interested in that Daryl guy?"

She should say yes, knowing it was the smart, prudent thing to do. Then he'd leave her alone and her common sense would start working properly again. She wouldn't have to worry he'd kiss her again and make her wish he'd never stop.

"If those old women you're sitting with told you about him,

they also had to tell you I'm not." She suddenly felt like the old moth rushing helplessly to the forest fire.

Trying to appear unaffected, she stressed, "Not that it's any..."

"Maybe I'm making it my business," he interrupted.

She pretended to scan the crowd while trying to ignore her racing pulse but he pulled her closer. She didn't doubt after the way they'd been dancing together, the town gossips would have ripped her up one side and down the next by morning.

As his cheek rested against her head, she began to mentally list the reasons this should be the last time she danced with him but they came to mind too fast to enumerate.

She had never felt this overwhelming attraction to anyone else before. That alone scared the hell out of her. Especially since he would soon breeze out of town and, by next week, probably wouldn't remember her name.

She knew the impossibility of a relationship between someone like her and someone like him. Mainly because someone like him wasn't looking for a relationship.

Besides, he's a rock star, for God's sake.

Oh, why couldn't he be just a plumber?

Someone tapped Matt on the shoulder, causing him to lift his head. He saw a tall, handsome guy smiling at Summer.

"Mind if I cut in?"

"Yes!" he snapped.

"Be nice." She gave him a disapproving look before stepping into the intruder's arms.

He decided two could play her game. He noticed a pretty brunette sitting alone and asked her to dance. Although he smiled and made polite conversation while keeping his gaze away from Summer, he didn't hold his new partner close nor did he linger with her when the song ended.

As soon as he sat down at his table, Lisa became almost as hard to get rid of as the smell of spoiled meat in a freezer. He danced with her once more while Summer remained with the jerk who had cut in on them.

Finally sensing his disinterest, Lisa momentarily gave up and turned her attention to Howard.

"Bob, who's that guy dancing with Summer?" Matt casually asked.

Bob scanned the dance floor until he spotted the couple in question. "That's Jim Townsend, the town doc. He's been after her, same as Daryl."

Giving him a nudge with his elbow, Bob goaded, "You wouldn't be jealous by any chance? Don't worry. She hasn't given any guy around here the time of day."

When she finally sat down, he briefly looked over and decided he wouldn't dance with her anymore. He didn't need to be panting after some hick chick.

Didn't he have enough aggravation in his life without inviting more?

He needed to regain the feeling of being in control, which he had lost somewhere between first hitting town and now.

He got up to ask the brunette to dance again. What was her name? Dana? Dawn? Debbie?

He glanced at Summer, who was watching him.

Their eyes met.

He walked right by Dana/Dawn/Debbie.

Chapter Eleven

"I'll walk you home."

She gave him a pointed look. "You're going there anyway, remember?"

When they started to cross the street, she stumbled. Grasping her arm to keep her upright, he accused, "You're drunk!"

"You think so?" she giggled. When he scowled at her, she assured, "I'm not. Really." She giggled again. "God! Calm down!"

They reached the house and started up the front porch steps. Gyp stopped barking as soon as she opened the door but immediately sat down and whined, his tail thumping against the floor.

"You didn't lock up when you left?" His mouth gaped open.

She waved a hand in the air. "Nobody 'round here locks doors."

"That's not a good enough reason. Don't you realize what could happen?"

"Here's my baby." She knelt down and hugged her dog. "What a good boy you are. Want to go out?" She rose and headed for the back door.

He slowly followed, feeling ignored.

She went out on the porch. Sitting on the swing, she removed her boots and socks, then wiggled her toes like a child. Sighing, she stared out into the yard.

He remained standing in the shadowy darkness as he watched her. The full moon's eerie light caused her to appear almost ethereal, as though if he blinked, she'd disappear.

He had the insane urge to strip off her clothes and dance naked with her in the moonlight. He wanted to lay her on the grass and make love with such wild intensity, it would take their breath away.

Most of all, he wanted her to want that too.

Moving slowly, he sat next to her.

They were silent as he gently set the swing in motion with his feet. The creaking of the wood and the wind passing through the trees and bushes were the only sounds interrupting the night's quietness.

All he could think of was how much he wanted her. He felt every inch of his body aching with wanting.

He made a weak attempt to get himself under control, but had no real desire to heed any warnings now. He hadn't wanted any other woman this much, in this way. He knew it wasn't horniness but something totally different and frightening, yet something he was powerless to resist.

"Summer?" He turned toward her.

"What?" she whispered.

She feared looking at him, thinking he'd be able to sense how much she wanted him to put his arms around her.

What could it hurt? He would be leaving town soon. Maybe tomorrow. She could give in and have one night of passion. he could worry about her broken heart later.

He reached out a hand to lift her hair off her shoulder. Bending toward her, he pressed his lips against her cheek, causing her breath to catch.

"I really like dancing with you," he murmured.

"I like dancing with you too." she whispered.

As he moved his mouth to cover hers, her breath caught in her chest. His kiss was gentle and slow, but powerfully seductive, making their contact the other night seem totally innocent. He deepened the kiss when she slid her arms around his neck.

"You're not drunk, are you?" His whisper sounded harsh.

"No." At least she hadn't felt drunk until he began kissing

her. The world now tilted crazily, making her head spin.

"You swear?" He moved his hand to her breast.

"I...Oh!...swear."

He slid her top up, exposing her lacy white bra. He nuzzled and kissed her breast through the material while rubbing the nipple with his thumb.

"Matt," she sighed out his name.

"What, baby?" He lifted his head. "God, don't tell me to stop."

She looked into his eyes, knowing that was exactly what she should do. And knowing she couldn't, she ran a trembling hand through his hair.

"You've been driving me crazy since the night we played cards. All I've been able to think about is how much I want you." His mouth returned to hers.

She arched her back when his hand slid between her legs. For the first time in her life, desire and passion became so overpowering, nothing in the world could make her alter the course he was charting.

"I want to be in you."

His words caused her to feel as though her heart and lungs had gone haywire. She couldn't get her breathing regulated.

Didn't he know he was driving her crazy with his hands?

He suddenly stood and grabbed her hand, roughly pulling her up. Wordlessly, he led her inside, walking briskly through the house and up the stairs. He didn't let go of her until they were in her bedroom, the door closed and locked behind them.

She wondered how he could maneuver around so well in the dark. He fumbled slightly but managed to turn on the lamp sitting on the nightstand.

He didn't seem to notice the antique cherrywood dresser and chest she had carefully restored. Maybe because his attention had been snagged by the double bed, covered with the homemade quilt she'd helped her grandmother make.

"I don't do this...I mean, I...," she stammered. She felt embarrassment heat her face, making her wish he hadn't turned on the light.

"Shh. You worry too much." He placed a finger against her lips. "Trust me."

She'd be a fool if she did.

Framing her face with his hands, he gave her a quick but tender kiss before lifting her top over her head.

He unfastened the front clasp of her bra with swift precision but she didn't want to worry and analyze anything but what was happening at the moment. She tugged at his white tee shirt until it was off.

When he pulled her close, she thought she'd die from the pleasure of their naked skin touching. She felt his heart pounding just as fast as hers. His hands glided over her back, then came around to cup her breasts.

"You're skin's so soft." He ran his thumbs over her nipples, his tongue over her lips. "I can't wait to taste you. All over."

He nudged her back against the bed just in time, for her bones had melted. His words, not to mention his touch, fanned the fire he had started inside her the other night.

Never mind that he was dangerous. He would break her heart and she knew it. He would leave, probably without a second thought, yet she felt powerless to stop him because first she'd have to stop herself. And she knew she couldn't. It was too late.

He joined her on the bed, taking her into his arms. He kissed her several times, each kiss becoming more urgent until his tongue parted her lips, seeking entry. She felt his erection stir as he made a trail of hot, terribly potent kisses starting at her mouth, running down her throat and ending at her breasts. His hips began to move suggestively against her, causing her legs to open as if she had no control. She moaned as his teeth gently tugged on her nipple.

"You're so beautiful," he murmured, reaching down to unfasten her jeans. When he couldn't fit his hand down the front of her pants, he impatiently lifted her hips, jerked the jeans and her panties down her legs and tossed them aside.

"You're skin's so soft." He ran his hands restlessly over her, only stopping long enough to quickly pull off his clothes.

Drawing her back into his arms, he began giving her hot, open mouthed kisses. Kisses that made her heart feel like bursting, her body weep even more with wanting.

His hand strayed down to her stomach and kept moving lower while he looked into her eyes. His fingers gently parted her, slowly slid inside and back out to tease her small feminine nub.

"Do you like this?" he whispered.

She opened her mouth but she couldn't speak. Shivering, she began experiencing sensations totally unfamiliar to her but, oh, so wildly sensuous she thought she would faint. Involuntary gasps and moans escaped from her mouth, and soon she made a low mewling sound as something began building inside of her, becoming more powerful with every rotation of his thumb. Her eyes couldn't focus, she couldn't think of anything except what he was doing to her.

She cried out his name. She thought she wanted him to stop because she didn't think she could bear the intense pleasure any longer but knew she'd die if he did.

Instead, he increased the pace of his stroking that little part of her he seemed to know too well.

He crooned into her ear, telling her everything he wanted to do to her. She didn't think she could get any more excited but she was wrong. Her body tensed right before all her control shattered as her entire being was caught up in a wondrously sensual explosion.

He held her close as she floated back to earth.

She wanted more and he didn't disappoint her. He began

kissing and fondling her all over again, coaxing her to run her hands over him as well. She hesitated only slightly but soon couldn't stop running her fingertips over his lean, muscular form. When she tried to put her hand around his erection, he was too big and so hard, for a moment, she was afraid.

"You can't do that right now or I'll never last," he harshly whispered.

He pulled her back into his arms and kissed her. His fingers glided down over her stomach and moved between her legs to toy with the dampness there. His thumb once again created wicked sensations, quickly arousing her until she was wild with lust.

He positioned himself to enter her but could only advance an inch at a time. Midway through, his progress became more difficult. His hips thrust forcefully against her until she felt something inside her tear, causing her to cry out.

"Summer?" Holding himself poised above her, he looked down at her with wide-eyed urgency.

She had instinctively wrapped her legs around his hips as she hugged him close. The pain had been sharper than she'd anticipated but was brief, already ebbing away.

She turned her head but urged in a raw whisper, "Don't stop! Matt, please don't stop!"

"Oh, God, I don't want to!"

He leaned his cheek against hers and closed his eyes, keeping his pace slow. She heard him groan as ripples of pleasure began erupting, causing her to strain her hips upward, wanting him deeper inside.

"Are you okay?" he whispered.

She couldn't speak, could only nod her head.

"Am I hurting you?"

"No. I love what you're doing."

"I'm trying to go slow. Be gentle. But I'm not sure how to...I mean, I've never been with a virgin. I don't know the right

91

way to...well, you know."

A shaky little laugh bubbled out of her. "You're asking the wrong person for advice."

Answering with a surprised chuckle, he lifted his head and looked into her eyes. She smiled up at him, and the awkwardness of the moment vanished.

His eyes darkened with passion as he slid in and then nearly out of her.

"I want this to be perfect for you. So you'll want to do it again as soon as possible. With me."

Sliding his hands under her hips, he lifted her so his thrusts went deeper. She heard her own heartbeat pounding in her ears, felt his heart thundering against her breast. His breathing became labored as he plunged harder and faster, increasing the intensity of the sweet torture until she thought she was on the verge of shattering into a million pieces.

"Come with me," he gasped. "I want you to come with me."

Seconds later, powerful waves of erotic pleasure engulfed her, carrying her to the brink of insanity. She mindlessly chanted his name while savoring every second of the sensual ride.

She became dimly aware he was following in her wake when he shuddered with what she now knew was sweet release.

So, this is what it feels like to give yourself to someone, she marveled. It had been so miraculous and humbling. Surely, it couldn't be like this with anyone else.

Wrapping his arms tightly around her, he rolled to his side, bringing her with him. He moved a hand up and speared his fingers into her hair, holding her head against his neck. They were both panting for breath, their bodies slick with sweat but still they clung to each other.

She wanted to permanently etch in her mind every detail

and sensation of this experience. But, then, how could she forget it?

The pleasure she derived from being held by another human being felt almost as incredible as the lovemaking had been, though in a different way.

It also glaringly pointed out just how lonely she'd been.

Chapter Twelve

"I can't believe you were a virgin." He brushed her cheek with the back of his hand. "Why didn't you tell me? Did I hurt you? I was too rough, wasn't I?"

"No. you were perfect."

"Are you sorry?" He truly didn't want her to regret what they'd just done.

"No. It was wonderful," she murmured against his neck.

"Yes, wonderful. Breathtaking. Awesome. Heavenly." He pressed a kiss into her hair.

He shifted his shoulders so she had to move her head and look at him. He thought he saw a trace of sadness and maybe longing in those beautiful eyes. An alien feeling of protectiveness stirred within him as he placed gentle kisses on her face.

"The next time will be even better."

He couldn't believe after what had just happened between them, her face turned pink.

While he moved one hand in gentle circles on her back, he asked, "How did you come to be the owner of this place at such a young age? Where's your family?"

"My grandparents raised me. My grandfather died when I was in high school and I lost my grandma almost two years ago. Since this place is too big for just me to ramble around in, I thought a bed and breakfast business was a good idea."

He rested his head against hers while considering what she had told him. He could sense she held some things back but he was in no position to criticize.

"Do you get many customers through here? You are off the beaten path."

"There are a lot of festivals and fairs throughout the area starting in spring and continuing all through summer. Since I advertise in the Missouri travel brochures, business is fairly good until late fall."

They were silent for a short while, holding each other close, still reluctant to break contact.

"What about you? Where are you originally from?" she asked, tracing light circles on his chest with her finger.

"Joliet, Illinois."

"Were you always interested in music?"

"No. I was about thirteen when I got hooked on the piano. The music teacher was a big influence on me. We still keep in touch."

He omitted the fact he'd bought Mr. Meyer and his wife a new house, just to show how much he appreciated his kindness throughout the years when he needed it most. God only knew where he would have ended up if that man hadn't taken him under his wing.

"Your parents must be proud of you."

She must not have seen his mother making the rounds on the talk shows. Rather than have the ugliness of his past intrude on the moment, he changed the subject. "Have you always lived in this town?"

She talked about going to college in Cape Girardeau, and then moving to St. Louis. He heard the grief in her voice when she said she'd returned to Haversfield to take care of her grandmother while she battled cancer, deciding to stay after her death because of all the memories the house held.

He gently glided his hand repeatedly over her head while she talked. He couldn't remember ever feeling the need to be tender.

It seemed a thousand different thoughts and feelings rushed through him in a split second. If he analyzed the situation, it would have scared him to death.

One thought kept coming to mind, refusing to be ignored. Years of rational action had gone up in smoke, burned away by the heat of intense desire.

He had used no protection. Hadn't even thought of it.

Violent thunderstorms blew into town before dawn. Lightning streaked across the darkened sky, followed by thunder powerful enough to rattle the windows.

The noise woke Matt. Without thinking, he reached for Summer but discovered he was alone.

A flash of lightning showed her standing by the window, naked. He felt instant desire so strong, it hit him like a sucker punch to his gut. He couldn't believe he wanted her again with an almost overwhelming intensity.

"Hey, you okay? C'mere."

"Come watch. It's breathtaking." She spoke without turning. "I'm glad you let Gyp in earlier. He's terrified of storms. Be careful if you get up because he's under the bed. Sometimes, he stretches his legs out too far."

Matt rose and walked up behind her, sliding his arms around her waist. The blue-white streaks in the sky were wondrous, but another act of nature attracted him more. He pressed his erection against her buttocks.

"You want to experience something else breathtaking?" he suggested. His hands moved over her breasts until he impatiently lifted her and took her back to bed.

He'd managed to find the condoms in his suitcase but the way things were going, he'd need to buy a crate of them. Making love with her was proving more addictive than he could have imagined.

His kisses became more passionate and needy, craving a like response from her. It thrilled him when he felt the pace of her breathing quicken and she gasped for breath.

"Are you too sore? Should we stop?"

She turned her head against his shoulder, as though it embarrassed her to say, "No."

She awoke to the warm feeling of his arm around her. Still enveloped in the heady afterglow of sex, she smiled and cuddled closer to him, thinking his soft snoring sounded comforting.

When she suddenly remembered the two guests, she started to sit up.

"What? What's wrong?" Keeping his eyes closed, he tightened his hold to prevent her from leaving his side. "Stay here with me."

"I can't. Those ladies will be up soon." she whispered.

He slowly opened his eyes. "Are you afraid of what they'll think?"

She sighed. "Not really. Besides, they think you're wonderful. I have to get up and have breakfast on the table. They're planning to be on the road at eight."

His sleepy eyes traveled over her face, noting the whisker burns on her cheeks and chin. Her makeup had either been rubbed or kissed off, causing her to look younger than her years. Her long hair was tangled but damned if he didn't think she was the most gorgeous woman on the face of the earth.

His hand strayed to her breast. "Okay. I'll help you."

"You don't have to." She sat up.

"We'll get rid of them quicker if I do." He pulled her back down next to him and pressed himself against her, giving her a slow, heart stopping kiss.

"Maybe not. Once ya'll start gabbing, they might decide to stay another day," she murmured against his lips. "Why don't you go back to sleep?"

"Right now, sleep is the last thing on my mind."

After she finally showered and dressed, she ventured downstairs to start breakfast, leaving him snoring in her bedroom.

Despite not wanting to think about him leaving, she could

think of nothing else.

Making love with him was a much more ground shaking experience than she had anticipated. He had fluctuated between being so achingly tender at times and then so wonderfully forceful.

Surely he couldn't be like this with every woman he slept with? He certainly didn't act like she was just a one night stand nor did he make her feel like one.

How could she ever have thought she could have one night of passion and then send him on his way?

She couldn't allow herself to fantasize he might be falling in love with her. It would only make his leaving more painful. They were from such different worlds, they may as well be from different planets. Their lifestyles were drastically opposite. She meant nothing to him except a temporary diversion. She could never have him. Even if she could, his interest would eventually stray.

He was just a milder version of her mother, wasn't he? And she didn't need someone like that.

She told herself all these things, but her heart begged for a second opinion.

When the guests came downstairs, it amazed her she could carry on a conversation and appear calm. Matt, thankfully, remained upstairs and hopefully wouldn't appear until the ladies left. Not that she feared they'd recognize him. She worried more about him grabbing her for a morning kiss right in front of them.

She had to keep her personal life private. Did he understand that? She didn't need departing guests telling others about the "hot little number" running the B&B in Haversfield.

After the women had checked out, she sat in the kitchen drinking coffee. She was on her third cup and still hadn't managed to swallow the lump in her throat brought on by the thought of him breezing out of town. If Harvey had returned, maybe today would be the day.

Why did reality always have to be so harsh?

When she began to make a fresh pot of coffee, he strolled into the kitchen. He came up behind her and kissed the top of her head.

"Morning."

"Morning." She tried to keep any hint of sadness from her voice.

Oh, this was a great mess she'd gotten herself into, wasn't it?

"There's a paper on the table, if you want to check out the news."

"I'd rather check you out."

Smiling, she asked, "Want some pancakes?"

"Sure."

She hid her feelings, but grew more worried about herself. She didn't want him to leave even though he wasn't anybody at all she could take seriously. Except in bed.

The longer he stayed, the harder it would be to watch him go. She was hanging on by her fingernails as it was.

And she had no one to blame but herself.

Chapter Thirteen

"I guess the rain's letting up. You'll probably want to find out if Harvey's come back."

He didn't respond as he slouched at the table, drinking his coffee while he watched her wash dishes. She had been quiet during breakfast. Too quiet. And it appeared her feelings for him had definitely cooled.

He wondered if he normally appeared this casual and aloof after a night of sex with his previous bed partners. Giving himself a mental shake, he silently chided, *what's wrong with this picture?*

"I guess I'll call him," he finally said. "You know his number?"

"It's written on that list next to the phone."

He walked over to the phone and looked for Harvey's number. Lifting the receiver, he punched out the numbers and didn't relax until he counted the tenth unanswered ring. He hung up keeping his voice neutral as he spoke. "No answer."

Someone knocked on the front door, causing Gyp to run and investigate. Summer followed.

"Sheriff Calvert. What brings you here?" she asked, holding the door open.

"I'm here on business. I need to question your guest, if you don't mind."

"What about?" She felt a tingling sensation on the back of her neck.

"Seems Lisa Harkiss was found dead in her car this morning behind Maisie's. We think she may have been raped. We'll know more after we get the coroner's preliminary results. Some people think this fella staying here may know something."

Matt heard their conversation as he sat in the kitchen. He

struggled to control his frustration. Was he going to be a suspect in every rape and murder committed in whatever state he happened to be in at the time, regardless of what name he was using?

"He couldn't possibly know anything about this."

The sheriff's eyes settled on Matt as he walked up beside Summer.

"You were in town last night, weren't you?"

"Yes," he responded, forcing himself to be polite.

"I can swear to you he was here in the house all night."

"Just because he's renting a room from you don't mean you can account for his whereabouts every second," the sheriff tiredly commented.

Matt remained silent, refusing to say anything that would put Summer in an embarrassing position.

"Oh, but you're wrong." She folded her arms across her chest. "He was with me every single minute of the night. All night."

Her bluntness made Matt wince. Putting a protective hand on her shoulder, he hissed, "Shut up!"

Calvert was momentarily speechless. Regaining his composure, he said, "I suggest you don't leave town. We may need to question you later."

"Fine," Matt coolly replied.

Calvert turned and left.

"What'd you go and say that for?" Matt's hands balled into fists at his sides.

She turned to face him, placing her hands on her hips. "Because it's the truth."

"Don't you know what kind of gossip you've just opened yourself up to?"

She waved her hand, dismissing his concern. "It won't be anything I'm not used to." She turned and headed back to the kitchen.

He slowly followed, wondering about her remark.

She started to dry and put away the dishes while he sat at the table, glaring at the newspaper.

His emotions were churning. Damn! Why the hell did he have to land in this town where everyone knows everything about everybody else? More importantly, why did he have such strong feelings of protectiveness toward Summer?

Most of all, he wanted to know why he was acting like some lovesick teenager who had just gotten his first taste of sex.

He roughly turned a page of the paper while cursing his car for breaking down. Well, it served him right. Instead of touring redneck America, he should have gone to Jamaica or Aruba and flopped his ass on some beach until his name faded from the headlines.

He glanced up from the newspaper he wasn't reading. He should have kept his damn hands off her. Now, the whole town will be talking about what a slut she is before the day was over.

Never mind she had given her wholehearted cooperation, eagerly participating in her deflowerment. Hell, she'd taken to sex as enthusiastically as a drug addict getting that first taste of heaven and anxiously looking forward to more.

The image of her with someone else after he left popped into his head. For a few seconds, he found it hard to breathe and his chest hurt. He had absolutely no explanation for the emotions he was experiencing. Or why.

She tossed the dishcloth onto the counter. Walking over to him, she slid her arms around his neck. "Let's go upstairs. You said you had more things to teach me."

His frustration, simmering since Calvert's visit, erupted. Rising, he pulled her roughly against him, crudely reaching a hand between her legs. "Sure, sweetheart. Maybe now that you know how much fun you can have in bed, you'll give some of the guys in town a chance after I'm gone.

"By the way, how come I'm the first man you spread your legs for? You're dazzled by my personality? Or is it my star status and big bucks that make you quiver?"

A shocked look appeared on her face as her mouth dropped open. He didn't think it was possible to look hurt and stunned at the same time but she did. Shoving against his chest to free herself, she stepped back, her arms rigidly pressed against her sides, her hands clenched into fists.

Before he knew it, her roundhouse punch caught him squarely in his midriff with more force than he thought her capable of.

He doubled over, hugging himself while gasping for air.

"Christ, Summer," he wheezed.

"You son of a bitch!" she spit out before turning on her heel and running upstairs.

Still hunched over, he sat down at the table and waited for the pain to subside. When he could breathe normally, he muttered, "Apparently, I don't need a scandal and reporters to screw up my life. I can do just fine on my own."

She remained in her bedroom for the rest of the afternoon. By evening, Matt, feeling more repulsive than a cockroach, went upstairs and knocked on her door. When she didn't respond, he tried turning the handle but it was locked.

"Summer, c'mon. I'm sorry. I didn't mean it. Please open the door." When she still didn't answer, he resorted to whining, "Gyp's hungry. I don't know where his food is."

After a full minute of silence, the door flew open. Her eyes were swollen from crying, her nose red from blowing. He suffered a fresh wave of guilt as she pushed by him and headed downstairs.

"Honey, c'mon! I'm sorry," he pleaded. Catching up with her as she walked into the kitchen, he grabbed her arm. "Damn it, I didn't mean it!"

"Keep your hands off me!" she snarled, jerking free of his

grasp.

"Well, at least you're talking to me."

He grinned sheepishly and leaned against the counter, quickly folding his arms across his chest. If she was going to punch him again, he was going to be ready this time.

She fed the dog and, without saying a word, grabbed her purse and keys before storming out the back door.

He ran after her, ordering, "Come back here! We need to talk! I apologized! What else do you want?" He caught up with her, grabbed her shoulders and turned her around to face him.

"I told you to leave me alone. I'll be more than happy to call Calvert back to drag your ass out of here."

Her menacing tone caused him to release her. He wasn't sure she would really call the sheriff but he was in no position to call her bluff. Feeling helpless, he watched her back out of the driveway and head down the street.

He scrubbed his hands over his face and wished he could start the day over.

As he walked back into the kitchen, Gyp looked up at him with what could only be described as an accusatory glare.

Chapter Fourteen

She'd been gone for over an hour. Matt knew it had been that long because he'd agonized over each minute as it passed.

She had to know she was making him crazy.

When he couldn't stand waiting any longer, he stomped over to Maisie's, mad at the world but mostly at himself.

Howard was there alone, eating dinner. Matt slid heavily into the other side of the booth.

As Howard shoved a fork loaded with chicken fried steak into his mouth, he studied Matt a short while before asking, "Why're you acting like someone just broke your favorite toy?"

He made a rude sound as an elderly waitress came over, slapped a menu down and left. Staring after her, he said, "You know, I'm thinking God must be a woman. Who else would make females so screwed up just to aggravate men to death?"

"I take it you and Sum aren't getting along?"

He glared at Howard, who stopped cleaning his plate long enough to laugh. "Okay. We won't talk about it."

After taking a cursory look at the menu, he shoved it aside.

"You hear about Lisa?" Howard asked.

"I not only heard about it, your sheriff considers me a suspect," he complained.

Howard frowned while he considered this bit of news. Waving his fork for emphasis, he said, "Oh, don't worry about that fat tub of lard. Calvert's been watching too many reruns of *Matlock*."

"Easy for you to say. He didn't come nosing around you."

"Daryl probably got him stirred up. Maybe he figures he'll get rid of you one way or another. He probably considers you a threat to his plans to get Summer. Even though that's never gonna happen 'cause she don't want no part of him. Townsend either." Howard turned his attention back to eating.

Matt motioned for the waitress. When she arrived at the booth with an attitude, he said, a little too sharply, "Give me what he's having," as he jerked his thumb in Howard's direction.

"You want a beer too?" she demanded, pushing her glasses up her nose.

"Yeah," he replied, but she was already walking away. "What's she so damn happy about?"

"Oh, that's Maisie's sister. She's just filling in until someone is hired to replace Lisa." Taking another mouthful of food, Howard added, "Even though Lisa was the closest thing to a town tramp we could come up with, it's still a shame what happened to her."

"Yeah."

"So you gonna tell me why you're acting like you been screwed and not even kissed?"

Matt hesitated. Did he really want to reveal anything about his personal life? His answer came when a strong feeling of trust, combined with the need to confide in someone, urged him to throw caution to the wind.

He spilled everything, starting with the death of the seventeen year old girl in his apartment and ending with the sheriff's visit.

However, instead of saying what he and Summer had really spent the night doing, he said they stayed up just talking. He told Howard they had gotten into an argument after breakfast over something stupid and she wouldn't listen to reason, which, he reasoned, was sort of the truth. He had said something really stupid and now she wouldn't listen to him.

"I might be a country boy but I'm smart enough to figure out there's more to just talking between you and Sum. Otherwise, you wouldn't be so pissed. Besides, I saw you two on the dance floor last night, rubbing against each other so much I was surprised sparks didn't set the damn place on fire.

Let me clue you in, so maybe you'll understand her a little. She and I are cousins so I know what I'm talking about."

Pausing to wipe his mouth with a napkin, Howard continued. "When her mother was nineteen, she quit college and ran away to San Francisco to become a hippie. She was a few years too late but, just like Timothy Leary had preached, she tuned in, turned on and dropped out. She had Summer when I was three years old. Anyway, her mother didn't know or care who the father was.

"When Summer was pretty young...maybe two months old...her mom hitchhiked from California and brought her back here, staying long enough to sign over custody to her parents. After that, she used to breeze through town once or twice a year and stay long enough until she'd sufficiently embarrassed her family by screwing anybody left that she hadn't screwed during her last visit. I think Sum was about seven when her mother overdosed on heroine."

Howard took a sip of beer. "Well, you can imagine the kind of scandal her visits always caused in a town like this. When she started school, most kids were kind of mean to her but she always held up her head and tried to ignore them. Poor Sum. She had a rough time but rarely complained.

"She was pretty even then. A lot of people always held her mother's actions against her and certainly never let her forget what kind of woman her mom had been. But Sum's the most decent person I know. She's got higher morals than those ladies sitting their asses in the pews over at Midwestern Baptist Church every Sunday." Howard paused to take a bite of food.

"Her grandparents raised her. They were good people and tried to make up for what she never got from her mom. That's their house you're staying in. Her grandpa died of a heart attack when Summer was in high school. Her grandma died about two years ago from lung cancer. Her grandpa was my grandma's brother. My parents and I are the closest thing to family she's got left, except for some guy who was present at her conception and don't even know he's got a daughter.

"I sincerely hope you haven't done something to upset her or anything. 'Cause I like you and I'd really hate to have to kick your ass," Howard added rather casually. The look in his eyes said he was serious.

"Hey, I don't want no trouble. I'm just passing through. And I certainly don't want to cause her any grief because you're right, she is a decent person." He took a slow sip of beer. "Besides, I don't want to end up fighting you. ne punch and you'd go down. Where's the fun in that?"

"Screw you, glamour boy." Howard resumed eating.

"I can trust you to keep what I told you to yourself, can't I?"

Howard gave him a disgusted look. "I ought to kick your ass for even asking that."

When Summer first left the house, her only desire had been to get away from Matt. If she didn't have a business to run, she would stayed away until he'd left town.

It served her right to be hurt like this. She had walked into his arms with her eyes wide open despite knowing she should never, never have let him touch her.

But the damage was done and she couldn't turn back time.

What had possessed her to think she could have one passionate night with him, no strings attached? And why had she thought last night meant more to him than just a night of sex? Just because she wanted it to?

She had learned at a fairly early age not to trust people too readily. Anytime she had let her guard down and thought she could be just like everybody else, the rug was pulled out from under her, tossing her on her butt, crying.

Throughout her school years, she had felt the tacit

implication by many of the town's people that, somehow, she was inferior and would probably grow up to be white trash, just like her mother. So, like a turtle, she had grown a hard, outer shell for protection.

She rarely had been invited by the other girls to sleepovers or parties. A lot of the boys had asked her out but, after too many times wrestling with a date who did not take her rejections seriously, she no longer dated. She had, however, developed necessary skills at warding off unwelcome advances.

The only time she ever felt normal was when she had been away at college, where she didn't have the cloud of her mother's past affecting her relationships. She had felt lighthearted and free, although she still held herself to a stringent moral code. She had dated frequently and even had a periodic boyfriend or two but had never fallen in love enough to engage in sex or even fantasize about marriage.

When she graduated with a degree in marketing, her four years away from town had foolishly given her the impression things would be different when she returned. But they weren't.

Her solution was to move. She got a job with an advertising firm in St. Louis. While living there, she kept in constant touch with her grandmother and they frequently visited back and forth since they were only two hours of highway apart.

It was devastating when her grandmother was diagnosed with lung cancer. Summer had quit her job and moved back home to care for her but it took less than a year for the illness to claim its victim.

And now she wondered what was wrong with her. After all the heartaches she'd been through during her life already, why had she set herself up to get her heart broken by Matt?

That question triggered a fresh supply of tears.

Matt Zeller, of all people. He'd probably screwed over half the women in the U.S. and, for all she knew, still had a thing going with Brandy Cole. He was probably used to breezing into town, grabbing the nearest agreeable female for some adult recreation and then blowing her off when he hit the road again.

How pitiful that she had willingly become just another conquest.

God, could she be more pathetic?

Without realizing it, she had driven to the isolated little cemetery surrounded by acres and acres of fields.

She parked her Jeep and walked over to the Taylor plot. As she knelt down to remove the wilted flowers she had placed on the grave last weekend, despair overwhelmed her.

"Oh, Grandma! Why didn't you ever give up those damn cigarettes years ago? I miss you so much."

She burst into tears.

Chapter Fifteen

Matt walked back from Maisie's and, seeing the empty driveway, felt even more guilt wash over him now that he knew about Summer's childhood.

He wished he had access to a car, although he wouldn't know where to begin to look for her. He ended up waiting on the front porch. Gyp acted reluctant to share his space but decided to wait there too.

He checked his watch, which he seemed to be doing every time he breathed. She'd been gone two hours and seventeen minutes.

What if something had happened to her? These dark, winding country roads could be dangerous at night. People drove with no regard to the speed limit. He imagined a dozen terrible scenarios that could have occurred until she finally pulled into the driveway.

She drove all the way to the back of the house. To avoid him, he guessed, as he opened the front door and went inside.

Too bad what she wanted. He had to apologize before he drove himself crazy.

When she walked into the kitchen, he and Gyp were there waiting. She petted Gyp briefly, completely ignoring Matt's existence.

"Summer, please. I'm sorry for being such an ass." Somehow he had to make things right between the two of them before he left town. He didn't want that wounded expression haunting him.

She placed her purse and keys on the table, refusing to meet his gaze. "The minute Harvey has your car running, I want you to leave." Her tone was listless, her face void of expression.

She turned and left the room.

"Please, just listen to me." He followed right on her heels but wasn't brave enough to reach out and touch her.

She rushed up the stairs and into her bedroom, slamming and locking the door.

He stood there in the hall, wondering what to do. Wishing there was someone to tell him, because he certainly didn't have a clue.

His experience with women didn't cover situations like this. If he'd ever made an ass of himself with a woman in the past, and he was sure he had, he never before had cared. Now, he did.

Returning to the kitchen, he took a soda from the refrigerator and sat at the table, hating the heavy silence.

A guilty conscience was one hell of a burden.

Matt tossed and turned all night, sleeping very little. He was too uncomfortable in the bed, more uncomfortable in his own skin.

He noticed the sun rise and light up the room since he had forgotten to pull down the shades last night.

It was useless to remain in bed, although he was exhausted. He wanted to see Summer yet dreaded another encounter.

Shirtless and barefoot, he went downstairs after shrugging on a pair of jeans. He found her sitting at the kitchen table, drinking coffee and reading the newspaper.

It was no surprise she didn't look up when he entered the room.

"Good morning." He thought he sounded calm. Reasonable. The exact opposite of the moron he'd been yesterday.

She ignored him.

He looked around. Obviously, she had no intention of making breakfast. There was no sign of any food. Just coffee.

How long was she going to carry this out?

Okay, he was a bastard for what he'd said yesterday and how he'd acted. As soon as Howard had told him about her past, he'd realized just how damaging his remarks had been. But he hadn't known at the time his comments would be so grossly inappropriate.

"Hey, this is a bed and breakfast place. Get it?" Maybe he could make her mad enough to argue with him. Maybe if she hit him, she'd feel better. He sure would.

She picked up her mug and took a sip, seeming completely deaf.

"Don't you think you may be over reacting?"

When she still didn't respond, he walked closer to her chair, softening his tone of voice. "Maybe I was a little upset yesterday because you seemed too anxious to get rid of me. You seemed disappointed when Harvey wasn't around to fix my car."

Since she hadn't punched him yet, he felt safe enough to edge closer. Lowering his voice again, he said, "Maybe I was hoping you liked the idea of having me around a little longer. Maybe I'm not ready to leave you even if Harvey does show up and fix the damn car."

Although she didn't speak, he knew from her expression she was listening. She had quit reading the newspaper and stared straight ahead.

He carefully took the mug from her hand and set it on the table, keeping his movements slow. "C'mon, Summer. Accept my apology. I'm really, really sorry."

She cleared her throat. "I don't know. Maybe..."

Moving as quick as lightning, he scooped her off the chair and threw her over his shoulder. She beat on his back with her fists, and yelled for him to put her down but he headed for the stairs.

Christ! She was deliberately aiming for his kidneys!

Matt cursed under his breath when he heard a knock on the door. Though she landed some powerful blows on his back, he refused to let her loose. Especially since she had started to laugh.

He stopped at the foot of the stairs and turned to face the front door, which stood open.

"Sorry to interrupt." Daryl's voice caused Matt to let Summer slide down his body until her feet touched the floor. "This is official business."

Looking through the screen door, he saw Daryl's uniform and disgustedly realized he must be a deputy.

"What is it?" He knew his tone was sharp but, damn it, he resented the interruption.

"Well, it seems we got a little problem that you may be able to help out with. If you would consent to some tests, then maybe you can clear yourself."

"Clear himself of what? Wait a minute, Daryl! I've already vouched for his whereabouts. I know exactly where he was and what he was doing when Lisa was killed." She then demanded, "And what kind of tests?"

Daryl stared at Matt. "We need samples of your semen and hair."

Her eyes flew to Matt's face when he said, "Sure. Take whatever tests you want to, cowboy. I got nothing to hide."

"No! Maybe you should see a lawyer first," she firmly suggested.

"I don't need a lawyer!" he exploded. "I haven't done anything."

Besides, if he spoke with a local attorney, his true identity might come out and then reporters would swarm into town like locusts. Prying into everyone's lives around here. Especially Summer's.

She stood on tiptoe and whispered in his ear, "I know you didn't! But he might try to pin something on you."

114

"Relax." He put a hand on her shoulder. "He's going to look like an idiot because I'm innocent."

"You want to accompany me to the doctor's office?" Daryl's tone was sarcastic.

"Fine." Matt stuck his chin out.

"No, I'll drive you," she insisted.

"No, I don't want you involved in this," he countered.

"Tough. I'm driving you," she flatly stated before she turned to Daryl and demanded, "Is he being charged with anything?"

"Not yet. I'm just checking out the possibilities," Daryl replied, an arrogant smirk plastered on his face.

Matt clenched his fist, wishing he could plant it in the middle of the deputy's face.

Though he quietly submitted to the tests at Jim Townsend's office, he was seething inside.

When Daryl wanted him to stop in at the sheriff's office and make a statement, Summer became belligerent, saying, "Then you must want one from me, too, since I can swear in court that he was with me. I'll even submit to a lie detector test."

"Okay, Summer, we need a statement from you, too!" Daryl snapped.

"Want some lunch?" she asked, when they finally returned to her house.

Matt had been silent during most of the ride back. Instead of brooding about being unjustly accused of the murder in New York and now here, he worried about keeping her from becoming fodder for the town gossips.

She'd suffered enough while growing up. He didn't want to cause her any more heartache.

"I thought you said you only provided breakfast." He decided to lighten the mood.

She shrugged. "I know what I said, but I'm hungry and as long as I'm making something, you might as well eat, too." She opened the refrigerator. "How about roast beef sandwiches?"

"Great." He had to admit she was one classy lady. Not only did it seem she'd forgiven him, but she'd readily verified his whereabouts to Calvert and that bastard Daryl, instead of protecting her reputation.

They shared a pained expression when someone knocked on the front door while they were eating.

"It's just me, Sum. I guess that dumb shit Daryl's busy trying to stir up some more trouble," Howard spoke as he made his way to the back of the house.

"Oh. I guess you heard." She watched her cousin enter the kitchen.

"You know gossip travels fast in this town. If someone belches, it's on the front page of the *Haversfield Times*."

Howard placed a six pack of beer on the table before he took a seat. "I figured you could use a couple of brews about now," he said to Matt as he eyed the food. "You got any more of this stuff, Sum? Think you could make me a sandwich?"

"Sure. I need practice in order to fulfill my lifelong dream of becoming a waitress." She wrinkled her nose at him before getting up and walking over to the refrigerator.

"What was I thinking when I told Matt you were nice? Uh, I mean Bill."

"You know who he is?" She spun around, her eyes wide with surprise.

"I told him," Matt calmly informed through a mouth full of food.

"Why?"

"Why not?" he shrugged.

"Don't worry. I ain't about to throw myself at him. Personally, I don't think he's that cute." Howard pulled out a chair. "Now, you gonna stand there and watch me starve to death?"

Howard hung around until early evening. His visit had lessened the tension considerably and, by the time he left, Matt and Summer were more relaxed.

She started cleaning up the kitchen while he watched.

"Hey, Summer?"

"What?" she answered over her shoulder as she rinsed off the dishes.

"Know what I thought of to help me give that semen sample?"

"I don't think I want to know."

"Your lacy underwear."

"Pervert."

He walked up behind her, reached over and turned off the facet. He bent his head and rubbed the side of his cheek gently against hers, while he slid his arms around her waist.

"I haven't thanked you for going with me today, although you really shouldn't have. I don't want you mixed up in this."

"No thanks is necessary." Her voice sounded shaky.

Moving his hands up to her breasts, he murmured softly against her ear, "Does this mean you've forgiven me?"

"I guess." She sounded breathless.

"You're not mad at me anymore?" He inched his fingers under her tee shirt and bra. Palming her breasts, he lightly flicked her earlobe with his tongue.

"No." he word drifted from her mouth.

He slowly removed his hands and turned her around to face him. Before she knew what was happening, he hoisted her over his shoulder and laughed.

"Isn't this where we were before being so rudely interrupted?"

While she slept peacefully in his arms, he tried to make sense of his emotions. He was rapidly developing feelings for her he had never felt for any other woman. Hell, he always preferred to keep his distance. Especially after sex.

Just that alone should have him running in the opposite direction. Instead, the thought of leaving her depressed him. It made no sense because he wasn't a forever kind of guy. But he still didn't want to leave her. Not yet.

Sex with her wasn't sex. It was paradise. He still couldn't believe he'd wanted her so much, he hadn't used any protection the first time. Passion, desire, lust -- whatever it was had driven all common sense from his mind. He'd been too anxious to put his hands and mouth all over her.

Magazine articles often referred to him as a womanizer. He couldn't disagree because, in truth, he'd earned the reputation since becoming famous. What was wrong with having a brief fling with any of the gorgeous babes he met? He wasn't against having a little fun in bed with an agreeable partner but if she wanted anything other than a short fling, forget it. He didn't trust women, an obvious aftereffect of his childhood.

His distrust had been reinforced when a couple of lawsuits had been filed at different times by women who'd claimed he had fathered their babies. Those obvious attempts to obtain money for nothing angered him. When he'd demanded to take a paternity test, each woman had backed off and disappeared. Because he always practiced safe sex, he was confident of any test results. Never forgetting from whence he came, he never allowed the heat of the moment to overpower the need to use condoms.

Until he'd met Summer.

He still couldn't figure out what had happened.

Long before the murder in New York and ensuing media madness, he had grown tired of meaningless affairs. Coming from such a background as his, he didn't have much faith in love but he'd learned recreational sex never brought lasting satisfaction. There was something missing in his life; he had a deep-seated hunger but hadn't been able to figure out what he wanted.

The only thing he did know was life had become very confusing. And, he again thought, he wasn't ready to leave her.

So, why go until it was absolutely necessary? What was wrong with staying right where he was until he had to be in New York for rehearsals before his tour started? By then, he and Summer would surely grow tired of each other and his thinking would return to normal, wouldn't it?

Believing he'd sorted his jumbled thoughts, he felt better. Yawning, he shifted positions slightly, bringing her closer to him until he drifted off to sleep.

Chapter Sixteen

Gyp pawed Matt's arm until he woke. Reluctantly, he left the bed, careful not to wake Summer. Pulling on his jeans, he went downstairs to let the dog out.

After he started a pot of coffee, he wandered out to the back porch, enjoying the peacefulness of the early morning. The breeze carried the sweet aroma of the honeysuckle blooming on the fence.

He chuckled, remembering how angry he was when his car picked this area to quit. He'd been enjoying himself ever since landing in Haversfield, except for the investigation into Lisa's murder.

Hanging out with Howard, Bob and Ernie had been an added bonus. He couldn't remember when he'd laughed so much. Those guys were great.

As for Summer, well, spending every day and night with her was becoming addictive. If he wouldn't be sued by the record company and wouldn't be letting the guys in the band down, he'd blow off the tour and stay here for however long he wanted.

He didn't want to think about what that meant.

He heard the kitchen door open. Turning, he watched her walk out onto the porch. He held his arms open and she walked right into them, laying her head on his chest.

"What are you doing up so early?"

"Gyp needed to go out. You looked so peaceful, I didn't want to disturb you so I got up." He kissed the top of her head. "Did you miss me?"

"No."

"Liar."

Smiling, she tipped her head back so she could see his face. "It's nice to wake up and smell fresh coffee brewing.   never would have thought you were so domestic."

"Well, I am a bachelor."

"Yeah, right. Like you don't have a dozen people waiting on you."

"I don't," he said, sounding defensive. "I have a cleaning lady but I don't like anyone else hanging around my place."

"Oh." She stepped away from him. "Coffee's done. I need a dose of caffeine."

He and Gyp followed her in.

"What made you tell Howard who you really are?" She asked as she poured two cups of coffee.

"He just seems like the type of guy you can trust," he shrugged, taking a seat at the table.

"He is." She handed him a cup before sitting next to him. I'd trust him with anything."

"He said he wouldn't tell anyone and I believe him." He sipped his coffee. After a short silence, he let out an exaggerated sigh. "I guess if I'm going to get any breakfast around here, I'd better make it. How about some eggs? And bacon?"

"That sounds wonderful. I kind of like being waited on. Do you need a job?" she teased.

"Sweetheart, you can't afford me."

Her laugh warmed his heart.

While he cooked, she asked, "Where does your inspiration come from?"

"I don't know. Sometimes, an idea comes out of the blue. I can't usually just sit down and come up with a song. It can't be forced. When I get a melody or words running through my head, I try to write it down and then work on it."

"Do you ever get stage fright before a concert?"

"Not as much as I used to. I get a little nervous right before we go on, but once we start playing, it goes away."

"Are you looking forward to your tour? Do you like

traveling?"

"I'm anxious to see if the ticket sales are down because of all the bad publicity. It's not the money issue that bothers me; it's the principle of the thing. It's one thing if your music loses popularity, but it's a whole different matter to have your career ruined by something you didn't do." He dropped bread into the toaster. "As far as traveling, I'm getting tired of it."

"Are you and the band members close? I mean, are you really good friends?" She got up to refill her cup.

"We're not good friends but we all get along fine. Vinny's my best friend. He's not in the band. He and Gina, his wife, are like family. Well, they *are* my family. As a matter of fact, I need to call them soon."

"How did you guys meet?"

Matt paused a moment, wanting to tell her the truth but still reluctant to share that part of his life with her. It still made him feel a sense of shame despite knowing he had no control over his parents' actions years ago.

"We met growing up. In the old neighborhood." At least it was the truth. Just not all of it.

"Vinny got my career rolling. He hounded me until I entered my band in a contest a radio station was sponsoring. We won and got a recording contract."

He piled food on two plates while she got out the silverware.

She buttered the toast. "What about your parents? I think I remember seeing something about an interview with your mother but I don't watch much television."

"That woman may have given birth to me but I don't claim her. I don't claim the man who fathered me, either." He put serious effort into eating, grateful when she didn't push the subject. "What about you? Are Howard and the guys your closest friends?"

"Here in town they are. Julie's my best friend. She lives in

Poplar Bluff. She thinks I should sell this house and move there because, according to her, there's nothing to do here but watch the grass grow."

She paused to take a bite of food.

"I used to have a really good friend that lived next door to Ernie. Grace Teasdale. Actually, she and Ernie were together constantly since they learned to walk and talk. You rarely saw one without the other. The three of us spent a lot of time together."

"What happened?"

"I don't remember everything but Grace's father caused a big scene when we all were in high school. He found Grace and Ernie alone at the clubhouse they'd built years before. I think they were making out and Mr. Teasdale barged in, drunk as a skunk. He wouldn't let Grace see Ernie after that."

"Why didn't Ernie see her when her dad wasn't around?"

"I don't remember all the details. I just know that Ernie never mentioned her after that. Grace never mentioned Ernie either. Personally, I think she's the reason he hasn't married or has seldom really dated anyone steadily. Anyway, Grace and I were friends in high school but she never talked about what happened. She would never come to my house because she thought Ernie might show up. She became kind of a loner after that. She hung out with me occasionally but that was the extent of her socializing. After graduation, she went to college in Chicago and stayed there after she got her degree. We used to keep in touch a lot but now we only exchange emails occasionally."

They lingered over several cups of coffee after they were finished eating, talking easily about anything other than family.

He took her hand in his. "Since you were a virgin, I guess you're not on the pill."

"No. I wasn't very sensible the first time we...," Her voice trailed off. As her face reddened, she stared down into her coffee.

"It was my fault." He put an arm around her. "Before I met you, I *never* forgot to use protection. I wanted you so badly, common sense flew right out of my head."

Summer gave him a shy smile.

"You don't have to worry about catching anything from me." He didn't know if she'd thought of it. "I was given a clean bill of health right before I started off on this trip and I haven't been with anyone else since I was tested."

She fiddled with the silverware, appearing uncomfortable with the conversation. Her inexperience and lack of guile charmed him. She was such a refreshing change from the women he usually encountered.

That must be the reason he was in no hurry to leave. It helped having a rational explanation for his emotions.

"I guess I need to go out somewhere and buy condoms. Want to come along? You might see something you like." He twirled an imaginary mustache.

She primly replied, "No, thank you."

"Can I use your Jeep?"

"Sure." She chewed nervously on her lip. "Please don't buy them anywhere in town or people will...well, you know. There's another drug store right off Route 17, about six miles south."

"Everyone already probably knows, thanks to you telling the sheriff we spent the night together." He dug into his back pocket, took out his wallet and checked his money. "You need anything?"

"Nope."

After he made the trip to purchase birth control, he decided to stop in and bother Howard for a minute, but spotting the florist across from the hardware store made him want to get something for Summer.

He parked but remained in the car, trying to figure out

124

what was happening to him.

They had known each other for just a few days. He'd never cooked for a woman before. The times he'd bought flowers for someone had never involved any desire on his part to please. There had always been a reason, like a forgotten birthday, and the flowers were just a means to get someone off his back.

He had a vast amount of sexual experience with women but he had had no emotional investment in any of those affairs. They were brief and forgettable.

Maybe that was why he felt so awkward sometimes with her. In many ways, he was no more equipped for a relationship than a high school kid.

He felt downright silly, so he went to see Howard, who was actually busy with customers.

Matt poked around, inspecting the selection of hand tools while he waited.

"What's up?" Howard finally walked over to him. "Summer throw you out or you ready to blow this town?"

"Neither. Just thought I'd drop in and nose around."

"In that case, make yourself useful and help me move this display rack up to the front. I'm running a sale on flower bulbs and topsoil so my dad doesn't have a coronary on the cruise ship."

As the men moved the cumbersome stand near the front window, Howard asked, "Harvey back yet?"

"No."

"I think you're glad."

"What do you mean by that?"

"Contrary to local opinion, I ain't stupid." Howard looked him in the eye. "She's growing on you. Admit it. If she wasn't, you'd be pulling your hair out because you're stuck in this town. Just remember, she's special. She isn't what you're probably used to. I don't think she's all that experienced and I think you're growing on her. Just make sure you don't hurt her."

"I have no intention of hurting her." His irritation was evident. "I have feelings too, you know."

"Hey, simmer down. I like you." Howard lightly punched him on the shoulder. "It's just that, well, I like her better. We're family, you know."

The moment Matt walked into the house carrying two dozen pink roses, Summer embarrassed herself by bursting into tears.

Oh, sure, she'd received flowers before, but these meant so much more.

"Oh, Sum," he murmured, wrapping her in his arms. "If I'd known you'd react like this, I would have gotten you a candy bar instead."

They spent the rest of the afternoon in her bedroom, making love and napping. When someone called to make reservations for the next two nights, he muttered an obscenity.

"Damn. I don't want other people hangin' around here." His dismal expression made her laugh.

"In case you forgot, I am in business to make money."

He studied her for a few seconds. "Do you make enough? Do you need anything?"

"No. I'm doing okay." She didn't know whether to be touched or insulted.

She didn't feel it was appropriate to exchange information regarding their financial portfolios. Her grandfather had left a sizable insurance policy when he died. Howard's father had talked her grandmother into investing it wisely and, as a result, she was comfortably secure. Not rich but comfortable.

"You're doing more than okay." Matt grabbed her and gave her a sloppy kiss, making her giggle. "You're just so damn cute."

"Who gave you your first kiss? How old were you?" he

126

asked, wrapping her in his arms.

The memory caused her to smile. "Larry Fielding kissed me during fifth grade recess. I gave him a black eye."

He laughed. "I mean, your first real kiss."

"Hmm. Keith Burke. I was fifteen."

"And?"

"He took me to a dance at school. When he brought me home, we sat in his car and he kissed me."

"Did you date him after that? What happened?"

Sobering, she said, "I went out with him a few times but that was all."

She wasn't about to volunteer the rest of the story. After a few dates, he had wanted to take their innocent kissing to a much too advanced level. When she refused, he taunted her with insults and said everyone knew she was just like her mom, so why was she holding out?

Just thinking about that made her angry. It had been the first time she fully understood how much her mother's reputation had impacted every phase of her life.

"How about you? Let me guess." She looked at him slyly, wanting to shift the focus away from her past. "You were probably around eight! You said you'd never been with a virgin, so just how old were you when you were led astray?"

"Thirteen."

"God! Thirteen? How old was she? Did you like her?"

"Sherry Lee Alvers was sixteen. Let's just say everybody liked Sherry Lee."

"Does that mean what I think it does?"

"Yeah." He nuzzled her ear and breathed in the scent of her hair. "I really like the way you smell." He lightly kissed her. "As a matter of fact, I kind of like you, Summer Taylor."

Chapter Seventeen

"This article says the response to the band was so favorable at the fundraiser that Maisie hired them to play every Friday and Saturday night. They started last night," he commented from behind the local newspaper.

"Gee. Progress comes to Haversfield. When will it stop?" She drained her orange juice and decided she'd eaten too much for breakfast.

"Want to go tonight?"

"I have to wait for the people coming sometime after dinner. But after that, sure."

She spent the rest of the morning getting things ready for the expected guests, while he cut the grass. She hadn't wanted him to, especially when he told her he'd never mowed a lawn before in his life, but he seemed so enthused, she didn't have the heart to refuse his offer.

She breathed a sigh of relief when he finished, thankful he hadn't run over one of his feet or destroyed her flowers.

When she started cleaning the kitchen, he went for a jog after complaining he'd been eating like a pig since landing in town and needed to work off some weight.

Just thinking about his inevitable departure brought tears to her eyes. Although they hadn't known each other very long, she had never felt this way about anyone else. She knew it wasn't because he was the only man she'd slept with. It wasn't that simple.

The reason was, despite every warning she gave herself, she had been helpless to stop herself from falling in love with him.

She was going to have to think of this time they spent together as just a brief affair, although it pained her to think of it like that. What choice did she have, though? She was sure once he left, he would continue his usual life style with no looking back.

Just thinking of him making love with someone else made her heart hurt. She wanted to howl with the pain of it. Somehow, she had to shove the thought aside because there was no room in Matt Zeller's world for someone like Summer Taylor.

She just hoped when he finally left, she wouldn't cry hysterically until after he was gone.

While Matt sprinted around town, he felt peaceful. Of course, being Bill Reese had a lot to do with it since he'd put the problems of Matt Zeller, the murder investigation, the media and his mother on the back burner.

He smiled and waved at the people he had become acquainted with.

Wouldn't the press get the disappointment of a lifetime if they knew he was happily doing such ordinary things as jogging around Haversfield and hanging out with the locals? Or that he wouldn't trade an hour of Summer's company for that of any other female in the world?

His pace slowed when he thought of his attraction for her. Attraction wasn't a strong enough word but he refused to believe he was falling in love. They didn't know each other very long or very well. They had opposite lifestyles. Each had a scarred childhood, which he was positive would eventually sabotage any relationship between them.

But what was he thinking, anyway? A relationship? He'd been avoiding those for years. They didn't really have a relationship. They had no future because he had always known he wasn't cut out for the happily-ever-after sort of thing.

He wondered if she'd be hurt when he left but already knew the answer. For her sake, he should pack his things and hitchhike out of town today.

The bigger issue was that he didn't want to leave.

The guests were a middle-aged couple traveling back home to Iowa after spending a week in Baton Rouge visiting relatives. They arrived right after dinner.

While Summer got them settled in, Matt watched television in the family room. As soon as she was free, they were going to decide what they wanted to do for dinner. Earlier, she had suggested driving out along the old County Road to a new restaurant everyone was raving about.

Gyp started barking before Matt heard a car crunch over the gravel in the driveway, making its way to the back of the house. A car door slammed, forcing him to get off the couch to investigate.

Just as he neared the back door, he was startled when a young woman walked into the house. She wasn't as tall or as beautiful as Summer, but she was attractive. Her short, dark hair emphasized the wonderful bone structure of her face but her eyes looked puffy, as though from crying.

"Julie!" Summer rushed into the kitchen and threw her arms around the woman. "What a surprise!"

Stepping back, she looked at her friend's face. "What's wrong?"

"John and I broke up," Julie set a small suitcase on the floor. She noticed Matt standing there and looked at Summer. "Oh, I'm sorry. You have a guest. I should have called first."

"Don't be ridiculous. Sit down. This is, uh, Bill." She bit her bottom lip, then quickly added, "Bill Reese! He's...he..."

"Her boyfriend," he interrupted, extending his hand. "Summer's told me about you. I'm glad to meet you."

He almost laughed at the stunned expression on Julie's face as she shook his hand. He glanced over at Summer but she looked just as dazed.

Well, he had surprised himself with the explanation of his

130

presence. The words had shot out of his mouth like a cannonball. It would make matters worse if he tried to take them back.

Julie released his hand and sat down at the table.

"Maybe you two would like to be alone for a while?" He looked at Summer, who nodded. "I'll be upstairs. I need to call Vinny, anyway." He gave them a quick smile before leaving the room.

"Do you want something to drink?" Summer finally regained her composure. After all, just because he said he was her boyfriend didn't mean he really thought he was. He was probably merely protecting his identity.

"Yeah. A bottle of bourbon and a straw." Julie sighed.

"What happened?" She poured a glass of wine and pulled up a chair to sit beside her.

"I was wondering why John never took me to his apartment. So, this morning I got his address from the internet and paid him a visit. He was supposed to be sick. At least that's what he told me last night when he called and said he wouldn't be coming over. Anyway, to make a long story short, a woman answered the door. She was wearing a man's robe."

"God! What did you do? Did you ask her who she was?"

"No. John doesn't have any sisters. And she sure wasn't dressed like a cleaning lady."

"Did she say anything? What happened then?"

"I heard John yell, 'Who is it, honey? Get rid of them. Come back to bed.' That pretty much said everything." Julie sniffled. "I just left."

"Oh, I'm so sorry. But you're lucky you found out what a louse he is now."

"How could he lie like that? It wasn't like I was madly in love with him. We hadn't even been intimate yet, thank God. I just feel like such a fool for believing anything he said." She got a fresh tissue from her purse and blew her nose.

"What's the deal with this Bill? You didn't mention anything about having a boyfriend. How long have you two been seeing each other?" Julie narrowed her eyes. "Why haven't you told me about him?"

"I...uh...we haven't been seeing each other very long. He doesn't live in town, so he's been staying here."

"He's really attractive. You know, he looks familiar. Did he go to college with us?"

"No." She deliberately changed the subject. "Are you hungry? I'm starving. Bill and I are going out to dinner and you're coming with us." She then said a silent prayer and hoped she wouldn't slip and call him Matt.

"Oh, no. I'll feel like a third wheel."

"Oh, bull."

Later, they ended up just walking over to Maisie's since it was well past eight o'clock by the time they were ready.

Daryl was eating dinner by himself. He nodded a stiff greeting as they entered the restaurant.

After they settled into a booth, Julie commented, "That guy over there seems to be smirking. What's his problem?"

Summer glanced over at Daryl, but then shrugged her shoulders. She didn't say anything about Lisa's rape and murder, but Matt did. He added, "Howard thinks Daryl wants to cause me grief because he wants Summer all to himself."

"Oh, let's change the subject," she suggested. Soon she and Julie began entertaining him by recalling harmless escapades from their college days.

Julie asked about his job. He briefly answered her questions but shifted the attention back to her by asking where she worked. She described her position in the Human Resources Department at Harkins-Meeker, a chemical company fifteen miles southeast of Poplar Bluff.

When they finished eating, Summer and Matt insisted Julie accompany them into the bar.

"I've already screwed up your date enough, haven't I?"

"Oh, shut up." Summer scanned the crowd, waving when she noticed Howard and Ernie. "Let's sit with them."

"Let's not."

"I don't know why you and Howard don't like each other but it won't kill you two to be polite for one evening," she scolded Julie.

"What've you guys been up to?" Ernie asked when they sat down.

"Not much," Matt replied. "Where's your girlfriend?"

"Who knows? And she's not my girlfriend."

"What brings you to our little one horse town? Slumming?" Howard taunted Julie. His voice held too much sarcasm to be taken for good-natured teasing.

"Yes. I wanted to see if you knew how to use your newly installed indoor plumbing," she retorted.

Howard shot her a disgusted look.

Matt said, "This one's on me," when their drinks arrived. After paying the waitress, he tugged on Summer's hand and led her away for a dance.

Just like the other night, even though the song wasn't slow, he pulled her close.

"What's the story with your friend and Howard? I take it they don't like each other?"

"I don't even know why. When I was in college, Howard came to visit a few times. The three of us spent a lot of time together and they got along great at first. But one time he showed up unexpectedly and I had a date, so he and Julie went out together. I don't know what happened, but ever since, they want to kill each other. Go figure." She shrugged.

"We didn't like each other at first," he reminded, then whispered something wicked in her ear. She was glad the lighting was dim so people couldn't see her blush.

After the song ended, they went back to the table but Ernie

133

and Julie joined the line dance to *Boot Scootin' Boogie*.

"Look at Ernie go!" Matt laughed.

Howard made a rude comment, then walked off and struck up a conversation with an attractive blonde.

Matt stared thoughtfully at him for a short while before turning his gaze to Summer. "Well, I think I know what's wrong. Howard's got a thing for Julie."

"Yeah, right. You're crazy."

"That may be, sweetheart, but I know what I'm talking about."

She looked at her friend on the dance floor and then over at her cousin standing by the bar talking to the blonde. "I don't believe it."

Howard danced several times with the blonde but didn't bring her back to the table. Meanwhile, Julie was asked to dance a number of times by different guys. During the entire evening, Howard and Julie ignored each other completely.

Around midnight, Matt and Summer wanted to leave. When they told Julie, she decided to stay and hang out with Ernie. They waved goodbye to Howard, who was on the dance floor with a brunette this time.

They made a point to be extremely quiet as they entered the house, even though Gyp was barking in the back yard. Summer went to let him inside.

She tried to stifle a yawn. "I have to get up early, in case the guests want breakfast. Maybe I'll go to the bakery in the morning for some sweet rolls."

"That's what you're serving them for breakfast?"

"That's basically what a lot of bed and breakfast establishments serve. See how lucky you are?" she teased.

They held hands while they climbed the stairs. He quietly closed the bedroom door behind them. "People around town probably know what's going on between us."

"So?"

134

"Doesn't that bother you?"

"No."

"I don't want to cause you any trouble."

You won't until you leave, she thought. Then, I'll probably be suicidal.

Chapter Eighteen

Sunshine streaming through the windows heated his face, rousing him from sleep. Looking at the clock, he saw through blurry eyes it was after nine-thirty. He remembered Summer had guests, which explained her absence.

After dressing, he went downstairs and found her in the kitchen, drinking coffee and eating Danish pastries with Julie.

"Morning," he said, leaning down to kiss her. "Where are the travelers?"

"They decided to leave early so they could spend a day or so in St. Louis."

He poured himself a cup of coffee and sat down. "Okay. Where's the real breakfast?"

She pointed to the bakery box on the table. "Those look real to me."

"So, did you enjoy yourself after we left?" he asked Julie. "How late did Howard and Ernie stay?"

"We all stayed until the place closed. I was telling Sum that Daryl came in and asked me to dance. He always gives me the creeps whenever I run into him while I'm here. He asked me all kinds of questions about how long you were going to be in town and if you and Summer were serious."

"He's an untrustworthy bastard." His lip curled in disgust. "I'm beginning to think he really does want to pin Lisa's murder on me. That'd be one way of getting me out of the way."

Summer waved a hand in the air, dismissing his remark. "Even if all the men in the world disappeared except for Daryl, I still wouldn't be interested in him."

"He makes my skin crawl." Julie shuddered.

"Why? What did he do?" Matt asked.

"He always looks at me as though he's imaging what I look like naked. I bet he looks at all women that way. Not that he's so different from most of you jerks but he's so obvious. Last night he made a few suggestive remarks I pretended not to understand." She made a face. "I wanted to smack him across the face."

As they watched Julie drive off later, Matt suggested they barbecue since the temperature had climbed to 80 degrees.

"Sure. Sounds good to me."

While they were at Farley's Grocery Store on the edge of Haversfield, he tossed his favorite foods into the cart as they strolled up and down the aisles.

The store hadn't changed a bit as far as Summer could recall even though it was well stocked with all the latest products.

She was surprised he seemed to be having as much fun as a child in an amusement park. He selected enough different kinds of food to feed a family of four for a month, not to mention a good supply of junk food.

Claire Hobsen, the cashier, raised a censuring eyebrow at her and took her time passing the items over the electronic scanner, the store's most obvious acknowledgment of advanced technology. Her pointed gaze drifted from Summer to Matt, then back to Summer.

Matt watched Summer, who, instead of looking the judgmental bitch in the eye, seemed to become suddenly absorbed in the latest issue of *People*.

She paged through the magazine but he would bet she was actually recalling painful incidents from her childhood. Maybe Mrs. Hobsen hadn't thought she was good enough to socialize with her daughter or date her son. He wanted to yell right in the woman's face for causing her even a moment of anguish but he knew Summer wouldn't appreciate it if he did.

He quickly fished money from his wallet to pay the tab despite Summer's repeated protests.

She was silent as they loaded the bags into the Jeep. When

137

they were on the road, he looked over at her. "Why do you let someone like her rattle you so much?"

"This is a small town." Looking down at her hands, she shrugged.

"So? You have nothing to be ashamed of." When she didn't respond, he continued. "There's always some people who think they're better than everybody else no matter what size the town is."

She still didn't say anything. He wished she trusted him enough to tell him about her background, even though Howard had already told him the vital parts.

He reached over and cupped her chin in his hand, turning her head so she was facing him. "Hey, c'mon. I've noticed there are a lot of nice people in this town who like you. Don't be so sad because of one woman's ignorance."

"It's okay. I'm fine."

By the time he had the steaks on the grill in the backyard, her mood had improved. A glass of wine had helped.

"We'll eat on the patio," she said, with the first hint of enthusiasm he'd heard in hours. "I'll set the table."

He looked over at the wrought iron table and chairs while she went inside. He turned his attention back to cooking. When it was time to eat, he saw that she'd placed a flowered cloth on the table, which was set beautifully with fine china and crystal candleholders. She'd also made a salad and baked potatoes.

He was extremely solicitous and entertaining throughout dinner, amusing her with several stories about different encounters with his idols in the music industry. She laughed when he spoke of being so nervous when he first met Eric Clapton, he'd called him "Ma'am."

He described the first time he was on stage with Robert Plant and Tina Turner at the Grammy awards. So awestruck in the presence of such great artists, he couldn't wait until the show was over so he could get their autographs.

"They had to think I was the biggest geek in the world," he laughed.

After they finished eating and fed the dog the generous scraps, they carried the dishes into the kitchen. When they went back outside and sat on the porch swing, he pulled her against him. They watched Gyp curl up in the corner.

Matt set the swing in motion with his feet, surprising himself by saying, "I used to wonder what it would have been like to grow up in a decent family and live in a nice neighborhood. Even a small town like this. I'd have given anything to have had a normal childhood with loving parents and maybe a brother or sister to fight with. A mom who baked cookies and chased away the monsters that hide in the closet at night. A dad who had coached the baseball or soccer team. Who had maybe taken me fishing."

She didn't turn to look at him, but cautiously asked, "What was your childhood like?"

"It was the stuff nightmares are made of. My mother was a prostitute, having the maternal instincts of a park bench. I don't know if she's still in the profession but, then again, I don't care. I was barely out of diapers when she started bringing men home, not caring what I might see. She didn't care if I'd eaten all day or had clean clothes.

"I learned early on -- I can't remember if I was three or four -- to keep quiet and not ask for anything. She didn't need much of an excuse to give me a busted lip or black eye."

She was horrified to learn when he desperately needed a mother's loving kindness, he'd received cuts and bruises. Once, a broken arm; another time, a cigarette burn on his chest. Tears came to her eyes as he continued.

"I guess you've wondered about my scars, though they've faded over the years."

"They aren't really noticeable." She softly asked, "What

about your dad?"

"My father, or what I remember of him, had worked to maintain a steady relationship with alcohol and other women. The main thing I clearly remember is he always smelled of cheap liquor and cheaper aftershave. He seldom was home and often disappeared for weeks at a time.

"The day he came home long enough to pack his clothes and leave forever was not any more memorable than any other. He hadn't bothered to say goodbye but that was fine with me because I'd been more acquainted with the neighbors than with him."

He breathed a little raggedly, as though recalling the experience was still too painful.

"I never understood why my parents had bothered to get married in the first place. Oh, I knew my mother had gotten pregnant with me, but, in retrospect, Dawn Weist and Jim Zeller never struck me as the kind of people concerned with appearances. They certainly hadn't been concerned about their marriage or me.

"They were my parents, yet I always felt so disconnected from them, I used to pray someone would tell me I was really adopted. But when the social workers came to remove me from my mother's custody, I was devastated to learn I really have their blood running through my veins."

"Did one of the neighbors complain? Was that why you were taken away?" she gently asked.

"No. I started running with a bad crowd. By the time I was seven, I was shoplifting and skipping school. When the authorities got involved, I thought somebody was finally going to make my mom act like she should. Instead, I was taken to my first foster home."

He described the heartache of dealing with the events in his life and how he always felt tainted, that somehow he didn't deserve anything better.

140

"She has a lot of nerve appearing on talk shows, saying I'm not helping her with her bills. One of these days, someone is going to confront her with the truth. Maybe then she'll crawl back under whatever rock she calls home." He leaned his cheek against her head.

"Obviously, she hasn't changed. Do you ever think about confronting her?" she asked.

"No. What would be the point? Besides, one good thing came out of living in foster care. I met Vinny there. His parents had been killed in a car accident when he was eight. He said up until then, they'd been so happy, Disney could have made a movie about them.

"His mother's brother and his wife took him to live with them but their two kids made Vinny's life hell. When he was around fourteen, he was in a gang that operated a car theft ring. That's when he was put in the same foster home where I was. At first, we hated each other but soon became friends. More like family, actually.

"Mr. Meyer, my music teacher when I was thirteen, noticed I had an ear for music. The first time I plunked out a tune on the piano in his class, I was addicted. He gave me free lessons for years. He kind of took me under his wing. I spent a lot of time at his house. I used to pretend he and his wife were my parents.

"Anyway, I was a few years out of high school with my own band when Vinny hounded me to enter a contest he heard about. I told you a little about this the other day. Each band had to have original songs and lyrics and I wasn't confident the ones I'd written would win. But we did win. The prize was a recording contract and the rest, so they say, is history."

When he finished speaking, Summer turned and rested her cheek against his chest. After a short silence, she unburdened the story of her own personal heartache.

He didn't mention that Howard had told him most of it.

Instead, he gently stroked her hair until she finished her account of growing up without the love of a mother and father and having to live down her mom's reputation. She said she was thankful to have had such wonderful grandparents and wished he had had relatives to provide the love and support every child needs.

When she finished, they silently remained wrapped in each other's arms, each lost in their own thoughts. After a short while, he wanted to lighten the mood. He actually did feel more at peace than he ever remembered feeling. Maybe talking about the darkest days of his life had lanced the wound and bled out the heartache.

"Say, let's break open the ice cream. Want to?" He gave her a light swat on her backside.

For the next week, the world was a perfect place. Although Summer had to tend to the details of her business as guests came and went, she still spent most of her time with Matt.

Their shared confidences brought a new dimension to their relationship. Fellow survivors of basically the same war, they had a better understanding of each other. It also made them freer to be themselves and the playful side of their personalities surfaced more often.

Whatever they did, they couldn't stop touching each other. Sometimes their lovemaking was tender, other times intense and erotic, but it was always incredible

With every minute of each passing day, she fell more in love with him.

Bob's wife, Ruth returned from St. Louis, so he wasn't seen much except for an occasional lunch at Maisie's.

Howard seemed quieter than usual, often ignoring opportunities to make one of his sarcastically funny remarks. When Summer commented on his behavior privately to Matt, he only said that further convinced him Howard was mooning over Julie.

As the week came to an end, Harvey returned to town.

And William Tyler Reese's placid existence ended.

Chapter Nineteen

They had just returned from walking Gyp when the phone rang. A feeling of dread danced over Summer's heart as she watched Matt take the jug of ice water from the refrigerator. She slowly picked up the receiver.

"Hello?" She listened briefly. "It's Harvey."

She handed the phone to him. Walking over to the counter, she adjusted the cover on the toaster before deciding to make coffee. Not because she wanted any but it was something to occupy her shaking hands.

She prepared the coffeemaker, then leaned back against the sink. She folded her arms and tried to smile when he looked at her but her face felt rigid with suppressed emotion.

She knew this day had been coming. And she had no illusions about what would happen. He'd leave, her heart would break and she'd spend the rest of her life trying to forget him.

"Okay. I'll be there in a little while." He gently placed the receiver on the hook. He stood for a minute, staring at the phone as though he'd just been informed of a death.

"Harvey fixed my car," he finally said. "I'll walk over and get it, okay?"

"Yeah." It surprised her she could speak. The lump in her throat hurt so much, it had to be as big as Texas.

When she heard the front door close, she let the tears fall from her eyes.

He's going to leave me. He's really going to leave me.

She allowed herself a few minutes to cry, all the while remembering the warnings she'd given herself and ignored.

She'd known the risks, known there was a price to pay for behaving so foolishly. Well, now it was time to pay the piper and she didn't want to.

144

Is this how you want him to remember you? You'll have years to cry after he's gone.

Forcing herself to get a handle on her emotions, she went over to the sink and splashed cold water on her face.

By the time she heard him return, she had better control over her feelings.

"Summer?" He called as he walked in the back door.

"In here." She had settled in the family room. Picking up the remote control, she turned down the volume of the television.

She hoped her face didn't look as ravaged as her heart felt. More importantly, she prayed he didn't suspect she'd just had a mini breakdown.

He entered the room and studied her face. Frowning, he sat next to her and pulled her into his arms.

As Sheriff Calvert looked over the test results, Daryl felt his opportunity to arrest Summer's playmate for the rape and murder of Lisa slip farther away.

"Maybe he had something to do with it, anyway."

"No he didn't. And if you go and question him one more time, he should hire a lawyer to charge you with police harassment." Calvert turned his attention to the ringing phone.

After a brief conversation in which he mostly listened, Calvert replaced the receiver.

"Seems the state's department of motor vehicles has a problem verifying the information on Bill Reese's driver's license and car registration. They claim William Tyler Reese, III is dead."

"I knew that bastard couldn't be trusted!" Daryl's exuberance launched him from the chair. "I'll go arrest him!"

"You'll do no such thing," Calvert warned, rising from his chair. He fished in his pocket for keys. "I don't know why your tail's in such a twist over this Reese guy, or whoever he is. But this all might be a mix-up. I'm going over to talk to him."

"At least let me go with you."

"All right. But keep your mouth shut," Calvert admonished.

Gyp's barking stirred Summer and Matt, who had been watching television before drifting off to sleep in the family room. When the barking continued, Summer groaned.

"I'll see if anything's wrong." Matt got up from the sofa and headed toward the front door.

When Summer heard voices, she tried to figure out who was at the door, prayed it wasn't someone wanting to rent a room.

After a short while, he returned, his expression grim.

"What's wrong?"

"Calvert wants to haul me in for having improper identification. Looks like my cover's about to be blown to hell."

He removed his wallet from his back pocket and took out a business card. "He and that jackass Daryl are waiting for me. I need to call my attorney."

A few hours later, Summmer watched the helicopter circle, then hover until it descended onto the field, the strong wind from the blades disturbing the tall grass. She had suggested this spot for secrecy because it was near the graveyard, an area she knew would be deserted.

She watched a sharply dressed, middle-aged man hop out as if he regularly made such a landing. It was at that moment the vast disparity in her and Matt's lifestyles truly hit her.

Oh, not that she hadn't thought of it before. She had spent considerable time thinking of the many ways their lives differed. She had told herself it was just a bizarre fluke he ended up in Haversfield. Ended up in her bed.

But somewhere in all her musings, against all logic, a seed

of hope had sprouted in her heart. Unrealistic hope that fate had led him to her. That he would fall madly in love with her. That he'd never leave. That he wouldn't want to.

Now, with each step Hugh Parker took toward her, reality doused that spark of hope.

Matt's identity would soon be discovered. Besides, he had to leave to resume his real life. Away from her.

"Ms. Taylor? I'm Hugh Parker." He stopped before Summer.

She nodded a greeting.

"It was kind of you to offer to serve as my chauffeur."

"Haversfield has no rental car agencies."

"So I discovered. As we discussed on the phone, it was important to get here as soon as possible and air travel, though faster, leaves me without transportation. I need to get Matt out of this mess as quickly and quietly as possible before the media finds out."

Mr. Parker gestured toward her Jeep. "Shall we get going?"

Sheriff Calvert listened to Matt, in the presence of his lawyer, explain his desire to obtain obscurity from the relentless media attention.

Calvert was no fan of rock and roll -- other than Elvis and the great Jerry Lee Lewis, of course. But, after the initial surprise over the suspect's true identity, he grudgingly sympathized with the star.

He wasn't buying the part about him not knowing the identity of the man who provided the falsified license and car registration. He didn't believe for one second he was some guy Matt allegedly met in a bar one night.

However, he was smart enough to know if he threw whatever charges he could at Matt, his high priced attorney would come up with a way to legally paint him as the biggest buffoon that ever walked the earth. Just thinking about that idiot Daryl up on the witness stand sent chills down his back.

To avoid a media frenzy, it was agreed Matt would be heavily fined.

When Daryl realized the bastard was going to breeze out of town after only having his wrists slapped, rage ate at his insides.

Or what was left of his insides jealousy over Summer hadn't consumed.

Murmuring an excuse about having to check on something, he left the room and walked out of the station.

Summer and Matt took Hugh back to the helicopter and stayed to watch it take off. Both were unusually quiet, not discussing the lawyer's strong advice that "Bill Reese" needed to leave town immediately before it was discovered he was Matt Zeller.

A heavy quietness engulfed them as they drove back to her house and continued after they walked into the kitchen.

He didn't have a clue how to handle this situation. He'd never had to say goodbye to a woman he didn't want to say goodbye to.

Was this love? No, it couldn't be. He cared for her but this wasn't love. He just wasn't cut out for that sort of thing.

"Unfortunately, Hugh's right. I should hit the road, otherwise reporters will soon be swarming all over the place. Good thing he talked Calvert out of confiscating my car."

He ran a nervous hand across his brow. Jesus, he felt like crying. He never imagined leaving her would be this hard.

"Yeah. Good thing," she softly answered.

"Then I guess I'll go upstairs and pack." He waited. He didn't know why because he didn't know what he expected her to do or say. Beg him not to leave?

She stood still, a slight smile frozen on her face.

Since he couldn't think of a better idea, he finally turned and went upstairs.

He felt as stiff as a robot as he mindlessly gathered up his stuff from the room he'd continued to rent to keep up appearances in front of the paying guests. He shoved his things into his suitcase. Before closing it, he went into her bedroom to check if he'd left anything.

He opened the door and, seeing the bed, wondered how long it would take before the memories of being with her would fade. How much time would it take to rid his senses of the feel and taste of her?

She was a floor away yet his loins ached with wanting her already. How many miles would he have to travel before this intense hold she had over him eased?

How much time would have to pass before he forgot what it was like to take an evening walk around town, her hand in his?.

Would he ever be able to dance with another woman without thinking of her?

Giving himself a mental shake, he removed everything that was his and returned to his bedroom, briefly wondering why they'd bothered to keep up the appearance of separate bedrooms.

He closed his suitcase.

He hadn't been prepared for such an emotional departure. Maybe becoming Bill Reese hadn't been such a great idea. He'd pretended to be someone he wasn't and now was mixing that someone up with his true identity. It had to be the reason he was experiencing such heartache.

He carried his suitcase downstairs, placing it by the front door before looking for her. Finding her in the living room, he stood in the doorway and watched her. She must have been deep in thought because she didn't notice him as she walked around, occasionally pausing to touch or pick up a photograph or small object on display.

"Well, I guess I'm ready," he finally said. The lump in his throat made his voice sound raspy.

Slowly, she turned to face him, tears shimmering in her eyes. "I hate good-byes."

He knew this had to be just as hard for her. Probably harder.

Crossing the room, he pulled her into his arms, breathing in the scent of her hair for the last time. Funny, he'd written dozens of songs dealing with a myriad of emotions but couldn't think of one damn thing to say right now.

He didn't want to leave her but couldn't bring himself to make empty promises. He wasn't a forever kind of guy, despite what Bill Reese may be thinking.

He felt certain once he was gone for a few days, the old Matt would be back instead of this sentimental sap who'd become attached to a woman and a town.

After a few weeks, he'd think of the time with her, in this town, and smile fondly at the memories. Hopefully, without having this heavy, almost unbearable weight on his heart.

But right now, he felt as though something was ripping away at his insides. He tried telling himself it was only because his idyllic life as a normal guy in Smalltown, USA was over.

He gave himself a harsh mental shake. All good things come to an end, right? What the hell did he think was going to happen?

Is it any wonder he enjoyed his time in Haversfield without the harassment of photographers? Without the false adulation of shallow people attracted to fame and fortune? Or of women who had no souls, loving to sleep with stars only for what they thought they may gain?

He'd needed a break and he'd gotten it. Now, he needed to go back to his real life with a clearer mind and lighter spirit and make some decisions about his future.

150

Delaying his departure would only make leaving more difficult. Rehearsals for his band's tour were scheduled to start soon and he had to be there.

He told himself all these things and, yet, it didn't change the fact it was torture leaving her.

"Do you want anything to take with you? A sandwich? Soda?" she asked, pulling away from him.

You. He cleared his throat. "I'll be okay."

She walked with him to his car. After he placed the suitcase in the trunk, he crouched down to pet Gyp one last time, scratching that favorite spot on his head.

Straightening, he said, "I left my phone number and my manager's number upstairs in your bedroom. In case you ever need me."

"I'll be okay." Her voice broke as tears slid down her cheeks.

"Take care of yourself." He placed his hands on her cheeks and kissed her one last time.

All the tears in the world wouldn't change things but she couldn't stop them from pouring from her eyes as she watched him drive away. She walked into the family room, dropped down on the couch and cried out her misery.

She'd survive, of course, as she had when each of her grandparents had died. Sure, she'd cry. Maybe forever. She might have to live the rest of her life with a broken heart but she'd survive.

She just wanted to know one thing. Wished she had the opportunity right now to ask God one question.

Is my life going to be nothing but one heartache after another?

Chapter Twenty

While Daryl cruised the streets of Haversfield, he spotted Mr. Rock & Roll himself heading out of town. He pounded his fist on the steering wheel and swore.

He'd alerted the media solely to make the bastard's life hell but those slow asses hadn't shown up yet. And now it looked as though it was too late.

That high priced lawyer had advised him to get out of town but Daryl never thought he'd move this fast.

And Summer, that bitch! Treating him like he was something to spread on the fields to make the crops grow. Pretending to be so pure. Why, he'd bet she'd spread her legs for Zeller the first night he came to town.

Well, he'd make her pay. Just like Lisa.

Oh, Lisa had thought it was hilarious the night at the fund-raiser when, while they danced, he'd suggested they go to his place and watch a porno flick. Hell, she practically did every guy in town and there she was, laughing at him. Making fun of him.

Well, he'd shown her.

He'd hidden in the backseat of her car and waited. He'd known she'd be tipsy; Lisa never left Maisie's sober. When he'd put his hand over her mouth and placed his gun against her head, she hadn't been laughing then.

She hadn't laughed while he'd made her drive to the graveyard. Once there, she had tried to wheedle her way into his good graces but it was too late. She'd made him feel like a fool in Maisie's.

He'd pulled her from the car and told her to strip for him. When she refused, he ripped off the skimpy top she was wearing. He still got hard when he thought about her underwear. Just swatches of lace barely holding up her big tits

152

and covering her crotch.

He'd made her go down on him twice. She'd tried to bite him but a punch to her head had improved her attitude. She'd behaved after that.

It had felt so good to rape her. Exciting. He'd never been so hard as when he'd shoved his dick into her. And she hadn't fooled him. He knew she'd gotten off, too.

That's what had made him so mad. When he was through with her, she had the nerve to scream she'd have Calvert arrest him for rape.

Well, he wasn't about to let her make a big ass out of him. It would be like her publicly saying she, who had willingly screwed everybody in town, drew the line when it came to Daryl. *He* had to use force.

He would have been able to frame Summer's playmate for the murder if it weren't for Doc Townsend's nosy assistant. Daryl had intended to switch Zeller's hair and semen samples with his own but that fat tub Betty Ann Dirkson never let those vials out of her sight. And once she'd put the seal on them, it'd be too obvious if they'd been tampered with.

It seemed like nothing could go right lately.

It still pissed him off that Summer thought she was too good for him or anybody else in town but she sure dropped her panties for the first stranger to come sniffing after her.

He smiled, willing to bet little Miss Priss wasn't feeling too superior after Mr. Rich and Famous just breezed out of town.

Without her.

Maybe he'd cruise on over to Taylor House now that she was alone.

Howard sat at the bar, brooding over a beer at Maisie's, wondering why he couldn't forget a certain woman after a certain night a few years back. She'd been tormenting him ever since he'd had a brief, unforgettable taste of what lay beneath her tough exterior. And since that night, he'd craved more.

But she didn't return his feelings, damn her.

He knew she wasn't worth it. She was sarcastic. Mean. Ornery. Hell, he could use an entire dictionary to describe all her negative traits but he still wanted her more than anything. When she wasn't being difficult, she was one sweet, intelligent woman.

She was beautiful, too. Sexy. Every time he thought he was over her, she popped into town and tormented the hell out of him.

She was making him mad right now because he, once again, couldn't forget her. This had been going on way too long.

Maybe Matt would have some advice he could use.

He slid off the barstool, thinking anything was worth a try at this point because he sure wasn't doing very well on his own.

"Daryl, what do you want now?" Summer spoke through the screen door. She knew her eyes were all red and puffy but she didn't care.

"I'm just checking on you. You know, there's still a murderer on the loose." He took off his hat and scratched the top of his head. "C'mon, I'm just doin' my job."

"Yeah, I guess you are."

"How about I come inside for a soda or a glass of sweet tea? It sure is hot out here."

"I don't think so. I'm about to call it a night."

He suddenly yanked open the door and stepped into the house.

"What the hell do you think you're doing?" she demanded.

He grabbed her arm and led her away from the door. "You don't have nobody to play with now that your lover flew the coop. Thought you might need somebody to scratch your itch."

He shoved her against the wall and crushed his mouth against hers.

She tried to turn her head, tried to put her hands on his chest to shove him away but she was no match for his strength.

Panic and revulsion caused her stomach to churn, along with the beginning of indignation.

Daryl finally lifted his head. "Why don't we go upstairs?"

"No! Get your hands off me!" She struggled to stay calm but he was still pressing her against the wall. "Get out of my house! Now!"

His short, surly laugh made her want to throw up.

"Not till I've had some of this." He roughly shoved a hand between her legs.

Her knee shot up and, thank God, made contact with the part of him she'd rather die than have in her.

"You bitch!" He bent over in pain but his hand grabbed her arm, stopping her from escaping. He shoved her back against the wall.

"Oh, no you don't, you little tease. All these years, you been trying to pass yourself off as a pure little virgin. Hell, you ain't no better than Lisa."

He grabbed her tee shirt and tried to pull it up but she was desperately fighting him. She began clawing at his face when he tried to hook his leg around hers and knock her to the floor.

He threw a punch at her head but since she was in motion constantly, his fist barely caught her on the ear.

Just when she realized she wouldn't be able to fight him off much longer, someone had him in a stranglehold.

"Howard! Oh, thank God!" She began to sob.

"Don't fall apart on me now, Sum! Take his gun!"

She did as she was told while Daryl struggled for air against the press of Howard's arm. Her hands were shaking but she aimed the gun at Daryl's head.

"I'm okay. You can let him go now. One of us should call Calvert."

"Give me the gun. I'm afraid you won't shoot him if he tries anything. But I will." Howard held a hand out, releasing Daryl only when he took the gun from his cousin. "You go call the sheriff."

It wasn't long after Calvert had hauled Daryl away when the events of the last several hours caught up with Summer. The shock of almost becoming a statistic like Lisa started a trembling in her that she couldn't stop.

"I still think you need to go to the hospital to get checked out."

"No. I'm just bruised, that's all." She couldn't stop thinking about what would have happened if Howard hadn't shown up.

He led her into the family room and made her sit on the sofa. "I'll be back in a second."

He returned with the bottle of bourbon she kept in the kitchen pantry. He made her drink two shots to steady her nerves.

When she began crying, he moved next to her and put his arm around her shoulders. He made soothing noises until she calmed somewhat.

"Where's Matt?"

"He left." She rubbed her eyes with her fists but more tears leaked out. "Calvert found out who he really is because his driver's license and other papers didn't check out. His attorney told him to leave town before the press got wind of it."

"Oh."

"Gyp really tore up the back door trying to get inside when Daryl was here." She stroked the dog's head, which rested on her lap. She didn't often allow him up on the furniture but the

156

dog needed reassurance that she was okay.

"Don't worry. I'll fix it."

"Matt warned me about leaving the doors unlocked. I should have listened, especially after Lisa's murder."

After a short silence, she asked, "Would you stay here while I take a shower? I can still smell Daryl's aftershave on me. I shouldn't be afraid because he's locked up, but..."

"Hey, what's family for?" he interrupted. "Take as long as you need."

A few reporters finally came nosing around but Howard slammed the door in their faces.

The only story they got from the patrons at Maisie's was the one about the capture of a rapist/murderer who happened to be a law officer. They would rather have gotten photos or an exclusive on the missing rock star but no one would even confirm Matt Zeller had ever been in town.

Chapter Twenty-One

Julie pulled into Summer's driveway. When she wasn't hoping and praying her friend was okay, she fantasized about what would be the best, and most painful, way to kill Howard.

He could have been a little more informative on the phone than just, "Get your butt up here. Summer needs you."

Then he'd hung up, the damn moron.

As soon as her feet hit the ground, she ran into the house, yelling, "Summer? What's wrong? Are you okay?"

Someone grabbed her from behind, clamping a hand over her mouth. She began fighting, trying to jab her elbow backwards into her assailant's rib cage.

"Shh! I finally got Sum calmed down enough to fall asleep." Howard spoke quietly into her ear before releasing her.

She turned, furious enough to bite his head off. "You son-of-a..."

He put his hand over her mouth again and dragged her into the kitchen. "Sit down and shut up while I explain everything."

She shot daggers at him until he began filling her in on what had happened. Her anger soon turned to shock. When he finished, her mouth hung open.

"Oh, my God! I've always known he was a creep. Why wasn't he included as a suspect in Lisa's murder from the beginning?"

He looked at her as though the words "mentally challenged" should apply to her.

"In case you forgot, this is Haversfield. The local law enforcement here makes Andy and Barney of Mayberry look like real professionals."

"Oh, that's right. Be your usual sarcastic, ignorant self," she huffed, crossing her arms in front of her.

He plowed a hand through his hair. "This town doesn't exactly stand on procedures and formalities. I don't know if there's ever been a murder committed here before. I'll bet it was the only time Calvert used handcuffs except when Jake Teasdale got drunk and started breaking the storefront windows on the Fourth of July years ago."

"Boy, Summer's sure been through a lot. You know, I thought Bill...I mean, Matt looked familiar. I think she really fell hard for him. Is he going to stay in touch with her?"

"She said he didn't say anything."

"Typical man." She snorted.

"What's that supposed to mean?"

She let out a little puff of air, indicating just how dense she thought he was.

"I asked you what you meant by that."

"Forget it." She stood up. She walked over to the sink and got a quick drink of water. Turning, she watched him walk toward her.

"Forget what?"

She felt her face grow warm.

"Forget we spent one incredible night together and then you acted like it never happened?" He stood before her, placing his hands on his hips.

"I acted like it never happened? You were the one that got involved with somebody else, hardware store boy. Not me!"

"Only after you told Sum you'd met someone you were crazy about."

"I meant you, you stupid jerk!" She stuck her chin out.

Howard looked as though he'd been shot between the eyes. "Me?"

"After that weekend you visited us in school, when Summer went out with the guy she was dating and you and I hung out together, I did tell her I'd met someone. Only I never told her it was you because I wasn't sure if you were going to call. Since you two are related, I would have been embarrassed had I said anything and then you didn't call. Which was exactly what happened." Julie crossed her arms and glared at him.

He scratched the back of his head. "I did call later that week. Summer told me you'd met someone. I thought she meant someone else."

"So you immediately began dating another woman. Until she ran off to Atlanta." She shrugged. "Well, all that's water under the bridge. History."

"Yeah. History." He slowly moved closer to her, as though he was scared to touch her. His hesitation lasted only a minute before he slid his arms around her waist. "And I've been wanting to go back in time ever since."

"You have?" Air filled her lungs and stayed there.

He answered by placing his mouth on hers. A soft, tentative kiss. As though he couldn't quite believe this was really happening.

His arms circled her, held her tightly while his mouth became more demanding. It amazed her how quickly passion flooded her senses.

His hands began to roam, seeming to want to touch every inch of her. He started to unbutton her top but she placed her hands over his.

"Wait."

"I have. For years."

"Howard, I mean it. I need to know what you want. What you expect."

"I want you to shut up. You talk too much." He attempted to undo her buttons again but her hands tightened their grip.

"I'm serious."

"And you think I'm not?"

She backed away and crossed her arms. She tried to look as though her bones were solid enough to support her, despite the fact this idiot had turned them into jelly.

"I would appreciate an honest answer. Well?"

"You want dinner first?" He raised his eyebrows.

She stared at him. She'd never dreamed he could be so cavalier. So crude. So incredibly obtuse. That was no head on his shoulders -- that was a concrete block.

For such a long time, she'd been tortured by the idea he thought of her only as a one night stand. And minutes ago, he had her thinking she'd meant something to him, after all. But that hope faded as quickly as it had flared.

She turned from him. Pride prevented her from revealing the tears in her eyes.

"I should check on Summer."

She felt his hands on her shoulders, halting her exit from the room. He turned her around.

"Julie, I'm sorry. I was only kidding." He brushed a kiss across her cheek. "You asked me what I want. Well, I want you. I want you to move here. You know I can't relocate because of the business."

"Move here? Haversfield? This backward town in the middle of nowhere?" She blinked a few times. A slow smile lit her face.

She placed her head on his chest and shocked herself by answering, "Okay."

Before Summer fully awoke, her heart ached, heavy with the knowledge that Matt had left.

Left town. Left her. Just like they both knew he would.

She next remembered Daryl had tried to rape her. Aside from a few body aches, this recollection caused less anguish than the first.

Although she'd prefer to stay in bed, she got up and walked to the window. Looking down at the driveway, she saw Julie's car and assumed Howard had called her. Her presence would be comforting, especially if she could stay for a while.

She walked into the bathroom, glancing only briefly at the mirror. As expected, she looked like hell. Her eyes were so swollen from crying, they were little more than slits.

When she finished her morning ritual, she left her room, wondering if Julie, who always stayed in the room directly across from her, was awake.

Knocking softly before opening the door, she stuck her head inside the room.

Evidently, the events of last night had stressed her out so much, she was hallucinating because she thought she saw Julie's head resting on Howard's shoulder.

She blinked repeatedly but the scene wouldn't change.

She couldn't be any more shocked if she'd discovered two aliens snuggled together under that quilt she'd helped her grandmother make.

Her cousin and her best friend. Obviously, without a stitch of clothing between them. And she hadn't had a clue, but Matt had.

How had he known?

She backed out of the room and quietly closed the door. As she went downstairs, she muttered to Gyp that nothing else could happen to rock her world. She'd gotten enough shocks lately to last a lifetime.

Matt landing on her doorstep, Daryl turning out to be Lisa's killer and Julie and Howard wrapped in each other's arms.

Whoever said life in a small town was boring?

She let the dog out before putting on a pot of coffee. She flipped on the radio and wasn't prepared to hear Matt's voice, singing the song he'd crooned into her ear the night they'd danced right here in the kitchen.

It wasn't as though she'd forgotten about him and needed a reminder. The broken heart laying heavily in her chest was reminder enough.

162

Glancing briefly at the phone, she wished with all her heart he'd call. She had known they wouldn't have a relationship or a happy ending. But just a call to let her know he was thinking of her. Maybe missed her a little. Before time and other women made her just a fading memory.

But she had the awful feeling he'd never be on the other end of the telephone. And that hurt so much more than she'd ever imagined it would.

She couldn't fault him because he hadn't made any promises. He hadn't in any way led her on.

Wrapping her arms around her waist, she walked to the back door. Leaning her head against the frame, she absently watched Gyp chase a squirrel and wondered how long would it take before she could think of him without tears filling her eyes.

Chapter Twenty-Two

Gina poured coffee into Matt's cup while he pretended to read the newspaper but she knew he'd been on the same page for the last ten minutes.

She also noticed he spent most of the time staring off into space.

Since landing on her and Vinny's doorstep a week ago, he seemed different. He was quieter than usual. More pensive.

Or was he brooding? She couldn't quite put her finger on it. If she didn't know better, she'd think he was lovesick.

Lovesick?

Yes. Now, everything made sense.

She set the carafe on the warmer and joined him at the table. "What's her name?" she asked.

"Summer," he absently responded. Realizing what he'd just said, he lifted his gaze from the paper. "I mean, who?"

"Is that the woman you're in love with? Summer?" She took a sip of her coffee.

"I'm not in love. What makes you think so?"

"Well, I can just tell. You can give Vinny that bullshit story about being at a crossroads concerning your career. Maybe you are but that isn't what's causing you to walk the floor at night and stare off into space ninety percent of the time."

She placed her hand on his arm. "So, tell me about her. My guess is she lives in Haversfield and she's the reason you stayed there."

"I'm not in love," he again insisted.

"Okay. Whatever. Tell me about her anyway."

He hesitated but began talking about Summer. He also described Howard, Bob and Ernie. He told her about Maisie's and the rest of the town. But the majority of the time, he talked about Summer.

He finished talking nearly an hour later. "I'm not in love with her. She's just...special."

"Hmm." She tucked her tongue around a back tooth, wondering how long it would take for him to discover, or admit, the truth.

Gina still wondered when she and Vinny left Midway Airport the following week after dropping Matt off to catch his flight to New York. He hadn't mentioned Summer again and she didn't ask any more questions. She didn't need to.

But she did have an idea. A plan that would satisfy her curiosity and maybe somehow help those two get together, although she hadn't worked all the details out yet.

"Matt was telling me about the little town he stayed in while his car was being fixed. Haversfield sounds like the perfect place to get away for a mini vacation."

"What are you up to?" Vinny briefly took his eyes from the road as he drove south on Cicero. He gave his wife a quick, suspicious glance.

"Nothing. I just want us to get away for a few days." She placed her hand on his thigh. "We could stay at the bed and breakfast place where he stayed. It sounds romantic."

"Matt at a romantic place?" He laughed.

She let a minute pass before saying, "Maybe I'll go by myself. Although I'd sure hate to be wearing my new teddy from Victoria's Secret and be all alone." She let out a deep breath.

"You are definitely up to something." He gave her another suspicious glance.

She started to move her hand further up his leg. It stopped just a heartbeat away from the part of him she could still get hard in record time.

"Christ, Gina! Not while I'm driving!"

"I can't help it! Just thinking about you and me getting away from our businesses for a few days gets me so excited!"

She didn't have to fake the breathlessness in her voice because she was still wildly attracted to her husband. He couldn't be described as terribly handsome, but his slightly hooked nose, golden-brown eyes and wide, thin mouth gave him a dangerous look she could never resist.

He clamped his hand over hers. "Behave."

"But that's exactly what I don't want to do." She smiled seductively.

"When do you want to leave?" he sighed.

While Matt unpacked, he realized he didn't even have a picture of her. Not that he needed one. Her image hadn't faded the slightest bit from his mind. He could recall every inch of her, right down to the wayward freckle on her right heel.

He'd thought miles of highway between them would put everything in perspective. That hadn't happened. Not during his drive to visit Vinny and Gina, not during his stay at their house and not during the plane trip to New York.

By now, he was supposed to have reached the conclusion they were just two people who had met and liked each other. Had a good time in and out of bed.

By now, he was supposed to have stopped missing her. Stopped missing hearing that endearing Southern drawl.

Since leaving Haversfield, he had stopped himself dozens of times from picking up the phone and dialing her number. Mainly because he didn't know what to say.

Excuse me, Summer, but I can't stop thinking about you. Can't stop wanting you. So, help me out here...what's going on? I'm not in love but what the hell is going on?

He tried to tell himself his strange moodiness was the result of indecision over his career. The desire to quit the band after the tour ended was growing. Going solo appealed to him. Professionally, that is.

Remaining the loner in his private life was less appealing, though he tried hard as hell to convince himself nothing had changed.

He paced the apartment, wondering why he always felt like a stranger in what was supposed to be his home.

Since returning to New York, he threw himself into rehearsals but instead of the music driving all else from his mind, it only seemed to remind him more of his emotional turmoil.

He seldom went out to blow off steam with the other guys, preferring to spend most of his time alone, working on material for another album.

He occasionally let himself get talked into attending a party but socializing really didn't appeal to him.

The females he encountered were too obvious. Too flashy. Too experienced.

Too not Summer.

He knew he was pathetic. And he knew he'd better snap out of it, whatever "it" was.

While Summer registered the couple seated across from her, she recalled Matt had a friend named Vinny. The likelihood of his friend and this man being the same person was too remote to consider.

Besides, why would his friends come to Haversfield?

"How did you hear about Taylor House?"

"A friend...," the man started to say.

"You advertise, don't you?" The woman quickly interrupted her husband.

"Yes, I do."

"I'm sure I read about your place in a brochure." The woman smiled.

Vinny frowned, looking over at his wife.

"Well, if you follow me, I'll show you the upstairs. You

have your choice of two rooms."

Normally, there would have been three rooms available but last weekend Julie had moved into one, announcing she would look for a job in or around Haversfield. And her boyfriend -- jeez, would she ever get used to Howard being Julie's boyfriend? -- had moved in with her, saying they couldn't very well live at his parents. Summer didn't think his parents would mind but Julie felt too awkward with that arrangement.

The woman chose the same room Matt had selected. "This is wonderful. In fact, the whole house is just beautiful. Did you decorate it yourself?"

"Most of it. I have relatives who are great handymen. They own the hardware store." She looked briefly around the room to make sure everything was in order. "I'll let you settle in. If you need anything, just let me know."

"Isn't this great?" Gina asked, after Summer left the room and closed the door.

"It's nice." Vinny placed his hands on his hips. "But when you gonna tell me what you're up to? Why are we really here?"

"What's wrong with wanting to spend time with my husband?" She started to unpack.

"Nothing. Except I happen to know when you're up to something."

"You're too suspicious."

"Oh, yeah? Then why don't you want her to know you heard about this place from Matt?"

"I don't want to make her nervous, that's all." She walked over and slid her arms around his neck. "We're here for a romantic getaway. This is cozier than some old stuffy hotel, don't you think?" She pressed her hips against his.

"I knew you were trouble the first time I saw you." His fingers went to the buttons running down the front of her dress. "You can get me to do anything, and you know it."

"He left his number, so why don't you call him?"
"Because."
"Well, that certainly clears everything up." Julie picked up another potato to peel.
"We've been through this before." Summer let out a tired sigh as she breaded the pork chops. "Things between us were brief and temporary. We both knew that. End of story."
"You never were much of a liar." Julie rinsed off the potatoes. "You're in love with him. Howard thinks Matt's in love with you."
"You read too many romance novels. And Howard is crazy. Always has been. Anyway, it's been weeks since he left. He hasn't called and I don't expect him to."
She couldn't admit that every fiber of her being longed to hear his voice. Missed him. Each time the phone rang, she prayed he was calling.
The pragmatic side of her knew it was unwise to entertain the idea he might be as miserable as she. Might be missing her so much, his heart felt as splintered as hers. But her heart was being unrealistic and stubborn, refusing to believe she'd never see him again.
"Instead of crying yourself to sleep every night, and don't even attempt to deny it because I hear you, why don't you show a little initiative and do something? Like call him. Maybe all he needs is to hear your voice," suggested Julie.
"I am doing something! I'm trying to forget him but it's impossible because *you* keep talking about him!" she snapped. "Well, somehow I plan to forget him just like he obviously has forgotten about m..." She froze, noticing Vinny's wife standing in the doorway.
"Am I interrupting?"
"No." She forced a slight smile, wondering how much of

the conversation the woman had heard. "Is there something you need?"

"Not really. My husband fell asleep and I was a little restless. But if I'm bothering you, I'll leave."

"Oh, don't be silly. We're just making dinner," Julie waved a hand in the air.

"Are there any restaurants nearby? We don't know where anything is."

"Maisie's is just down the street." Julie put the potatoes on to boil. "But we're making enough food to feed an army unit. Why don't you join us?"

She could have hit Julie, who knew dinner was not included in the price of the room.

Aside from that, she didn't feel like making polite conversation with strangers over the dinner table. It would distract her from figuring out how to get over Matt.

"Oh, that sounds great! We'd be willing to pay for our meal. I mean, not to insult you or anything, but I remember you said breakfast was the only meal you provide. Are you sure you don't mind?" The woman directed the question at Summer.

"I'm sure." Trapped, what else could she say?

"Vinny, what do you think of Summer?" Gina stood in front of the mirror, checking her appearance before they went downstairs. "I mean, besides the way she looks."

"She's okay, I guess. A knockout." He frowned. "Why?"

"Matt's in love with her."

"You're crazy!" he laughed. "I mean, I know he was here, but I think your imagination's been working overtime." He laughed again. "In love? Not Matt. Besides, she'd not his type."

"We don't know what his type is because this is the first time it's ever happened." She turned and faced her husband.

170

"I know I'm right. Just don't tell her we know him. Not yet."

"That's why we're here, isn't it?" He lifted an eyebrow. "You somehow connived an invitation to dinner, didn't you? You're meddling."

"Am not!" she huffed, the picture of righteous indignation. Judging from the look on his face, he didn't believe her.

"Oh, all right," she shrugged. "I wanted to come here and meet her so I could think of some way to get them together again. Matt's been so good to us, I just want him to be happy. And you have to admit, he just wasn't himself when he stayed with us."

"That doesn't prove anything."

She put her hands on her hips and glared at him. "Vincent Carbone, you saw how miserable he was! I can't believe you're so blind! He spent an hour trying to convince me he wasn't in love.   But the whole time, all he talked about was how wonderful Summer is!"

"Okay, I admit it sounds like he might be hung up on her. But I don't think he'd want you interfering."

"He's a man. He doesn't know what he wants." She flapped a hand in the air.

Summer looked across the dining room table, feeling more uneasy toward the couple who had arrived earlier that day. Maybe uneasy wasn't the correct word. Suspicious wasn't right, either. She couldn't say why but sensed it was no coincidence they ended up in her house. Not that she thought they were up to something sinister. After all, this wasn't an episode of *CSI: Haversfield.*

"Gina, honey, pass me the biscuits."

Her fork stopped halfway to her mouth. She set it down.

Gina. Vinny. Suddenly, she connected the dots.

How stupid of her not to catch on right away. These people were definitely friends of Matt's. But he had ended up here out of necessity. Why were they here?

She moved mechanically through the rest of the meal. She picked at her food, not really hungry but then she seldom was lately.

After the table was cleared and the dishwasher was turned on, Howard and Vinny headed for the television to watch a ball game. Julie went downstairs to iron an outfit she planned on wearing to an interview the next morning.

Summer got Gyp's leash, hung it around her neck and started toward the back door when Gina asked, "Mind if I come along?"

"I guess not." She did, but couldn't bring herself to be rude.

As they left the backyard, Gina said, "If your dog doesn't need a leash, why bring it?"

"Because he knows I'll put him on it if he starts running around like a maniac."

"Oh."

They walked in silence until Gina asked, "Are there any malls around? I wouldn't mind doing a little shopping."

"Millbrook Court isn't too far away. You can get there in about twenty minutes."

"Sure is hot and sticky. Is the summer always like this?"

"Not always."

The tension between them mounted during another period of silence. She knew she wasn't imagining it. Finally, she blurted, "You and your husband are Matt's friends, aren't you?"

She knew the question came out sounding more like an accusation.

Gina gave her a wary glance. "Yes."

"You're not just passing through town. Why are you here?"

"Hmm. Well, I could make up something but then I think you're smart enough to recognize a lie when you hear it. The truth is, Matt's in love with you so, naturally, I wanted to meet you."

Those words shocked her, causing her to trip over her own feet. Her heart started pounding after a second of inactivity. "Did he tell you that?"

"Not directly." Gina continued walking.

"What does that mean?" She forced her feet to start moving.

"He came to our house after he left here. During the weeks he was with us, he was withdrawn. Moody. Definitely not his usual self."

"He was probably concerned about ticket sales for his concerts. Just worried about public opinion of him after the murder in his apartment," she rationalized.

"Matt wouldn't be that concerned over what the public thinks of him." Gina looked up at the sky and casually commented, "The stars look so much brighter in a small town. And you can see hundreds more of them."

"I know." Summer's voice was tight. She wanted to shout she didn't give a damn about the stars. She only wanted her to explain why she had said what she said. About Matt loving her.

An eternity seemed to pass before Gina picked up that thread of conversation and continued. "Matt claims he's not in love with you. But he talked about you as though you're an angel. And he's been miserable since leaving you. He's trying to convince himself he's not in love but he couldn't fool me."

"That's awfully shaky reasoning." Her heart started to dance with hope but she was afraid to believe Gina was right. "No, I think you're wrong. I haven't heard a word from him."

They walked in silence for a short while until Gina remarked, "Funny, isn't it, that he tries too hard to believe he's not in love with you. And you haven't denied you're in love with him."

She honestly couldn't speak. She didn't know why but she

couldn't lie about her feelings for him.

But...Matt in love with her? Her heart pounded when she considered Gina's words.

They walked in silence for a few minutes until Gina softly remarked, "I appreciate your honesty."

Chapter Twenty-Three

Gina turned a page of the paper and sipped her coffee. Although she and Vinny had been in Haversfield for just three days, she was discovering why Matt had been so reluctant to leave the town. And Summer.

Much to her delight, she and Summer were developing a friendship. They genuinely liked each other and had started sharing confidences.

Summer spoke of the time she and Matt spent together but was careful not to reveal what her heart wished for the future. It didn't matter because Gina was good at hearing what people didn't say.

She hadn't known what type of woman would eventually steal Matt's heart, only that he'd never fall for anyone pretentious. Or wild. Since getting to know Summer, she decided she could not have chosen anyone more perfect for him. And she wasn't about to let him blow this once-in-a-lifetime chance.

"I have an idea," she said, shifting her gaze from the newspaper to Summer, who stood at the stove frying eggs. "Let's go shopping. You need a dress. A killer dress."

"Why?" Summer gave her a puzzled look.

"Because you're going to New York. With Vinny and Me."

"Why on earth would I go to New York? Besides, I can't just leave my business." Summer turned her attention back to cooking.

"Sure you can. Julie can handle things for a few days."

"She's got her head up in the clouds now that she and Howard are involved. Or in love or whatever."

"It'll be fun. There's a big awards dinner. You might run into someone you know," she coaxed. "Wouldn't you like to see him again?"

"I'm not about to throw myself at him," Summer flatly stated. "If he wanted to see me, wouldn't he call or something?"

"Not necessarily. I think he's a little confused and doesn't know what to do next. He's always sworn he's a confirmed bachelor but he's never fallen in love before. There's no harm in helping things along. Listen, girlfriend, get out of the Dark Ages. Women nowadays go after what they want. You're no shrinking violet, anyway."

Summer suddenly rushed over to the sink and threw up.

Gina rushed to her side. "Are you okay?"

"Yeah." Summer turned the water on and washed out the basin. "Lately, my stomach's really been queasy. I must be coming down with something. Sometimes, just the smell of food makes me sick."

Gina studied her pale face, her slim form and flat belly. "Maybe. Or maybe you're pregnant."

Summer turned and stared at her. Her face whitened even more, her eyes filled with horror. "No! I can't be!"

"Have you had a period since Matt left?"

Color came back into Summer's face as she shook her head.

Gina slid an arm around her shoulders and guided her to a chair. "I'll go pick up a home pregnancy test. Where's the nearest drug store?"

"I'm supposed to be a responsible adult. I always swore I'd never end up like this." Summer covered her face with her hands and began to cry.

"Is that blue? What does it mean if it's blue? I forgot." Summer nervously babbled while praying for a negative reading.

Gina put her hand on her shoulder. "It means you're pregnant. And it means you're definitely going to New York."

"No! I can't! I don't want Matt to know!"

"But it's his! You have to let him know! He has that right!"

"No," she insisted. "I don't want him to feel forced into doing anything. He told me about his parents. I think he's determined not to follow in their footsteps."

"Oh, that's just plain bull. He isn't anything like his parents." Frowning, Gina bit her bottom lip. Finally, she asked, "Is abortion an option?"

If someone had asked that question before she became pregnant, she would have expressed uncertainty over a decision. Now, she flatly stated, "No."

"Good." Gina hugged her. "Don't worry. Everything's gonna work out."

"No, it won't. You have no idea how horrible it will be for me to be pregnant in this town."

"Why?"

She looked at her new friend. "He didn't tell you anything about my mother?"

"No."

"Well, it isn't a pretty story."

"Why don't we go into the family room and you can tell me about it."

Summer chose the overstuffed recliner while Gina arranged herself comfortably on the sofa. She told Gina about her childhood and the damage her mother caused. By the time she spoke of losing her grandparents, both women were teary eyed.

"It must have been terrible for you. But times are different now. Women have babies without husbands every day," Gina insisted.

"Not in Haversfield."

"Aren't you jumping the gun, anyway? Who says you won't have a husband? Do you think Matt will throw a check at you and disappear? I know him well enough to safely say that isn't a possibility."

"I don't want him to do anything just because I'm pregnant. Maybe I'm immature or impossibly romantic, but I wanted him to come back just because he loves me." Tears dropped from her eyes.

"Who says he doesn't? Maybe all he needs is a little help. Which is why you have to go to New York."

Warming to her cause, Gina added, "You're a strong woman. You survived your childhood and the death of your grandparents. You started your own business. Now's not the time to let your backbone slide out of your spine. Besides, you have someone else to think of. Someone who's going to need a daddy."

She wiped her eyes with the back of her hand. Standing, she began pacing the room. "He could be involved with someone by now."

"No way."

"He'll think I'm chasing him. Just out for his money."

"No way."

"We...you might be misinterpreting his feelings for me."

"No freaking way. So, as I was saying, you need a dress."

Summer looked at herself in the dressing room mirror, doubt clearly written on her face. Sure, the dress was elegant. Sexy. Black usually was. Expensive, sheer black lace began at the daringly low neckline, ran up to her neck and down her arms, not really concealing her skin. The same lace made up the entire back of the dress and connected to plain black material inches above the waistline.

"It's perfect," sighed Gina. "He'll take one look at you in that thing and want to rip it right off."

A deep blush heated her face. "You don't think it's too wild?"

"Definitely not! You couldn't find a more perfect dress.

178

Unless it's long, white and comes with a veil."

Summer rolled her eyes.

"I'm not sure about any of this. I may end up looking like a fool." She nervously pulled at the left sleeve. "Aren't there going to be a million women hanging all over him? Glamorous women?"

"As opposed to you, who's direly in need of plastic surgery to fix that deformed face of yours," Gina quipped.

She made a rude noise.

"C'mon, get real. You're gorgeous. That's how Matt described you. And that was before he ever saw you in anything like that."

"I just hope you know what you're doing." She turned and faced the mirror again for one last look. "Because I sure as hell don't."

After she paid for the dress, they leisurely made their way through the mall, stopping occasionally to look at things on display in the shop windows.

"Look at that darling little pink dress! It's so tiny!" Gina turned to look at her. "Do you want a girl or a boy?"

Her gaze traveled to the dress and her eyes suddenly misted. "Oh, God, Gina! I'm going to have a baby!"

Since taking the pregnancy test the preceding day, she thought she had accepted the fact. Obviously, she hadn't because now the full weight of reality -- the harshness of it -- seemed heavier.

Gina draped an arm across her shoulders and squeezed slightly. "You need to make an appointment with a doctor."

"I know. I'll have to go to one of the neighboring towns. I know this can't be kept a secret forever but I don't want to be the topic of local gossip any more than I already have been. I just couldn't deal with it right now."

She looked so sad, sympathetic tears formed in Gina's eyes. "I wish you'd believe me when I say things will work out.

I truly believe they will."

Summer carefully placed the dress she'd bought on a padded hanger and hung it in the closet. Opening the shoe box resting on her bed, she looked hatefully at the spike heels Gina had strong-armed her into buying. Sure, the black suede, strappy things were just as sexy as the dress but she'd bet her feet would scream in protest the entire time.

She had just two weeks. Two weeks to get herself together. To practice being so sophisticated, so irresistible and self- confident, people would be awestruck by her grace and beauty. Two weeks to pray Matt would do just as Gina claimed he would. Take one look at her and never let her go.

Gina and Vinny were leaving in the morning. In two weeks, she would meet them in Chicago and they all would fly to New York.

A bubble of panic gave her the jitters until she reminded herself she could always back out. She didn't have to go. Nobody was holding a gun to her head.

But when she thought of the child she had so thoughtlessly made with Matt, she knew she had to. She owed her son or daughter at least that much, if not more.

She hadn't told anyone else she was pregnant. Not even Julie. She dreaded how people would react, especially if her trip to New York was a disaster. If that happened, she'd have plenty else to think about. Like where she would move because she wasn't about to let any child of hers be subjected to the gossip and scorn Haversfield could produce.

Placing a hand over her still flat stomach, she wondered what this baby would look like. It surprised her she already felt powerful feelings of love and protectiveness for her child.

Her child. And Matt's.

When should she tell him of her pregnancy? Biting on her lower lip, Summer hoped he'd be so happy to see her, he'd...what? Profess his undying love? Propose?

It sure would make things a lot easier.

Would he hate her when he found out? Resent her? Reject her?

Chapter Twenty-Four

Matt watched the stripper shake her hips as she removed her top. Until recently, he would have been determined to find out if those large breasts were the work of God or a doctor. Since landing in Haversfield and having his entire world turned upside down, he glanced at his watch and wondered how soon he could leave without appearing rude.

It was the bass guitarist's thirtieth birthday party but Matt would rather be anywhere else.

No, he took that lie back. He'd rather be with Summer, watching her cute little rear end shake while she took off her top.

He didn't know exactly when he'd capitulated and accepted reality. Although he could put everything he knew about love into a thimble and still have room to spare, he knew he loved her. He just didn't know what that meant.

He already figured he'd be no good at it. In that area, he believed his genes guaranteed failure. But he'd rather cut off his arm than hurt the woman who had found a place in his heart and wouldn't get out.

He'd tried for weeks to convince himself if he did nothing, he'd get over her in time. As though he had the flu or a sprained ankle. Well, his damn symptoms just wouldn't go away.

The guys hooted as the stripper straddled Artie, the birthday boy, and gave him the lap dance of his life while Matt stared pensively off into space.

He needed a solution to his dilemma. Now that he'd admitted what he felt for Summer was love, he had no idea what to do next or if he even should do anything.

Given their histories, what were the odds the two of them could create a lifetime of happiness?

Slim to none. They'd had no examples to follow.

On the other hand, he had been so miserable since leaving her, he couldn't imagine feeling any worse. With each passing day, he missed her more instead of less. And each time he thought of the possibility of her meeting someone else...well, the scenarios of what he'd like to do to his replacement would have impressed Stephen King.

He now understood why those sniveling poets wrote such drivel. He knew exactly what they meant.

He couldn't go much longer without seeing her. He didn't want to. However, he was stuck on tour, in Memphis, at the moment. The band had to be in New York for the awards show Friday night. It was going to be televised and he'd given his word he would perform.

The only bright spot in all this was he'd invited Vinny and Gina to accompany him. Recalling that Gina had instantly figured out what took him weeks to muddle through made him laugh.

Until he also remembered how obnoxiously smug she became whenever she was right.

He consoled himself with the fact Friday was only two days away, then the band then had a few weeks off before resuming the final phase of the tour. A trip to Haversfield was definitely on his agenda.

He glanced at the stripper, who had removed her G-String and, if she wasn't actually screwing Artie, was simulating the act to perfection.

He looked around the room, wondering who most of the people were. He did, however, know the man who was emptying a small bag of white powder on the coffee table.

Rick Teak had been the band's drummer from the beginning. His drug addiction had caused problems before. He'd been warned more than once to get help until he was finally given an ultimatum -- choose the band or drugs.

Matt had been under the impression Rick had been clean for the past few months but the truth was displayed right before his eyes.

Disgust prodded him into leaving the party.

He headed down the hall, becoming angrier with each step. Passing his room, he continued on to the bank of elevators. He needed to clear his head, walk off his anger.

The fear of being recognized no longer prevented him from venturing outside hotel rooms. Weightier issues now created havoc in his life.

The night air was cool but thick with humidity. Still, it felt therapeutic.

Those few weeks in Haversfield had caused such disruption, such confusion in his personal life. Every philosophy and conviction regarding his future had been shot full of gaping holes.

Who would have thought a woman would have him so tied up in knots?

Though no one else knew, it embarrassed him he'd actually been daydreaming about living happily-ever-after with Summer.

Despite the confusion in his mind, he had finally made a firm decision about his career. Touring no longer appealed to him. Temper tantrums and various addictions of the band members had taken their toll. It was time to part company.

In the past, he had always dreaded the day when they would go their separate ways. Now, he couldn't wait.

As he continued walking, it crossed his mind, not for the first time, that Rick might know who killed the young girl in Matt's apartment months ago.

After all, it was Rick who always invited the people who brought the drugs to the parties. Like tonight.

An uneasy feeling sent a chill down his spine.

He turned around and headed back to the hotel.

184

"You think you know everything," Julie huffed.

"No, it just seems I do because you know so little." Howard dipped his spoon into his bowl for another taste. "I told you this stew needed a little more salt."

"Don't try and change the subject." She grabbed the salt shaker and banged it down in front of him. She began circling the table as she spoke. "I think Summer's making a mistake. Matt hasn't bothered to contact her in all this time and if he really loved her, he would have."

"Excuse me, but weren't you the one that kept hounding her to call him?" He salted his food.

"This is different. You and Gina filled her head with a bunch of nonsense and now she's probably halfway to the airport. If she gets hurt, it'll be all your fault!"

"She loves him, he loves her. Any fool could figure that out by the way the two of them acted around each other. Hey, c'mon. You know I'd never encourage her to do anything if I thought she'd get hurt." He waved his spoon in the air. "Anyway, they aren't as stupid as we were."

"You mean you were," she corrected.

"Quit trying to start a fight." He finished eating while she continued her restless pacing.

"Don't forget Bob and Ernie are coming to play cards tonight," he reminded. He picked up his dishes and took them to the sink.

"I know." She murmured, rather absently. "Maybe I should have gone with her."

He walked over and pulled her into his arms. "You couldn't. She's counting on you to take care of things around here. She's got some people scheduled to check in tomorrow."

"I know." She rested her head on his chest. "I just want her to be happy."

"Me, too. Quit worrying. Everything's gonna be fine." He

kissed her cheek. "When she gets back, we're going to have to find a place to live. We can't stay here forever."

"I know," she sighed, "but I was hoping to land a job first. I'm getting tired of going on interviews and not ending up with a job. Especially since I have to drive so far to these appointments. I wish Haversfield had more employment opportunities."

"You could always work at Maisie's."

"That was a joke, right?" She tilted her head back and raised an eyebrow.

"Yeah. You're not nice enough to be a waitress." He tweaked her nose. "I've got to get back to the store before my dad calls Calvert and reports me missing. Walk me to the door."

Summer looked at the sign indicating the exit for St. Louis International Airport. She wended her way to one of the parking lots that offered shuttle service back to the terminal.

Although she was early, it seemed to take an unusually long time to complete the paperwork. When she was transported to the terminal, she was afraid to check her bag at the curb.

As she walked toward the correct concourse, butterflies tickled her stomach. Or maybe the baby was the culprit. At any rate, she was thankful her nausea -- morning sickness, according to the doctor -- had subsided.

It was too late to worry if she was doing the right thing. Indecision and worry had driven her crazy for days but when Gina had called that morning to touch base, she knew she couldn't possibly back out. Not when she'd been fantasizing about the moment she and Matt would come face to face.

Not once, in all her imaginings, was he not ecstatic to see her.

She continued the long walk to the departure gate,

recalling Howard had been just as positive as Gina that Matt had fallen in love with her. It was what she wanted to believe. What she wanted to be true more than anything.

Arriving at the gate, she checked in and prayed the airline would not lose her bag. This was no time for her clothes to get lost. Especially that little black dress.

She glanced at her watch, calculating she had ninety minutes before passengers could board the plane.

Several people were seated in the bar across from the gate area. She noticed some had plates of food. She'd been too nervous this morning to eat much more than toast. Maybe a sandwich would settle her insides. She knew it wasn't good for the baby to go so long without eating.

She walked by the newspaper machines, unaware of the bold headlines on the various front pages.

ROCK STAR SOLVES MURDER!

ZELLER'S ZEST FOR JUSTICE NABS MURDERER!

BAD BOY OF ROCK A HERO!

"I'll kill him!"

"Who?"

"Your friend! Listen to this...'Brandy Cole couldn't be reached for comment but her publicist confirmed she's en route to join Matt in New York.' Wait until I get my hands on him," seethed Gina. "And that silicone stuffed bimbo."

"Settle down, hon. You know half of that crap isn't true. I talked to him right before we left the house and he didn't say anything about Brandy." Vinny looked around. "Shouldn't Summer be here by now? We board in just twenty minutes." He checked his watch. "Maybe she saw the papers and backed out."

"Maybe not. We'll just have to keep her from reading this trash." She carelessly folded the newspaper and offered it to the person seated on her right. She turned back to Vinny. "Is

Mr. Big Shot still planning to meet us after the awards show?"

"Yeah. There's a party in the ballroom. He said our names are on the list of guests the doorman will have. I told him we're bringing your sister. Summer will have to use Joanie's name at the door."

"If tonight doesn't go like I hope, I'm going to be responsible for her getting her heart broken." She took a deep breath. "He couldn't possibly have started up again with that porno pig."

"I doubt he did." He picked up his wife's hand and held it tightly in his. "You know, at first I didn't think you should meddle in his life. But after getting to know Summer, I agree that they're right for each other."

"There she is!" Relieved, Gina stood and waved. "Remember, we can't let her near the newspapers."

Chapter Twenty-Five

Summer's heart started beating more rapidly with each step they took toward the entrance to the ballroom. Taking deep breaths, she tried calming herself because all this excitement surely couldn't be good for the baby.

While she and Gina had dressed, they'd giggled like schoolgirls but now her emotions flip-flopped between anticipation and fear.

"Are you sure I look okay?" She touched Gina's arm.

"Okay? You're not okay, you're gorgeous! I wish I could take credit for all those beautiful ringlets but God deserves the applause."

"You look pretty wonderful yourself." She loved the midnight-blue color of Gina's simple dress. The stretchy material gently emphasized her generous bustline and narrow waist. She had watched Gina fashion her natural blonde hair into a French twist, completing the process in just a few seconds.

"C'mon, you two. I smell food with my name on it," Vinny linked arms with the women. "What a lucky guy I am. A babe on each arm."

He gave their names to the doorman, who efficiently scanned the list. He politely allowed them entrance and discreetly pointed in the direction of Matt's table.

Summer's heartbeat drummed in her ears, almost drowning out all other sounds. Shaping her mouth into a nervous smile, she searched the crowd for that one familiar face.

It seemed to take forever for them to make their way through the mass of people. The air rang heavily with the buzz of conversation, shrieks of laughter and the distinct sounds of numerous crystal glasses coming together for gestures of greeting and congratulations.

They finally neared their table. Summer's eyes at last spotted the only man who had managed to capture her heart. And who was now putting it through a meat grinder because the very blonde, very notorious Brandy Cole sat, or, more accurately, partially lay across his lap. Her champagne colored, skimpy dress left little to the imagination. Her breasts were all but falling out of the material.

Summer's eyes met his for the first time in nearly two months. She saw surprise reflected there, turning to what appeared to be shock.

When Brandy snaked her arms around his neck and pressed those well photographed breasts to his face, she felt as though shards of glass were ripping open her heart.

Brandy turned to view the three people who stood before them. Her gaze turned brittle when it landed on Summer. Brandy glanced back at Matt but his eyes were riveted on the woman in the black dress.

Although Summer had learned long ago to lift her head and stand proudly amid adversity, that was the last thing she felt capable of at the moment. She turned, ignoring Gina's hand on her arm.

What did she expect? That he'd been picking petals off daisies, wondering if she loved him, too? That he'd been celibate? So in love with her, he couldn't bear to touch another woman?

Evidently, the answer was yes.

She begged God to grant her the dignity of controlling her tears until she was alone. Moving as quickly as she could manage in her flimsy heels, she pushed through the crowd until she at last reached the doorway.

"Leaving so soon?" the doorman asked.

Her throat hurt so much from the strain of holding her tears in check, she couldn't speak. She nodded briefly and rushed toward the elegant lobby. At least she'd had enough sense to put money in her tiny, fashionable handbag.

As soon as she reached the curb, a taxi slowed to a stop in front of her.

"Need ride?" the cabbie asked in broken English.

"Yes."

The cabbie jumped out and opened the door for her.

Once she settled in the back of the taxi, it was a relief to let the tears fall.

She dug into her purse for a tissue, thinking that she'd probably need a case of them. The humiliation she'd just experienced in the ballroom made all the incidents in her childhood seem trivial.

While she'd been getting dressed this evening, she had tried to prepare herself for disappointment, telling herself Matt may not be happy about her sudden appearance. She had naively thought she could handle the situation should he have a date.

She couldn't believe her stupidity.

She wished she had worried more about being devastated. Maybe then she would have stayed in Haversfield where she belonged.

The sad part was she'd brought this on herself. She couldn't blame Gina or Howard. They had only urged her to follow her heart, certainly meaning no harm.

She couldn't even blame Matt because he really had done nothing to mislead her.

No, she had chosen to believe he loved her without hearing a word of encouragement from him.

And reality was a bitter pill, as usual.

Summer had no way of knowing Matt, once he'd recovered his senses after she'd turned and fled, had abruptly stood, causing the curvaceous Ms. Cole to hit the floor, landing in an ungracious sprawl.

The string of curse words Brandy screamed had no effect on his desire to catch up with the woman he'd been fantasizing about for weeks.

He still couldn't quite believe she'd actually come to New York to see him.

And in that dress.

God was certainly showing him no mercy.

How she had ended up arriving with his closest friends was a question his brain couldn't even tackle at the moment. His only goal was to catch up with her. Stop her from leaving.

He'd seen the pain in her beautiful blue eyes and knew he'd put it there. Though it was unintentionally inflicted, guilt still twisted his gut.

He never thought she could move so fast through a mob of people. By the time he reached the outside door, she was swinging a shapely leg into the cab before closing the door.

"Summer!" he shouted, pushing through the crowd on the sidewalk as he ran toward the vehicle but the taxi sped away from the curb. And, of course, there were no other cabs in the vicinity.

For a split second, he thought he could sprint as fast as the cab but traffic was light and the car was already out of sight. He had no idea where she was going.

"You mean you didn't go after her?" Gina chided when he returned.

"I don't know where she went!" He lifted his hands, palms up.

"Who are you people?" Brandy put her hands on her hips.

"None of your business." Gina gave her a dirty look before turning her attention back to Matt. "Did you come here with this..."

"Gina," Vinny warned, "calm down."

"You can't talk to me like that." Brandy snarled.

"Oh, I'm sorry. I meant, none of your business, Ms. Slut," She replied sweetly. Turning her back on Brandy, she reached up and twisted Matt's ear, hanging on to it despite his yelp.

"Let's go somewhere and talk."

"Get your hands off him!" Brandy shoved her, causing her to lose her hold on Matt. He stepped between the two women and received a knee to his groin at the exact second flash bulbs blinded him.

"Ommph!" He doubled over.

"Get outta my way or I'll do it again!" Gina warned, stretching to take a swing at Brandy's head.

Vinny grabbed her around the waist, holding her tightly against him. Now that she wasn't a moving target, Brandy attempted to land a furious blow on her jaw but Vinny, reacting quickly, turned and her fist instead connected with his shoulder blade.

"Let me go! I'll kill this bitch!" Gina struggled but her husband wouldn't let her loose. She glared at Matt. "This is all your fault! Tell me you're not stupid enough to have come with this piece of...."

"No, I didn't," Matt interrupted.

"Then why the hell didn't you stop Summer from leaving?"

He regained his composure enough to usher his friends out to the lobby, unaware Brandy trailed behind.

"Jesus, this woman can't take a hint!" Gina turned to face the intruder. "Will you get lost? Isn't there a party you're supposed to be stripping at somewhere?"

"Brandy, I think you'd better go join your friends," Matt advised.

"But, honey, I...."

"Get the hell out of here. Gina's right, you can't take a hint. I told you the only thing between us was sex and that was over months ago. You shouldn't have shown up here anyway, much less planted your ass on my lap. Please, just go away and

193

stay away."

Brandy felt anger and frustration color her face. For months she'd been trying to reel this man in but he had remained cool and detached. She was the object of millions of men's fantasies but she couldn't even get Matt to even call anymore.

She was pushing thirty and knew the fame and fortune she'd acquired baring all as a centerfold model wasn't going to last forever. Her problem was the very rich, very talented rock star hadn't cooperated with her plans for the future. Oh, sure, she could snag some other wealthy guy but her tongue was hanging out for him.

Despite the situation, just the thought of sex with him made her quiver. Not only had he found her G spot, he'd discovered letters on her that weren't even in the alphabet.

But his gaze was not heated with desire, only disgust. And it was directed at her. Brandy had no choice but to accept the fact this man would never be hers. The unwanted, unmistakable realization had been when she saw the way he had looked at the woman named Summer. Brandy had pushed the truth aside but it had ended up defeating her.

She straightened her dress, fluffed up her hair. Turning with enough haughtiness to choke an elephant, she walked back into the ballroom.

"I can't believe I got into a brawl in a room full of stars and photographers," Gina groaned.

"I wonder if the folks back home will recognize your face when the National Enquirer plasters it on the cover." Vinny commented. "Won't your parents be proud?"

She shrugged. "I'll worry about that later. What's important right now is your jackass friend is the reason Summer is probably crying her eyes out back at the hotel while we're standing here."

"I can't help it! Why didn't you tell me she was coming?

Vinny told me you were bringing your sister!" Matt angrily retorted.

"Because it was a surprise!"

"That's why you didn't want to stay at my apartment! We have to find her! Now!"

"Why *was* Brandy on your lap?!" She punched his arm.

"She showed up a second before you guys! Before I could push her away, I saw Summer and I froze! I couldn't believe she was here!"

"All right, you two. Yelling at each other isn't going to do anything except attract more attention." Vinny gave each a gentle push toward the exit.

Summer looked around the room once more but it appeared she had packed everything. Although she wanted to throw herself on the bed and cry for hours, she forced herself into action.

She'd already changed clothes. Wadding up that black dress Gina had sworn was going to change her life, she shoved it and the high heels into the suitcase.

She couldn't wait to put distance between herself and New York City. Thankfully, it hadn't taken long to reach the hotel to get her things.

Grabbing the suitcase and her purse, she headed for the elevator. As she rode down to the lobby, she congratulated herself on not fantasizing about Matt rushing after her, begging her to let him explain why Brandy Cole had been plastered over him like a second skin.

Her fantasizing days were over. From now on, her feet would stay firmly planted on the ground. She'd leave the daydreaming to her child.

Hopefully, her son or daughter would be luckier. Have a happier life. She was determined to do all she could to make that a reality.

She wanted to hang on to that belief because it made the present easier to bear.

Vinny paid the taxi fare while Gina and Matt rushed into the hotel.

"Would you please phone Summer Taylor's room?" Matt asked the desk clerk while Gina paced the marble floor.

"I'm sorry but she checked out."

"How long ago?"

He thought of every oath he'd like to scream. Why hadn't he grabbed her the second he spotted her? Instead of acting like he'd been immobilized by a stun gun? But, no, he'd let her go running out into the night, assuming he was with Brandy.

"Maybe twenty minutes." The clerk checked his watch.

"Do you know if she went to the airport?"

"No, I don't. Sorry."

"Thanks." He wanted to hit something. Preferably, Brandy for showing up tonight and planting herself on his lap seconds before Summer appeared.

Most of all, he wanted to punch himself for being the most stupid man on the planet. He'd wanted to call Summer a hundred times but hadn't. He'd been too afraid to face reality. He could have sent her flowers, could have asked her to go with him on tour. But he hadn't.

Guilty again.

"Vinny's right, I shouldn't have meddled." Gina's bottom lip quivered. "This is my fault. I want to go upstairs."

"It isn't your fault." He draped an arm across her shoulders and pulled her close.

"You two mind company?" Vinny's sarcasm did nothing to change the mood as he entered the lobby. "So, is Summer upstairs?"

"She checked out. She could have gone to a different hotel or to the airport. How do I know where to look?" He ran a hand through his hair. "Christ, I'd never be able to find her at the airport! This is New York! And I'll bet my bank account she sure as hell wouldn't answer any page."

"Wouldn't she go home eventually? I don't think she's the type to hop on the Concorde and tour Europe right now," reasoned Vinny.

"Yeah, you're right." He sighed.

"Let's get some food," Vinny suggested. "I'm starving. You can explain how you became a detective and caught a murderer over dinner. Then we'll figure out what you're going to do about Summer."

Chapter Twenty-Six

"Hey, finish the story," Vinny urged while cutting into a steak the size of Rhode Island.

Matt stopped picking at his food and looked up. "I told you I got thoroughly disgusted when Rick dumped that cocaine on the table. Rather than confront him, I left the party and walked around in the night air to clear my head. I was thinking about Summer, thinking about my decision to quit the band. But Rick kept coming to mind. For some strange reason, I got an uneasy feeling even though he'd been cleared, he might know who was responsible for that girl's death months ago.

"I'd probably been gone about an hour when it was almost like something was forcing me to return to the party. So I headed back to the hotel." He took a sip of water.

"The door wasn't locked so I went in. There were only a few people still there. Artie was passed out on the sofa, a redhead snoring alongside him. It was actually kind of dead so I started to leave to go to my room when I heard some odd noises. Like a muffled scream coming from the bedroom. No one else seemed to hear. Or care. So I went to check it out.

"I couldn't believe what I saw. Rick was injecting some kind of drug into the stripper. Her arms were tied to the bed with pillowcases. Another guy was screwing her. Her eyes pleaded with me for help. I didn't think, I just grabbed Rick's friend first. I don't know where I got all this strength, but I threw him across the room.

"Rick came at me. All of a sudden, he had a knife in his hand and started slashing at me, threatening to kill me."

"Oh my God!" Gina interrupted, her eyes wide with horror.

"Good thing he was so wasted or I'd never been able to overpower him," continued Matt. "I yelled for someone to call the cops and, thank God, one of the guys in the other room was coherent enough to do that. It turned out the semen and hair samples from Rick's friend matched those taken from the corpse found in my apartment.

"Evidently, Rick had given the girl at my party enough dope, too much dope, it turned out, that she didn't care if his friend raped her. Rick evidently likes to watch a rape while he jerks off. Uh, sorry Gina. Anyway, Rick wasn't a suspect because he never had sex with the girl. And he wasn't about to turn his friend in to the police and implicate himself.

"Those bastards." He shook his head, finding the events that occurred still unbelievable. "I think they would have killed the stripper so she couldn't go to the cops. But it would have seemed like an accidental overdose, just like before."

"Maybe they paid her for sex but then got carried away." Gina shuddered. "How disgusting. Thank God you went back to the room or she might have not made it out of there alive."

"Yeah. But it wasn't like I solved the crime of the century. I was glad, once and for all, my name was finally cleared without a shadow of a doubt. This is one time the reporters actually did me a favor."

"Did you have trouble getting a drummer to replace Rick?" Vinny asked.

"No. I had a guy already lined up because I didn't know if Rick was going to straighten out or not. He fit right in from the start." Matt pushed his food around the plate with his fork. "I hope Summer's okay."

"Me, too. All this turmoil can't be good for the ba..." Gina clamped her teeth down on her bottom lip. She reached for her glass and took a sip. "This wine is really good."

"What? What did you say?" Matt sat straight up.

"I said this wine is good." Gina ducked her head and took another sip.

"That's not what I meant and you know it. 'All this turmoil can't be good for the ba...' that's what you said." His eyes

199

narrowed. "Is she pregnant?"

Gina fidgeted with her napkin.

"Is Summer pregnant?" He was almost shouting.

Her nod was quick, almost imperceptible. "I promised I wouldn't say anything."

"Well, your loyalty is certainly touching. What else are you not supposed to tell me? I realize we hardly know each other, but..."

"Don't you dare try and make me feel guilty! You were the one with the bimbo on your lap, remember?" she snapped.

"I swear, one of these days, I'm going to deck the both of you." Vinny threw his napkin on the table.

Matt reached for his wallet, took out enough money to cover dinner and tossed it on the table. He stood. "My treat."

"Where you going?" Vinny asked.

"Where do you think?"

The "ding" sound indicated it was time to fasten the seat belts.

"Ladies and gentlemen, the captain asks that all seats be put in the upright position and fasten your seatbelts as we are about to enter our final approach into the St. Louis area. Please remain in your seats until the plane has come to a complete stop at the gate. Thanks for flying with us."

Matt only half listened to the stewardess as she gave the instructions for landing. The other half of his mind kept chanting, YOU'RE GOING TO BE A FATHER.

It was enough to make his knees knock together with fright.

He'd barely gotten used to the idea he was actually in love. That was scary enough. Now, fatherhood loomed menacingly over his head.

What kind of father would he make? He felt certain he'd be nothing like the man who impregnated his mother. That at least was a step in the right direction.

He already knew Summer would be an excellent mother. If she was so protective and loving toward Gyp, she'd be wonderful to her child.

Her child. His child. Their child.

He checked his watch as they hit the runway. By the time he rented a car and drove to Haversfield, it would be around four in the morning, if he was lucky. He didn't know what would happen when he got there but at least she wouldn't be able to run from him.

It surprised Summer she'd slept like the dead. She had been right to get a good night's rest instead of driving last night. She'd been too tired after flying into St. Louis to get her car and make the two hour trip to Haversfield. As exhausted as she'd been, she could have had an accident and harmed the baby in some way.

After taking a long shower, she ordered breakfast from room service and turned on the television, listening to the morning news as she dressed.

"People are still talking about the heroic actions of Matt Zeller," the commentator informed. "We now go to correspondent Ginny Doyle for a live interview with Erica Linden, the woman whose life police are claiming the rock star saved."

Summer yanked the sweatshirt over her head and gaped at the television as Erica articulated the chilling events of that night. The woman couldn't praise Matt enough as she described how he saved her from an almost certain death.

As the report continued, she learned the drummer in his band and his friend were being charged with the murder committed in New York months ago. They would also be charged with the rape and attempted murder of Erica Linden.

"Thank you, Erica." The camera focused back on Ginny

201

Doyle. "Back to you, John."

Matt a hero? She shrugged.

He certainly isn't mine.

Hours later, she pulled into the driveway behind a new Buick, wishing she could wipe the trip to New York from her mind. Better yet, she would give anything to go back in time and never let Matt set foot in her house.

At least she was home. Anxious to get inside and take comfort from familiar surroundings, she grabbed her suitcase and headed for the back door.

The kitchen was empty, the house unusually quiet.

Where was Gyp? And Julie?

She carried her bag upstairs. All the bedroom doors were closed, but that was standard procedure when there were paying customers.

When she opened the door to her room, she found it odd the shades and curtains were closed, making the room entirely too dark. And someone was snoring. Someone here in her room.

She yanked open the curtains and raised the shades. Spinning around, she thought her heart would jump out of her chest when her eyes focused on the man in her bed.

How in the hell had he beat her back from New York?

Sleeping next to him was her traitorous mutt she'd been so anxious to see.

Gyp's tail softly thumped on the bed as he lifted his head and gave her a sleepy glance.

Matt had just assumed he could stay in her room. That she'd welcome him back into her bed.

He had to have an overly inflated ego or else he was incredibly obtuse.

She wanted to grab the covers and dump him on the floor but had no desire for a confrontation at the moment. She needed to calm down, be sensible.

Most of all, she needed to stop shaking.

Why was he here, anyway? Oh, of course. How stupid of me, she thought. Mr. Hero probably needs another break from the news media.

She motioned for the dog to follow her out of the room. He stretched, yawned, then stretched again before jumping off the bed.

"Whose dog are you, anyway?" she muttered as they descended the stairs.

When she walked into the kitchen, she heard a car door slam. She looked out the window and saw her friend getting grocery bags out of the car. She turned toward the back door and waited.

"What the hell's going on?" asked Julie as soon as she entered the house and placed the bags on the counter.

"I was going to ask you the same thing. Why is Matt sleeping in my bedroom?" She placed her hands on her hips, taking an accusatory stance.

"Because he showed up before dawn, wanting to know if you were here. Howard and I said we thought you were with him. Then he just said he was tired and went upstairs. He hasn't come down yet?" Julie walked over to the table and sat down. She took the newspaper tucked under her arm and set it down.

"No."

"Well, wait till you see this." Julie spread the paper on the table.

"I really don't feel like reading..."

"You have to see this," Julie emphasized. "You won't believe it."

Annoyed, she walked over and looked where Julie's finger pointed. The headline CATFIGHT OVER HERO couldn't fail to attract anyone's attention.

"That's Brandy Cole shoving Gina." Her eyes grew round

with surprise. When she came to the sentence describing Gina as Matt's new love interest, she snorted in disgust. The reporter obviously didn't care about the truth in the rush to get the story printed.

"Yeah, but look at this one of Gina throwing a right hook. Were you there? Did Gina clock her?"

"I don't know. That had to have happened after I left," she murmured.

"Why did you leave? Wasn't Matt glad to see you? Or was he with Brandy?"

"I was very glad to see her. She left because of a misunderstanding," Matt spoke from the doorway.

He cautiously entered the room, his arms slightly crossed over his midsection as he warily glanced at Summer.

"I didn't misunderstand anything. My vision is excellent. I just realized as soon as I saw you with Brandy that I was intruding. It was foolish of me to show up to surprise you. And I'd appreciate it very much if you'd leave as soon as possible." She refused to look at him.

"I'm not going anywhere."

"This is my house. I'll call Calvert." Even to her own ears she sounded childish.

He made a rude noise. "Quit acting like a child."

His comment made her mad enough to turn around and face him. "What makes you think you can barge in..."

"Julie, would you please give us some time alone?" he interrupted.

"Uh, sure. Right. Actually, I'm supposed to take Howard lunch. I better get over to Maisie's and get it. Today's fried catfish day." She smiled sheepishly before hurrying from the room.

Once they were alone, Summer folded her arms and stood silently waiting. For what, she didn't know. Since he'd never offered any words of commitment or love, he didn't really owe her an explanation.

Besides, she didn't need one. Her vision was excellent, still 20/20, according to her last eye exam. Hadn't she seen Miss Yes-I'll-Take-Off-My-Clothes-For-Anyone, commonly known as Brandy Cole, plastered all over America's Hero? She was perfectly able to connect the dots without assistance.

He could certainly carry on with anyone he chose and, obviously, he fully intended to. She had been the one who'd barged in without an invitation. Traveling all the way to New York without any encouragement from him, just to make a fool of herself.

"I need coffee." He walked over to the counter, plucked a mug from the rack and poured himself a cup. He seemed to stall for time, taking a couple of slow sips before finally turning to look at her.

"Brandy was not with me. She didn't come with me, I didn't invite her. I didn't even know she'd be there or care. It was only a second or two before you walked in that she just plopped herself on my lap. My only mistake was waiting too long to toss her butt on the floor. But I was so shocked to see you, I wasn't thinking."

"Whatever."

"Listen, why don't we sit down? We need to talk."

"There's nothing really to talk about." She remained standing.

"Sit." He pulled out a chair.

She appeared indecisive but finally gave up and sat down.

He pulled a chair close, too close, she thought, and sat down.

"When were you going to tell me about the baby?"

She felt the breath just stop in her lungs until she forced herself to let it out. "Who told you?"

He started to put his arm around her but she flung it off. "Gina let it slip."

"She promised she wouldn't say anything." A stab of betrayal made her voice waver.

"Don't blame her. She feels bad enough. But don't I have a right to know?" He gave her an expectant look, waiting for her to respond. When she didn't, he took a sip of his coffee before blurting, "Don't worry. I'll marry you."

She had been avoiding eye contact since they sat down but now looked at him as though he'd said something extremely distasteful. And insulting.

"I want to do the right thing."

"No, thank you," she responded, a sliver of sarcasm in her voice.

"No? What do you mean, no?" he demanded.

"It's a simple enough word to understand." She stood. "When will you be leaving?"

"Damn it, we have a child to think of!"

"That's exactly what I'm doing. Excuse me, but I have things to do." She stood and walked out of the room.

As she went upstairs, she heard, *Don't worry. I'll marry you,* echo in her mind. Certainly not the words she had hoped he would say. Not even close.

He hadn't mentioned love. He hadn't said he'd been thinking of her, missing her. Couldn't forget her.

Nope, nothing like those words. Instead, it sounded as though she and the baby were an obligation. He'd made a mistake and was willing to accept the consequences and do the right thing.

After all, he was a hero, right?

Well, she might be impractical or overly emotional but she wasn't about to marry anyone who didn't love her, with or without a baby. A marriage like that was doomed for failure and she wasn't about to made a bad situation worse.

She had told him she had things to do, and she did. Like taking a nap. And having a good cry. She wasn't sure which would come first.

Chapter Twenty-Seven

Matt didn't stop her from leaving the room only because he was afraid he'd say something else to make things worse.

He knew he'd already said the wrong things. He clumsily had given the wrong impression about his feelings.

He had intended to ease into the subject of the baby instead of blurting it out, acting like a bull in a china shop. But the emotional roller coaster he'd been on since last night was playing hell with his nerves.

Could he blame his ineptness on jet lag?

Lack of sleep? Inexperience?

Hell, he *was* new at this love stuff.

She'd be doing him a favor if she got a gun and shot him because it certainly seemed like he was too stupid to live.

Matt had given dozens of interviews, been on *Sixty Minutes* and *Dateline* and not once had he sounded like the village idiot. He knew he could talk intelligently. String enough words together to impress people. Just not today.

He scrubbed his hands over his face. If he went after her, told her he loved her, she'd probably punch him in the head.

He left, not knowing what else to do.

Summer felt uncomfortable in her room. Probably because it looked like her and Matt's room. His things were strewn all over, as though he lived there, too. She had tried resting on the bed but the scent of his cologne lingered on the pillows.

She went into the hall, took clean linens from the closet and changed her bedding. Despite her efforts, sleep was still elusive. Surprisingly, so were tears.

Her life had become a soap opera. A trashy romance novel gone bad and it was her own fault. Since seeing Brandy on Matt's lap, she'd realized how foolish her expectations had been.

How can you expect anything from a man when he'd never offered anything?

It was too late to chide herself for making love with him without a condom. No, she corrected, she had made love. He'd had sex.

He would probably breeze in and out of the baby's life. Maybe after a time, his visits would dwindle because his demanding career would require more and more of his time. He had records to make, tours to do. Whatever.

The hell with him. From now on, she would concentrate on her baby. She would make her child feel loved and wanted every day of its life.

She hadn't gotten that from her mother but at least she had from her grandparents. The lessons she'd learned from them would guide her.

Tears did form in her eyes when she thought of her grandparents. What would they think of her now? If they knew of the mess she'd made of her life, would they be heartbroken? After all they'd been through with her mother, wouldn't they have been devastated?

Hugging a pillow tightly, Summer wished things were different. She had no one to blame but herself. She had been grossly irresponsible and gotten pregnant. Plus, the father of the baby didn't love her.

It was fashionable, even accepted, in today's world to have children without benefit of marriage. She had never condoned that behavior because of what she'd had to deal with growing up.

She'd never thought she'd ever place herself in that position. But that's exactly what she'd done.

Autumn had painted the leaves so beautifully, turning Haversfield into a scene worthy enough to be duplicated on a postcard. Though the day was sunny, Matt was glad he'd grabbed his jacket before leaving Summer's. The wind had a kick to it, signaling winter wasn't far off.

As he walked through the downtown area, he briefly wondered why more businesses hadn't opened. The area had potential for growth but no one seemed to have the energy or interest.

Pushing open the door of the hardware store, he stepped inside and spotted Julie sitting at the checkout counter with Howard. "What's going on?"

Howard put down his sandwich to run a napkin across his mouth. "Suppose you tell me. Just what the hell happened last night? And don't try to bullshit me."

He would have been insulted had he not realized Howard was merely assuming the role of Summer's protector.

"I had no clue she was going to show up in New York. Gina and Vinny never said a word about bringing her, but that's a whole different issue. I didn't have anything to do with Brandy Cole being at the party. And, pain in the ass that she is, she planted her butt on my lap right before Summer walked in." He stood with his hands on his hips.

"Summer jumped to conclusions and broke the speed record leaving the place. Just for the record, there is nothing going on between Brandy and me. I ended things with her before I ever set foot in this town and met your cousin. Besides, there was never anything between us except sex."

"Between who? You and Summer or you and Brandy?"

Taking a measured breath, he wondered if Howard was deliberately trying to provoke him. "Me and Brandy. As for Summer, I tried to talk to her a little while ago. I told her she doesn't have to worry, that I'll marry her. But she turned me down."

"Gee. How can any girl refuse such a romantic proposal." Julie rolled her eyes.

210

"Hold on. What's that supposed to mean? She doesn't have to worry about what?" Howard demanded.

"You know! The baby!" Exasperation caused Matt to snap out the words.

No one said a word for several seconds. Too late, Matt realized they didn't know. Otherwise, they wouldn't have shock registered on their faces.

"No, I didn't know, you son-of-a..." Howard lunged across the counter, both hands gripping his jacket.

"Stop it! The last thing Summer needs right now is the two of you acting like Neanderthals!" Julie admonished, prying Howard's hands off Matt.

"Oh, damn," he groaned. "Me and my big mouth."

"Let's discuss this as adults. If that's really the way you proposed to her, then you're incredibly stupid. No woman wants to feel like a man is marrying her because he has to. No wonder she turned you down," Julie scolded.

"If you think you're going to blow out of here and leave Sum in a jam, think again. Because I'll kill your sorry ass," Howard warned. "I know it takes two to make a baby and my cousin is old enough to handle her own life. But I'll make damn sure you don't walk out on her."

"I'm not going to leave her!" He glared at him. "How could you even think that?"

"You left out of here before without so much as a backward glance! If you had stayed, then Daryl wouldn't have been brave enough to try to rape her! But, hell, you wouldn't know about that because you haven't bothered to call or see her since you tore out of here! If she wouldn't have shown up in New York, she still wouldn't have seen hide nor hair of you!" Disgusted, Howard added, "I feel bad for encouraging her to take that trip."

"Daryl tried what?" Matt's face paled.

"Oh, I forgot. How would you know about that?" Howard

sneered. "He tried to attack her but lucky I dropped in before he did much damage."

"Where is he? I'll kill that bastard."

"He's locked up. At the preliminary hearing, the judge refused to allow him out on bond," Julie interjected. "He killed Lisa."

Matt turned away from them. He ran a hand over his face and realized he was trembling with rage. He took a few deep breaths, struggling to deal with the guilt he felt. If only he'd stayed in town or taken her with him like he should have.

"Listen, let's all calm down. Hasn't she been through enough? She shouldn't be upset," Julie urged, placing a hand on Matt's shoulder to turn him around.

"I've been touring with my band but there's a two week break now. I swear I was planning to come back! Despite what you might think, it was hard for me to leave her. She's been on my mind constantly." He lifted his chin a notch. "Your cousin didn't even bother to inform me she was pregnant. Gina let it slip."

Frowning, Howard picked up his napkin and carefully wiped his hands. "Well, Romeo, I advise you to get your sorry self back over there and straighten this out right now. One way or the other, you're gonna talk Summer into marrying you."

Matt let out a relieved breath when he didn't see his suitcase packed and thrown on the front porch. He went through the first floor of the house and out on the back porch, looking for her. Unsuccessful, he went upstairs and knocked on her bedroom door before opening it, surprised it wasn't locked.

He saw her standing by the window. She glanced over her shoulder as he entered the room but turned back to continue gazing outside.

"What's going on?" He kept his voice soft.

212

Julie had warned him again before he left Howard's store that all this commotion wasn't good for Summer in her condition. No matter what she did, he was determined not to argue with her.

Although he was annoyed she was totally ignoring him. And being unreasonable.

"I wish I had been here when Daryl tried to attack you."

"Howard was, so everything turned out okay. And if you don't mind, I don't want to talk about it." She added, "Shouldn't you be getting ready to leave?"

"We...uh, we need to talk." He wished she'd meet him halfway. He was so out of his element when it came to expressing his emotions. He could write award-winning songs but couldn't tell Summer what was in his heart.

"About what?" she dully asked.

"About getting married."

"Already have."

"No, Summer, we haven't. We need to discuss this calmly and rationally." He walked over and sat on the edge of the bed. "Do you think you could turn around and look at me?"

She let go of a long sigh but she did face him. He saw the blank expression on her face and would have preferred an indication of what she was feeling, whether it was anger or indifference.

"Why did you come to New York?"

She cleared her throat and looked away. "When Gina and Vinny arrived here to spend a few days, Gina and I became friends. Oh, I like Vinny, too, but Gina and I spent a lot of time together. She thought it would be fun if I went with them. And then I took a pregnancy test and Gina said I had to tell you."

Matt scratched at his chin, thinking. If she just wanted to inform him of the baby, a phone call would have done the job if she didn't really care about him.

A moment of clarity made him realize she had traveled all that way to see him because she must love him. If she didn't, she wouldn't have gotten so upset over Brandy, would she?

The inept way he'd proposed had no doubt planted the idea in her head that he felt trapped. If he tried to tell her any different, he doubted she would believe him right now. Most likely, she would prefer to blacken his eyes.

"Gina was right. You should have," he softly admonished. "You have my number. I check my messages daily."

"I don't want you to think I expect anything from you. I don't want any of your money." She looked him in the eye as she spoke.

"I never thought that. Still don't. But you're carrying my child." He thought it was a reasonable thing to point out.

"I'm carrying my child."

He had to remind himself that he wasn't going to argue with her and she obviously wasn't going to rationally discuss anything with him right now.

Apparently, a different approach was needed for the time being.

"You have a week to plan the wedding. I have to resume the tour after that." He stood up. "I want us to be married by then."

Her head snapped up. "You have a lot of nerve! Just because I'm carrying your child doesn't mean you can order me around."

"We can have any kind of wedding you want." He kept his voice calm.

"I don't want any!" she shouted.

He ignored her anger, flatly stating, "My child will be born to parents that are married. People in this town are not going to treat my child like they did you."

It was an ace up his sleeve. It was also a low blow, but he had to use anything he could think of to get her to marry him.

If she wasn't so obstinate, they could be in the bed he was looking at right now and having a much better time.

"I don't have to stay here in Haversfield. I can move. Raise the baby in another city." Defiantly, she lifted her chin. "Things are different nowadays. Women are having babies without being married."

"That's a crock and you know it. Why the hell would you move? This house is part of our child's heritage. The only connection with your grandparents." He questioned, "Are you saying you don't want your baby to have a better childhood than you had?"

Judging from the sudden slump of her shoulders, he had just seen the wind go out of her sails. Mentally, he patted himself on the back for gaining the upper hand. He just didn't know how long he'd be able to keep it.

"I hope you consider a church wedding. I would like to see you walk down the aisle with your head held high in front of everyone in this town. For our child's sake." *And yours.*

"All right, but I want a pre-nuptial agreement. I don't want your damn money. We can get a divorce after the baby is born," she insisted.

"We'll worry about that later."

A divorce? Not in this lifetime, sweetheart.

Chapter Twenty-Eight

"I can't believe she didn't tell me she's pregnant. We're supposedly best friends. She told Gina instead." Julie slipped her hands into her pockets.

"I know. My nose is a little out of joint over that, too." Howard locked the store up before they headed home.

"Do you really still think he loves her?"

"Yeah. He just went about things the wrong way. Hopefully, by now he's sweet talked himself back into her good graces." He put an arm around her shoulders as they walked.

"But what if he hasn't?"

"Then I'll rearrange his face," he simply informed.

She laughed as they neared the house. "Some guests are scheduled to check in today. I forgot to tell Summer."

"Shoot. I was hoping to have some peace and quiet tonight."

As they went inside, he said, "I don't see any blood anywhere. That's a good sign."

They walked into the kitchen and found Summer, standing at the stove stirring a pot of soup.

"Hey, cuz. What's up?"

"Nothing." She wiped her eyes with the sleeve of her shirt.

"Where's Matt?" Julie asked. "Everything okay between you two?"

"He went to Bob's to shoot pool. Everything's just w-w-wonderful," she sniffled.

Julie grabbed a paper towel and handed it to her. "Sit down. Tell us what's wrong."

"We're getting m-m-married!" Summer began to cry as though her heart were breaking.

"You and Summer are getting married?" Ernie repeated the

216

words he'd just heard. "Next week?"

"Yep. Nine ball in the side pocket." Matt leaned down, took his time and made the shot.

"Well, you're just full of surprises. I still ain't over the fact you're a rich and famous rock star," Bob remarked. "Or that you saved some woman's life. You sure are a busy guy."

"I guess you guys will be moving away." Ernie took a drink of his beer.

"Not really. I wouldn't mind living right here." If Summer would quit locking him out of the bedroom, that is.

"We should throw you a bachelor party," Ernie suggested.

"Now there's an idea. Maybe Maisie will even strip for us." Bob chalked his stick.

By the time they'd played a few games, Matt was less tense. He'd rather have stayed with Summer but thought maybe they needed a little break from each other since things hadn't gone well. Which was why he'd come to Bob's.

Getting married and becoming a father were two things he never expected to do. It surprised him he wasn't shaking in his Nikes.

He did know one thing. He was pretty damn happy to be back in town.

When he returned to Summer's, he wandered into the kitchen, wanting to see her but fearing another confrontation. The back door was open. He could hear the porch swing creak as it moved back and forth.

Like a magnet, she drew him outside. He sat next to her, afraid to get too close, afraid he'd never get close enough.

"You doing okay?" he softly asked.

"Fine."

"You feeling okay? I mean, with the baby."

"I'm okay."

"Morning sickness?"

"It's going away."

217

"Been to the doctor?"

"Yes. My pregnancy has been professionally confirmed, in case you're wondering if there's a chance this is a false alarm. But I told you we don't have to get married," she said through clenched teeth.

"I wasn't looking for a way out." He took hold of her arm and made her face him. "I just wanted to know if you're okay."

She freed herself from his grasp and stood. "The guest rooms are all filled because two couples checked in earlier. I guess you'll have to share my room but I don't want you to touch me."

He watched her turn and walk into the house. He wanted to follow her and give her a piece of his mind but things were already screwed up enough.

He sighed as he propelled the swing into action with his legs. The night air he breathed in was cool and crisp.

He was scared of marriage. The thought of becoming a father terrified him. Even so, he knew they belonged together.

How odd that for months he had denied what he felt for her and now couldn't be more determined to put a ring on her finger.

And it wasn't just because of the baby, like she thought. If she pushed aside her anger and hurt, she'd realize if he didn't love her, nothing on earth could make him marry her.

He wished he could change things. Go back to the day Calvert discovered his true identity. He would have said and done all the things he should have. He would never have left and not talked to her for months. He would already have been back here several times. And he would have killed Daryl the minute he tried to touch her.

Since that wasn't possible, he decided he'd just have to start over. Only this time, he would court her. Which was going to be hard since she'd just ordered him not to touch her.

Not touch her, he scoffed. He vowed he'd soon have her

218

eager for his touch. As eager as he was to touch her.

He didn't know how long he'd stayed outside but when the mosquitoes tried to make a buffet of him, he went indoors.

The house was quiet as he made his way upstairs. He cautiously opened the bedroom door, praying he wouldn't be hit by any thrown objects. He breathed a sigh of relief when he discovered Summer sleeping in bed, a paperback lying beside her. Instead of resting peacefully, the low lamplight showed her forehead creased with worry lines.

He quietly undressed. He placed the book on the nightstand, turned off the lamp and slid into bed. He gently pulled her into his arms and smiled when she snuggled next to him, though she remained asleep.

Everything about her appealed to him. Her warm body, the soft scent of her perfume. Her mind and spirit. He always wanted her sexually but for now it was enough just to hold her.

He wanted to run a hand over her belly and breasts and learn what changes their child had so far caused. If he didn't fear her reaction should she wake, he would have.

He consoled himself with the thought that soon he would be able to do much more than just run his hands over her.

He felt peaceful, filled with a strong sense of rightness about their future. He wished she did, too.

Before long, he drifted off to sleep with her still in his arms. They both slept deeply and soundly for the first time in months.

Summer felt his leg between hers, felt the heat of him against her back. Her eyes fluttered open.

Why couldn't she turn over and wake him with a kiss? Slide her hands over him, reacquaint herself with his body. She wanted to. Her physical desire for him was intense. Relentless. But she couldn't allow herself that lapse.

Despite the fact they'd soon be married, she refused to set

herself up for another heartbreak. One day, he would leave her again and return to his world.

If only he had tried to contact her during all these weeks. Then it would be easier to believe he cared enough about her to maybe even fall in love. No, she had to protect herself from these foolish dreams. If he hadn't found out about the baby, he wouldn't be sleeping in her bed at that moment.

They didn't have a relationship, didn't have a future. They'd only had sex.

She never had thought such a cold, practical discussion about a wedding would ever occur in her life. But then she'd been so wrong about everything else, why not this, too?

It was enough to make her cry again except she felt drained. Her emotions were so chaotic.

She gently pushed herself out of bed and walked into the bathroom. She pulled off her nightshirt and turned on the shower.

The pipes sang for a moment, just enough to wake Matt. It only took a second to realize where he was.

He could hear her in the shower. Against his will, he imagined the water running down her bare skin.

Quit torturing yourself, he warned. He was already hard enough. What would she do if he just stepped into the shower with her? Just grabbed her and kissed her until...

A knock sounded on the door, right before Julie stuck her head in. "Sorry, but I need to talk to Summer."

"She's in the shower."

Julie gave him a sheepish grin as she walked to the bathroom door and opened it. "Summer, the guests want to know if any fall festivals are going on around here. What should I tell them?"

"There's a stack of brochures on the desk. All the information's in them," she responded.

"Okay." Julie turned to leave. Before she walked out, she

told him, "Howard said if you get too bored, go see him."

"Okay."

After a few minutes, he heard the water shut off. It seemed to take forever before she walked out of the bathroom. A dark blue thick robe covered her from her neck down to her ankles.

He watched as she walked to the dresser and picked up a wide toothed comb.

"Have you called Gina about the wedding?"

The question slowed her hand as it gently worked the tangles from her hair. "No."

"Okay. I will. I'd like Vinny and her to be here. And Dave and Lil Meyer."

She nodded. Her eyes met his in the mirror, watched as he threw off the covers and rose from the bed, naked. Her hand faltered but she didn't look away. Even when her gaze drifted down to his erection and her face flushed.

"Guess I'll take a shower." He feigned calmness as he crossed the room.

Chapter Twenty-Nine

"You have to get busy. A wedding doesn't just happen," Julie chastised.

"I know." Summer took a deep breath and savored the aroma of coffee brewing. She wished she could have a cup but her caffeine days were temporarily gone.

"Yeah. Pick out a church and let's go talk to the minister. Today," Matt ordered between bites of scrambled eggs and sausage.

"I guess St. Matthew's is okay. We used to go there. That's where my grandparents' funerals were. I like the minister, Tim McAllister." She had the feeling she was sleepwalking and couldn't wake up. She still couldn't believe they were really planning a wedding under these circumstances.

"You need invitations. There won't be time to order and mail them. We'll have to make them and deliver them ourselves. You need flowers." Julie stood. "I'll go get some paper and a pen. You need to make a list and start arranging things right away."

"Okay, so after we eat, we'll go talk to McAllister." Matt sipped his coffee.

The morning was hectic but a lot was accomplished. After arrangements were made at the church, Summer and Matt went to get the marriage license. As they got into the rental car, he said, "Rings."

"Rings?" she echoed. She had hoped they'd accomplished enough for one day because she was ready to nod off.

"Is there a jewelry store in town?"

"There's one around the corner from Howard's store. It opened a few years ago." She yawned. Okay, she told herself, how long could it take to pick out some gold bands?

Forever, she realized an hour later. She never would have

dreamed he would want to talk about clarity of diamonds, weight and whatever. Wasn't a diamond a diamond? And why didn't they just get simple gold bands and be done with it so she could have a nap?

"Try this one on," he finally suggested.

She looked down and saw the most beautiful ring in the world. The marquise shaped diamond was surrounded by smaller ones. A simple wedding band completed the set.

"There's also a matching band for the groom," the jeweler pointed out.

Matt slipped the engagement ring on her finger. "Do you like that? How does it fit? Is there something else you want to try on?"

"It fits perfectly. It's the most beautiful ring I've ever seen," she softly answered, her eyes misting.

Why couldn't things be different? Why couldn't he love her?

"We can get just plain gold bands. You don't have to buy me anything like this."

Amused, he asked, "Don't you think I can afford it?"

"I know you can. But I didn't expect..."

"Okay, we'll take it." He slid his wallet from his back pocket and pulled out a credit card.

After he signed the bill, the jeweler handed him the box containing their wedding rings while she gazed at the diamonds on her finger.

As they walked toward the car, she asked, "Now can we go home? I can't help it but I'm so tired."

"Sure. I'm kind of tired myself." He muttered under his breath, "Tired of keeping my hands off you."

"What?"

"Nothing. I'm just mumbling."

When they pulled into the driveway, he asked, "Whose car is that?"

"It looks like Ruthie's. She's Bob's wife. Normally, I'm always glad to see her but right now I'm so tired, I could cry. I guess it's because I'm pregnant."

He covered her hand with his. "You can still take a nap. I'll talk to her."

"Thanks." Her eyes met his. When her heart started to pound, she reminded herself they were not in love. Well, at least one of them wasn't. Reluctantly, she turned and opened the door.

They went into the house and greeted Ruth, who immediately noticed Summer's ring. "My, isn't that the most spectacular thing in the world?"

"Wow! Is that a ring or a television set?" Julie exclaimed. She elbowed Matt. "You did good, Zeller."

"Have you gotten your dress yet?" Ruth asked.

"No."

"We'll have to do that tomorrow," Julie cut in. "Howard said Ruth was a calligrapher, so I called her to come over. We have to get started on these invitations," she reminded. "She has a few samples for you guys to choose from."

Summer thought she'd fall asleep over the different designs but Matt helped her choose one rather quickly. The front was plain but had a border consisting of a cut out lace pattern.

"I hate to be rude, but I need a nap. We've been running around for hours." Summer hoped Ruthie didn't put two and two together. The quick wedding, her tiredness. She hoped to keep her pregnancy a secret as long as possible.

"Why, sure, honey. You look all tuckered out. All this planning and excitement is rather tiresome. Julie and I can work on these while you rest," Ruth assured her.

She went to the bedroom, walked out of her shoes and crawled into bed. Though her eyelids were getting heavier, she couldn't help looking at her ring again.

Why was Matt going through all this trouble for a pretend marriage? To fool the people in town? The press? Or maybe he felt guilty about taking her virginity.

She finally drifted off to sleep without understanding anything.

Matt's fingers softly played part of a song he'd been working on for the past hour. He had the house to himself. The guests had driven to the next county for the Pumpkin Festival and weren't expected back until late evening. Julie and Howard had gone out for dinner and a movie.

After running to the store for a couple of things, he had decided to take advantage of the quietness and work. Gyp had curled up on the floor nearby and was now snoring, apparently unimpressed a so-called superstar was plunking at the piano keys.

He paused to check his watch, calculating Summer had been sleeping nearly three hours. He guessed he should check on her.

As he went upstairs, he wondered if it was normal for a pregnant woman to be so tired. Maybe he should scan the paperback about pregnancy she had been reading in bed the night before.

He opened the door. The darkening sky allowed little light to filter in the windows but it was enough to see her still sleeping. Backing out of the room, he went downstairs and returned to the piano.

He didn't know how long he'd been working when he noticed her standing in the doorway, her hands on her hips. She still looked sleepy, but mad enough to fight.

Warily, he turned to face her. "I'm sorry. Did I wake you?

"No," she snapped.

"What's wrong?"

"Ha," she snorted. "I've been in the kitchen!"

He rubbed his chin, sensing anything he said was going to be wrong. "Yeah?"

"Yeah! You're not supposed to be buying me flowers! I bet you didn't even call Hugh Parker to draw up that pre-nuptial agreement!"

While she'd been sleeping, he'd gone and bought her deep pink roses. He'd even been clever enough to write on the card, *Mommy, you should be nicer to daddy. Love, the baby.*

Because of that, she was mad? How was he going to romance her if everything he did ticked her off?

"Well?!"

"Well, what?" he asked.

"Did you call Hugh Parker?" Exasperation made her speak slowly and distinctly.

"Uh, no. There's plenty of time for that."

"No, there isn't!" She shouted. "One week from tomorrow, we're getting married! I don't want anyone throwing it in my face that I married you for your money! I don't want to have to worry about things like that! Because when we get divorced, I'll have enough on my mind!"

Her words made him furious. She evidently had no intention of even trying to make their marriage work.

Standing, he walked and shook a finger at her to emphasize his words. "Okay, fine! You want a pre-nup, you'll get one! I'll call Hugh in the morning!" he fumed, adding, "You're so impossibly bull-headed!"

He strode determinedly into the kitchen, picked up the roses and threw them into the trash. He grabbed his jacket from the chair, where he'd tossed it earlier.

"Where are you going?" she demanded, following him as he went to the front door.

"Out," he snapped, before shoving the door open.

The sound of the door slamming seemed to echo a couple

of times.

She walked into the kitchen and slumped onto a chair. The ticking of the clock on the wall seemed to emphasize the loneliness of the house when she was the sole occupant.

She laid her head down on the table and cried.

She hadn't really wanted to argue with him. She was just frightened. When she'd woken up a while ago, all she could think about was how much she wanted his arms around her. How much she wanted him.

If she felt this way again after spending only one day with him, how could she let him go after the baby was born?

She'd told him she intended to get a divorce.

She was beginning to think she opened her big mouth way too much.

If only he loved her.

But he didn't. He was doing the right thing and even being nice while he did it.

That made her cry even harder.

"Well, look who it is. I hear them wedding bells'll be ringing next Saturday morning. Ruthie's at home tonight working on the invitations. Said I was driving her crazy, so I came here," Bob remarked, a toothpick sticking out of his mouth.

Matt slid onto the stool next to him. "Yep. Next Saturday." He drummed his fingers on the wooden surface. When the bartender approached, he said, "Bourbon. Straight up."

"You sure look glum for a guy getting ready to take the plunge. What's the matter, kiddo? Fighting with the blushing bride? Don't worry. That's natural."

"I guess." Toying with the ashtray, he wondered why he was going to marry someone who was already planning their divorce.

"Just relax. Have a few drinks, kill some time. In the

morning, things will be better," Bob patted his shoulder.

"Yeah." He doubted that very much.

He hung out with Bob until the bar closed. Although he'd had a few, he didn't even have enough of a buzz going to feel good.

He walked slowly back to Summer's, half expecting to be locked out. When he stepped inside, he could hear the television in the family room.

Maybe it was the strain of the past few days, but he suddenly felt so tired, he wanted to lay down and sleep for days. Or years.

He started up the steps.

"Matt...I'm sorry."

The softness in her voice stopped him. Looking down, he saw her standing by the stairway. He noticed her eyes were puffy, indicating she'd spent the evening crying.

That tore at his heart.

He turned and retraced his steps until he stood facing her. "About what?"

"About the way I acted. Everything. I don't know why I'm so out of control."

He saw her bottom lip quiver. Without thinking, he pulled her into his arms and kissed her. He thought he intended the kiss to be comforting but, boy, was he ever wrong. Parts of his body suddenly had other intentions.

Her response was right up there with his own, which was all the encouragement he needed. Lifting her in his arms, he carried her upstairs.

Inside the bedroom, he untied the bulky robe she wore, pushed it off her shoulders. She didn't need any skimpy little lacey thing to drive him crazy. At the moment, nothing could compare to the tee shirt and boxer shorts she had on.

Shrugging out of his jacket, his fingers couldn't work fast enough to remove the rest of their clothing, so she helped.

He briefly looked at her growing breasts and slightly thickening waist, knowing he was the cause yet not feeling one bit of regret.

Uncontrollable desire demanded they hurry. When they hit the bed, he couldn't wait; she didn't want him to. He slid into her, careful despite his need. His hands locked with hers above her head. Looking into her eyes, he smiled as he led her into that magical, erotic place where lovers go.

When they floated back down to earth, he realized he'd been holding her hands the entire time.

Drained, he didn't have enough energy to roll off her.

Her arms held him tightly, telling him she wanted him just where he was.

Chapter Thirty

She felt his breathing even out until he finally dozed off. She couldn't blame him. They had come together with such emotion and passion, she felt totally drained.

She felt him roll to his side. Opening his eyes, he smiled briefly and pulled her closer before drifting back to sleep.

Summer wondered why she felt so safe with him when he was the one man on earth who could break her heart.

All she knew was that she was calmer now about the future. There would be no pretend marriage. It would be the real thing because she would do her best to make it work. She was no quitter.

Despite the hard blows life had thrown her way, her grandparents had taught her to fight back. That's just what she was going to do. Fight to win Matt's love.

He might be marrying her because of the baby, but he would stay because he loved them both.

She let out a contented sigh and rested her head against his chest.

"We have to find a place to live," Howard pointed out. "I think Matt's planning on them staying here. They don't need us interfering with their privacy."

"I know." Julie stuck a spoonful of butterscotch sundae into her mouth.

They had gone out to dinner and seen a movie so awful, they walked out before it was half over. They decided to take home dessert.

The house had been dark and silent when they returned. Assuming everyone else was in bed, they sat in the kitchen and tried to be quiet.

"I heard the Sullivan house is going up for sale. Tom got a

job in Memphis, so he'll be moving his family there." He scraped the bottom of the container that had held a mountainous banana split a short time ago.

"The house two doors down? The brick Tudor? I love that house! It's kind of big, though."

"Sure, it's big for just two people. But by the time we have kids..."

"Wait! Back up. Did I miss something?" She held up her hand.

"What?" He gave her a questioning look.

"Was I sleeping when you proposed?"

"Probably," he shrugged.

"Howard Erikson, if that's the best you can do, then you can forget it! Boy, you're about as romantic as the farm report!" she huffed.

Standing, she snatched up the empty ice cream containers and threw them away.

He looked at her and, in that moment, saw his future. Their future. He imagined her wearing a simple gold band, but wouldn't be surprised if she wanted the Hope diamond. He could picture her belly growing round with his child. A couple of times. He didn't doubt she was the kind who'd brag about how she wore the pants in their family.

Was she ever in for a rude awakening.

When she stomped by, he snagged her arm and pulled her onto his lap. "Now, you listen up. If you think we're not getting married, you're as crazy as my Aunt Dorothy was when she told everyone that three Martians had knocked on her door and offered to buy her farm.

"We love each other." He softened his voice. "You want sweet words and a diamond? Then you'll get them. Because you mean everything to me. You are the first thing I want to see in the morning and the last thing at night. I can't imagine my future without you in it."

231

"It's not that I need a flashy ring on my finger." She slid her arms around his neck. "I guess being taken for granted isn't so bad. But, sometimes a woman wants a little romance."

"That doesn't sound like anything I can't handle." He nibbled at her lips. "Want to continue this discussion upstairs?"

"I'd love to."

Summer stepped into the shower and reached for the shampoo. It was still early but she'd slept soundly and felt full of energy. Happiness made her giggle, because she and Matt were getting married one week from today.

Before she'd gotten out of bed, she'd been tempted to wake him with a kiss but he was sleeping so soundly, she didn't have the heart.

Humming softly, she massaged the shampoo into her hair. She heard the shower door open, turned her head and watched him step in behind her.

"Hi." He kissed her shoulder, slid his arms around her waist.

"Morning." Her voice faltered because his hands had moved to her breasts. "Don't forget, this morning you..."

"If you mention that damn pre-nuptial agreement, I'll throw you out the window!" he growled.

She laughed. "I was just going to remind you to call Mr. and Mrs. Meyer."

"Oh." He continued exploring how pregnancy had changed her body. He turned her around and took his time. One thing led to another until the water became cold, forcing them to hurry from the shower.

By the time they went downstairs, everyone else was in the dining room having pastries for breakfast.

"I'm sorry. I should have come down earlier." Summer smiled at Julie.

"That's okay. Howard and I got up early and we both were craving cheese Danish." She motioned to the two couples finishing their coffee. "We're losing our guests today. Their bags are already in the car. Want me to check them out?"

"That's okay. I'll do it."

A short time later, Summer accepted praise for the accommodations as she said goodbye to the guests while Matt made a few phone calls.

When she returned to the dining room, Julie reminded, "We have to find you a wedding dress today."

"Actually, I need to go up in the attic and see if my great-grandmother's dress is in good enough condition. When I was a teenager, my grandmother had gotten it out. It only needed cleaning, so she had that done and repacked for storage. She wore it when she and Gramps got married." She took a seat next to Matt.

"You're not climbing around in an attic," he warned.

"There's stairs, silly. You can come with me."

"Okay." He set down his coffee cup. "Let's go."

When they went upstairs, she led the way to the end of the hall and opened a door.

"I thought this was just a closet," he said, following her up the steps. It surprised him to see everything was stored in a neat and orderly fashion. "It's so clean up here."

"It's just a little dusty." She glanced around, then pointed to the right. "My grandpa built those shelves. I think that big blue box on the top is the one. Can you reach it?"

"Sure." He walked over and stretched until his hands gripped the large box and lifted it off the shelf. "Anything else you need?"

"No."

He followed her downstairs and into the kitchen. When he placed the box on the table, she said worriedly, "I hope it fits. There isn't much time to do any alterations."

233

She took a pair of scissors and cut through the heavy tape. After opening the lid, she carefully removed the tissue paper from a lace veil and set it on the table. She took out the ivory satin gown and held it up.

"It's simple but I think it's so elegant. I love it."

As a young girl, she dreamed of wearing the dress when she married her Prince Charming. Although the reality of her situation had little in common with those long ago dreams, she harbored the secret hope a happy ending was still possible. She refused to believe it was childish to think Matt would eventually fall in love with her. Anything was possible.

"You're going to look beautiful." He smiled.

"I don't think the groom's supposed to see the dress before the wedding. It's supposed to be bad luck." Blushing, she lowered her gaze. "I supposed I should try it...oh!" A sudden gripping pain in her stomach took her breath away. She carelessly dropped the dress over a chair.

He watched her suddenly hunch over and place her hands on her lower abdomen.

"Something's wrong!" She gasped. A painful cramping began and she felt a strange dampness between her legs.

"Howard!" he yelled, trying to steer her to a chair. "Hurry!"

Howard came flying into the room, Julie on his heels. "What?"

"It's Summer! What's faster around here? An ambulance or driving to the hospital?"

Matt had never been a particularly religious man but during the ride to the hospital, he prayed intensely while trying to comfort Summer.

"I'm losing the baby," she cried. She was curled up on the backseat of Julie's car, laying partially on him.

"Shhh. Try and calm down, sweetheart. It'll be all right." He held her tighter, wishing he could believe his own words but there was a dark stain spreading between her legs, making him feel helpless.

The drive seemed to take forever despite Howard speeding like a maniac. It felt as though hours had passed before they finally pulled in front of the emergency entrance.

"She's pregnant and bleeding!" Carrying her inside, Matt spoke to the first nurse he saw.

"Follow me." The woman led them into an examining cubicle.

From that point, events seemed to happen in a hazy, surrealistic manner. The room soon filled with hospital personnel, moving quickly and efficiently.

He was asked to step out into the hall. He complied only because he knew he was in the way.

Julie had gotten Summer's insurance information from her wallet and was handling the paperwork at the front desk. She turned and gave him a sympathetic pat on the arm.

"They say what's wrong yet?" Howard had just returned from parking the car.

"No." Matt began pacing, wondering if their night of passion had brought this on. He'd never forgive himself.

Finally, a man in green scrubs came out. "Mr. Taylor? I'm Dr. Rawlings."

"Zeller. We're getting married next Saturday." He didn't know why he felt the need to explain their unmarried status. "How is she?"

"I'm afraid she's miscarried. I'm sorry."

Despite somehow knowing for the last hour that Summer was losing their baby, it still rocked him back on his heels. "Is she all right? Can I see her now?"

"Only for a minute. She's going to be prepped for a D and C."

Miscarried. D and C. He knew what those words meant. He just didn't know they would ever make him feel like crying.

He felt numb as he walked to her bedside. She was so pale, her face ravaged by tears.

"I lost the baby."

He took her hand and kissed it. "I know."

Chapter Thirty-One

Summer opened her eyes. Nausea from the anesthesia made her dizzy, temporarily crowding out the heartbreak over the loss of her baby. The inevitable loss of Matt.

She wanted to go back to sleep and escape her misery.

Dr. Rawlings had said it wasn't unusual for first pregnancies to end in miscarriage. His words were no source of comfort.

"Good. You're awake." A nurse appeared, speaking too cheerfully. "The nausea and dizziness will be gone in a few hours. The best thing to do when you get home is to rest as much as possible."

The woman helped her sit up and get dressed. It did no good for Summer to protest, saying she was still woozy and sick to her stomach. She found herself hustled into a wheelchair and steered toward the lobby.

"I know how you feel. I've been through this," the nurse said.

She wanted to slap her face and scream at her but didn't have the energy. This woman had no idea how she felt.

Howard and Julie waited in the front seat as Matt helped her into the car. During the ride home, she let him hold her only because she was too weak to push him away.

Tomorrow would be soon enough to deal with distancing herself and facing another harsh reality.

Once they were home, he carried her upstairs. Neither spoke as he helped her change into a nightgown and settled her in bed. He sat at her side, took her hand in his and silently watched her drift into a sound sleep.

He stood, removed his shoes and got in beside her. He lay spoon fashion behind her, slipping an arm around her waist.

Once again, he hadn't known what to say to her.

Why did words fail him around her?

237

She was hurting; he was too. They had just lost a child. Medical science referred to it as a fetus, but it was still their child.

How could a day that had started so happily end like this?

It was dawn when she awoke. She looked at him, sleeping on his side, facing her, and felt such a powerful sense of loss engulf her, she struggled to breathe.

The rose colored glasses she had recently chosen to look through were gone. Smashed and broken, just like her dreams.

They were not going to marry. There was no reason because their child was gone.

All the crying in the world wouldn't change things.

Dr. Rawlings had instructed her to rest for a few days and soon she'd be fine. But she knew better.

Life had thrown her another cruel, heartless punch and, this time, she was down for the count. She had no desire to get up.

She thought of the plans that needed canceling and didn't want to deal with any of it. Closing her eyes, she wondered if Julie would mind taking over.

She fell back into a troubled sleep and the next thing she knew, she heard someone enter the room. She turned over and realized she was in bed alone. Opening her eyes, she saw Julie standing by the bed.

"Hey, Sum, you okay?"

"No." She hugged a pillow.

"I know. I wish there was something I could do to make things better." Julie sat on the bed and took her hand.

"Actually, there is. Could you call Ruth so she doesn't go through all that trouble of making the invitations? And the minister...let him know the wedding's canceled."

"What are you talking about? Matt said the wedding was still on."

238

"He's wrong." Pulling her hand free, she struggled to a sitting position. "We don't have to get married now and we're not."

"Maybe you need to talk to him before you do anything rash." Softly, Julie added, "I think he really loves you."

"The only reason we were getting married was because of the baby. Now, we need to get back to our separate corners of the world and stay there."

"I was thinking...there's a saying that things happen for a reason. Maybe your pregnancy brought you two together because you were meant for each other."

"You must have been reading one of those romance novels Gina left behind. Real life doesn't work like that," she sharply remarked. "If you'll excuse me, I need to use the bathroom."

A short time later, Julie resumed her argument while she slipped on a robe.

"I know you love him. If he didn't love you, what other reason would he have for still wanting to marry you?"

"Maybe he feels obligated. Or he's got a martyr complex. But once he hits the highway, I'm sure he'll breathe a sigh of relief. I'll soon be a fading memory. Just like I was the last time he left." She turned and discovered him standing in the doorway, his hands on his hips.

"Could you give us a minute?"

"Sure." Julie left, shutting the door behind her.

Summer felt the room spin and quickly sat on the bed.

"Are you okay?" His voice was filled with concern.

"Yes. Just a little weak."

"Do you want something to eat? You might feel better."

"I'll eat later." She cleared her throat. "I want you to leave."

"Okay. Rest for a while and I'll check on you..."

"I mean, I want you to leave here. Leave Haversfield. I want you to go home." She spoke as though her lips were lifeless, her body wooden.

"I still want us to get married," he insisted.

"Well, we're not. You need to get back to your life. I need to get back to mine."

"Listen, this has been hard on you. On us." He sat next to her. "But we need to talk. I love you."

Why hadn't he spoken those words before when she so desperately wanted to hear them? She stared at him for a long moment, wishing she could believe him but she guessed he was just feeling sorry for her right now. Slowly, she shook her head.

"I don't think that's true. In fact, I'm certain it isn't. If I hadn't gone to New York, I'd still be waiting to hear from you. That sure doesn't sound like love to me."

"I was planning on coming here right after that damn awards show!"

"Stop it!" She didn't want to hear any more of his excuses. "I don't want you here! I don't want to marry you! I just want you gone! I want to forget all this ever happened!"

"Quit yelling." He tried pulling her into his arms but she pushed him away.

She rose and walked to the door. She didn't turn around, but spoke over her shoulder. "It's for the best. My best. It's what I want, so, please, just go!"

She opened the door and cautiously made her way down the hall despite desperately wanting to turn back and throw herself into Matt's arms. But that would be a mistake.

He'd said the right words too late. She'd never again attempt to build a future on shaky ground. It would probably take her lifetime to get over him but that's what she had to do.

She entered the kitchen and joined Julie at the table. Her expression was bland, her movements very controlled.

"Want some tea and toast?" Julie touched her shoulder.

"I guess."

Julie went to fill the kettle with water before dropping bread into the toaster. "I really think you're making a mistake. Don't let him leave now. Not like this. You need to talk to him."

"No offense, but I'm no longer accepting advice from other people."

Matt's footsteps could be heard as he descended the stairs. The sound of the front door slamming made her feel as though a bullet had just tore through her heart but she stared straight ahead, sipping her tea.

"He's leaving! Are you just going to let him go like that?"

"Yes." Again, she reminded herself it was what she had to do. Let him go.

Only a fool would marry a man when she wasn't sure if he loved her. There would always be that doubt.

How could anyone be happy in that kind of marriage?

She forced herself to take a few bites of toast and tried to ignore Julie's anxious glances.

When she heard his car start and back out of the driveway, her heartache didn't ease in the slightest. It only increased.

Losing the baby and the illusion that Matt might love her caused such deep, unbearable grief at that moment, she wanted to die.

Too deep for tears. That phrase ran through her mind. Some emotions really were too deep for tears.

Everyone tiptoed around her for a few days, giving her time to get a grip on her fragile emotions. Though she kept insisting she was fine, no one believed her.

Julie had no choice but to cancel the arrangements and repack the wedding dress so it could be taken back up to the attic.

Howard took a turn at trying to talk some sense into her but she refused to listen to his advice.

She retreated to her room and spent most of the next few

days there. The river of tears finally broke free and her crying bouts lasted until an exhaustive, troubled sleep would finally overtake her. When she'd awaken, the cycle would begin again.

She ate only when Julie or Howard forced her to.

Everything reminded her of Matt. It seemed everywhere she looked, she expected to see him.

They'd made too many memories in the time they'd had together and she couldn't forget even one of them.

When she finally slid the engagement ring off her finger, she told herself she couldn't honestly blame him. She'd known all along she'd end up like this. Alone, with a broken heart.

Oh, God, how will I live without him?

A few days later, Julie came in and tossed a thick envelope onto the bed. "It looks official. Scary even."

She frowned and opened it.

Julie watched her facial expression turn from puzzlement to sadness.

"What's the matter?"

"It's the prenuptial agreement I asked for. But it's wrong. I didn't want anything and it says here that I would get sixty percent of everything in the event of a divorce."

Shaking, she held the papers out to her friend.

Julie briefly scanned the legal jargon. Looking up, she pointedly asked, "And you think he doesn't love you?"

Summer really didn't know what to think.

Chapter Thirty-Two

She still didn't know what to think a week later when the mailman rang the doorbell.

"Hey, Cliff, what's up?"

"Hey, Summer, you need to sign for this letter. Must be important." He handed her a pen.

"Wonder what it is. Maybe I won a sweepstakes." She scribbled her signature.

"I'll be your best friend if that's the case." He tore a section off the label before handing her the letter, along with the rest of her mail. "Have a good one." He gave her a little wave.

"You too." She watched him leave the porch.

"Who was that?" Julie asked as she came downstairs.

"Mailman." She looked down at the letter, noticing Hugh Parker's return address. She tore open the envelope, wondering why he was sending her anything. Surely he knew by now a pre-nup was no longer necessary.

She read the letter in disbelief, unaware she had uttered a few vicious curse words.

"What's the matter?" Julie asked.

"This is from Matt's attorney. He's threatening to sue me for breach of promise. I don't believe this! Do people even do this anymore?" Her hand trembled as she held the letter out. Anger made her face feel hot.

"What?" Julie angled her head to get a look at the paper.

"Matt! He's suing me for breach of promise! The bastard!"

After a few moments of stunned silence, Julie burst into laughter. "And you say he doesn't love you?"

"Will you stop that cackling? What the hell am I going to do?"

"Gee." Julie put her finger to her head, feigning stupidity. "Why ask me? You're the one with all the answers."

She made an obscene gesture and stomped away.

Julie couldn't wait to tell Howard. She grabbed her jacket and walked to the hardware store.

"What are you so happy about?" He pecked her on the cheek despite a store full of people eyeing the Pre-Winter Sale items.

"Matt's threatened to sue Summer for breach of promise," Julie whispered in his ear. "She got a letter from his lawyer."

"Oh."

"Oh?" Her eyes widened. "That's all you've got to say?" Frowning, she gave him a suspicious look. "Come to think of it, you don't look too surprised. What's going on?"

"We've been in touch." He scratched the back of his head. "Don't tell Sum or she'll kill me."

"Why didn't you tell me?" She punched his arm.

"Look, it's a guy thing. Besides, I promised him I wouldn't tell anyone."

"Oh? I'm just anyone?"

"No, you're her best friend. You think I'm stupid?"

She sputtered with indignation for a few seconds. "Are you saying I can't keep a secret?"

"No, but I promised Matt. And I don't break my promises."

"Howard, can you show me how to work this damn thing?" An elderly woman pointed to a snow blower on display.

"Sure, Mrs. Dario. Be right with you."

Turning his attention back to Julie, he lowered his voice. "We'll talk later. He isn't doing this to hurt her. You know I'd never let anyone hurt her."

He gave her a quick kiss. "See you at home."

"Men!" She muttered to herself as she walked out of the store.

She took her time getting back to the house, figuring Summer would still be raving like a lunatic.

When she finally walked through the front door, she heard

her talking on the kitchen phone.

"No, Mr. Parker, it wasn't like that...yes, but..."

A few seconds of silence, then, "Well, yes, we did pick out the rings and talk to the minister but...yes, we got the marriage license."

More silence.

"Fine. I'll be there."

Julie heard her groan as she placed the receiver on the hook.

"What now?"

Summer took a soda from the refrigerator and sat at the table. "I have to meet with Matt and his lawyer. Well, I don't have to but I sure don't want to end up in court."

"What is he asking for? Money?"

"No. I don't know what he wants."

Julie slid into a chair at the opposite side of the table, clasping her hands in front of her. "Maybe this is his way of proving he loves you. You know, going through all this trouble. Just think how humiliating it would be if the tabloids get wind of *this* story. They'd make him look like an idiot."

"What about me?" Summer lifted her chin a notch. "I do have a business to run. People come here for peace and quiet. The quaintness of a small town and all that. If this goes to court, it'll end up in the papers and all kinds of creeps will come nosing around. It would be a circus. No decent people will want to come here."

"Hmm. Maybe. But what motive, other than love, would cause him to do this?"

"I don't know," Summer slowly answered. Her shoulders slumped. "I don't know anything anymore."

"When are you meeting them?"

"This Friday in Springfield. It's supposed to be an informal discussion to resolve this mess. Matt's in Shreveport for a concert tonight and has one Saturday night in Kansas City so I guess Springfield's on the way. Whatever. Anyway, Mr. Parker is sending a helicopter to pick me up at noon. I asked him if I needed a lawyer and he said only if I wanted one. I guess I won't need one if I don't sign anything."

"Howard, let's take Gyp for a walk." Julie dried the last plate and put it in the cabinet.

"I will. I need the exercise." Summer took the leash from its hook. "Guess I need a jacket."

When Julie heard the front door close, she turned to Howard and said, "Okay. Explain what Matt's up to."

"You can't tell her. Swear?"

"Yes."

"Hold up your right hand."

"Howard!" she warned.

"Okay. He loves her." He stood up, leaving the paper he'd been glancing at on the table. "Want to go shoot a game of pool at Bob's?"

She blinked. Frowning, she asked, "Aren't you leaving something out? Like the whole story?"

"No. The threat of a lawsuit is just his way of making her see him. Pretty clever, huh?"

Frustrated, she was positive he knew more than he was saying. She also knew he wasn't going to tell her.

"Yes, she agreed to meet with us. It's set for Friday. Are you sure you want to do this? I can understand your motives but you know how I feel about your tactics."

"Don't worry, Hugh. They're working so far."

"I suppose. Well, I guess I'll see you on Friday."

Friday couldn't come soon enough, Matt thought, hanging up the phone. It already seemed an eternity had passed since he'd seen her.

Howard had assured him she had recovered physically

246

from the miscarriage but had been withdrawn and quiet since he'd left.

Well, he hadn't been himself, either, since leaving her.

He rose from his chair and went to the window. At night, the view of Shreveport resembled dozens of other cities.

It didn't matter where he was because he was miles away from where he'd left his heart.

He hadn't wanted to leave but she'd been so unreasonable. He'd wanted to stay and comfort her, seek comfort from her. After all, he'd lost a child, too. He'd let her chase him away only because he thought it was what she needed.

He wouldn't make that mistake again. He knew she loved him. It was no wonder she doubted his love after the way he'd bungled things from the beginning.

Thank God, he was a quick learner. Well, maybe he'd been slow but at least he'd learned.

As he was growing up, he'd learned to bury his battered emotions and, over time, convinced himself he really didn't need anyone. He'd consistently avoided emotional entanglements with women, too afraid of letting anyone get close. Until a certain woman and town made him want things he never thought he wanted. Like marriage to a woman he was crazy about. And children.

His own family.

He'd ripped off the bandaid on his wounded childhood and realized by facing his past, he could finally heal. No more thinking he wasn't entitled to happiness with a woman who loved him. And he knew she loved him, despite his past and all of his flaws.

No more handling situations by avoiding them. No more walking away when the going got tough. And won't his mother be surprised tomorrow to come face to face with him?

He was a man on a mission. No longer would he allow the past to interfere with his life. Not if he expected to have a future with Summer.

He felt only slightly guilty about deceiving her now. Since she wouldn't give him a second chance otherwise, he'd resorted to desperate measures.

In this case, he felt a little deceit was justified.

Summer looked up at the night sky and wondered what was causing Matt to do this? Could Julie be right? Did he really love her?

If so, he had an odd way of showing it.

Why did they both have to be so handicapped when it came to love?

She realized now she'd been rather cruel the day he left. No, she shamefully admitted, the day she threw him out. Had he been grieving too over the loss of their baby?

Could that be the reason behind the letter from Hugh Parker? Revenge because she'd added to his misery?

She really didn't think so but she'd been wrong before.

Gyp rushed the Henderson's fence, barking and growling at George, the family dog. The collie snarled out insults of his own until they both tired of their usual game.

"It's a wonder he speaks to you," she admonished but Gyp strutted ahead, his tail held high.

Her thoughts returned to Matt. Damn it, she did miss him. She didn't want to but she did.

Friday was two days away. She didn't know what was going to happen when she saw him, other than her heart probably would suffer another huge break.

How would he act? Would he be angry?

What should she wear?

If this was going to be the last time he saw her, then she wanted to look so sexy, so desirable, she'd knock his socks off.

Chapter Thirty-Three

Matt was sitting in a chair, waiting for the last swipe of the makeup artist's brush, when Kayla Thomas, the newest rising star of the talk show circuit, strolled in.

"Good morning! It's great to finally meet face to face."

He'd wondered if she was as beautiful off the air as she was on her television program, "Inside the Story." Now he knew she was. Not that he was interested. He wasn't. His heart already belonged to someone. He smiled.

"Thanks for getting me copies of all the paperwork from the state of Illinois. I've read through the reports over the last two days and, knowing what I now know, I'm dying for the chance to get Dawn in front of a rolling camera. It's remarkable you haven't come forward sooner."

"I guess I was hoping someone would confront her with the truth and she'd go away." He straightened his tie after the makeup artist whipped the protective smock off his shoulders.

"She probably will after today." The reporter took out a notebook and sat in the chair next to his. "I thought we'd go over a few things. I read that she never called or tried to see you once the state placed you in its custody. Is that true? You really haven't seen her in twenty-two years?"

"Yes."

"Before she appeared on the Sara Kell show, she never tried to call you, right?"

"Right. Now that I'm rich and famous, she wants to play Mommy."

"She sounds like a horrible woman. Are you nervous?"

"Maybe a little," he replied. "I'm just anxious to get this over with."

While he'd been still young - maybe ten or eleven, he'd often fantasized his mother would come looking for him. She would fall to her knees, hug him and beg his forgiveness. But he'd given up that fantasy long ago.

Since Dawn had spent the past several months making the rounds on the talk shows, claiming her son refused her calls and didn't care if she starved to death, he knew things would probably get ugly today. Especially when her lies were refuted on national television.

Two hours later, after he and Kayla had discussed his childhood at length, he was led to one of three chairs on the set. The makeup artist reappeared, looked at him critically while she blotted his face with a sponge. He was glad when she finished.

Kayla sat to his right, in the middle chair. "She has no idea you're here. My assistant is getting her from the green room."

His pulse started to race. He told himself she could no longer hurt him; he was no longer a defenseless child. He then thought of how she'd been cashing in by spewing lies, trying to paint him as a selfish monster who ignored his devoted mother.

There had been so many times he'd wondered about meeting her face to face. How would he feel? Would he be nervous? Frightened? Angry? Want revenge?

As Dawn stepped into his line of vision, he felt all those emotions until anger became the dominant feeling. Her blonde hair was cut in the newest style, her face artfully made up. He supposed a stranger would find her attractive. He knew she couldn't have picked out the sedate blue suit she wore. It was too classy.

Once the initial shock of seeing her passed, he was ready.

Kayla motioned the crew to begin filming and gestured for Dawn to take a seat. When she noticed him, her step faltered as her mouth dropped open. "What the hell...I mean, what's he doing here?"

"In the studio today, we have Matt Zeller, one of the

biggest superstars in the rock industry." Kayla smoothly began the show. "He's had to deal with a lot of bad press recently until he helped solve the murder committed in his apartment months ago. Our audience is probably aware his mother Dawn Zeller has appeared on different programs lately, claiming her son won't see her or support her financially."

Turning to Dawn, she said, "Let's start with you. What kind of boy was Matt when he was little?"

"Uh, he was...he cried a lot. He was a lot of trouble."

"What kind of childhood did he have? What kinds of things did you do with him? You know, did you sit down with your son and watch *Sesame Street*? Take him to the park?"

Dawn looked stumped for an answer, clearly not expecting this line of questioning. Her eyes darted nervously around the room.

After a few awkward moments, Kayla briefly looked at her notes. "Let's talk about your career when your son was living with you."

"I worked in a bar, trying to make ends meet. It was hard. My husband ran off with another woman and I tried to provide for Matt the best I could," Dawn answered, trying for the role of martyr and failing.

"You worked as a prostitute?"

"I did not! I was a barmaid!"

"Really?" Kayla responded. "Are barmaids usually arrested seven times for prostitution? And what about all those drug charges?"

"You bitch!"

"I've been doing some research and have a few questions," the reporter interrupted. "Is it true the child protection agency removed Matt from your care when he was seven?"

Dawn's face hardened but she remained silent.

"Because of abuse? And neglect? One of the reports states he had scars on his back and cigarette burns on his chest. Most of our viewing audience probably feels a woman who does that to a child deserves to be behind bars and not on a talk show."

Dawn's face went from white to red but Matt doubted it was from embarrassment.

"They couldn't prove I did it," she retorted.

"Furthermore, once Matt was removed from your custody, you never inquired about his welfare, never attempted to see him, although supervised visitation was possible."

Kayla turned to Matt, softening her voice. "I know this has to be difficult to confront the woman who treated you so horribly, who failed you so miserably. In a very public way, she's accused you of being ruthless and selfish. She's said you refused to pay her bills. Would you care to comment?"

"This ain't the way this is supposed to go! You're supposed to nail that bastard for not giving me some money!" Dawn shrieked. "You can go to hell! You all can kiss my ass!"

She stood up and stormed off the set.

"Can you tell us what you're feeling at the moment?" Kayla asked, unruffled.

"Like a hundred and fifty pound weight has been lifted off my shoulders." He couldn't help but smile. He'd faced the monster and survived.

"What was it like to have a mother like that? Tell us, if you don't mind, about your childhood."

He did so, only briefly wondering how his fans would react. He recalled being terrified whenever he was left home alone when he was much too young an age. He described how he'd felt living with a mother who showed him no affection, only rage or indifference. How he'd felt when his alcoholic father, who'd been home so little, went away and never returned.

It wasn't as difficult as he'd thought to speak of the physical and emotional abuse he'd experienced. He'd been right to confront the woman who'd caused him such pain. By doing so, he'd taken away her power to affect him.

The damage was done, the nightmare of having his life exposed to the world had become a reality and he'd lived through it. It had been on his terms and he felt better because of it.

"I'm sure there are many children who consider you their idol. What advice can you give those who are living in abusive homes? I can only imagine how terrifying it must be."

"Tell someone. Tell everyone. Tell your teacher, tell a friend's mother. Tell a policeman. Don't be afraid no one will believe you. Most of all, don't feel like you've done something wrong. It isn't your fault, it's the fault of your mother or your father or the person who's abusing you. You have to tell someone so it will stop."

Matt took a sip of water. "As I got older, I was very fortunate to have a music teacher recognize my natural talent for the piano. Dave Meyer was wonderful. He and his wife played a major role in steering me in the right direction, away from the streets. They and music saved me."

"Tell me, how has your childhood affected your life as an adult? Are there any lingering problems?" Kayla asked.

"Just recently, I realized I never thought I deserved to be happy. Deep down inside, that little boy of long ago still existed, believing he wasn't worthy of love. I'd gotten so used to hiding my feelings, I grew up unable to express my emotions. I was so afraid of getting hurt, I didn't want to get close to anyone." He smiled wryly. "I've learned that's no way to live."

"And now? What do you think will be different in your life?"

Kayla's question was easy to answer. "Everything."

"We wish you all the best. Thank you for sharing your story with us."

When the mikes were unhooked, Kayla sighed. "That went really well. I think you've just become a much needed role model for a couple of million kids. I hope the ones who need to take your advice do speak up about being abused."

"Me too."

"Thanks again for giving me this interview. Now can I ask why? I mean, why did you choose my show?"

"Because you have a reputation for honesty. While everyone else was trying to link me with the murder in my apartment, you never joined the feeding frenzy."

"You have no idea how many arguments I had with my producer over that." She grimaced. "I've been walking on thin ice ever since because of it."

"Well, now you've got this exclusive, so you get the last laugh."

"I sure do. It was truly a pleasure meeting you. The car will take you back to your hotel."

As Matt rode in the quiet limo, he wished Summer was sitting beside him. She didn't know it but just by loving him, she'd given him the strength to go public with his story. He still found it amazing that he was head over heels in love with her.

He couldn't wait until Friday. Even more, he couldn't wait until they started the rest of their lives together.

Not that he thought it'd be easy to sweep her off her feet. She could be difficult at times. She might even break one or two of his ribs before he convinced her they belonged together.

Now that he knew what he wanted out of life and who he wanted to spend it with, he couldn't wait to see what would happen next. He felt like a kid anticipating Christmas.

Chapter Thirty-Four

Summer checked her appearance in the mirror, wondering if the black suit she'd bought the previous day was too sedate.

"I don't know. I look boring, don't I?" she asked, nervously fidgeting with the lapels of her jacket.

Julie rolled her eyes. "No. You look dignified, yet elegant. Classy."

"Boring."

"Then why don't you wear pasties and a G-string?"

"You're no help!"

"You really look great." Julie sighed. "There are tons of women who'd kill to look boring like you."

"Oh, well, it's too late to change, anyway." She grabbed her purse. "Okay. Let's go."

They drove to the same location where Hugh Parker's helicopter had landed when Matt's identity was discovered by Sheriff Calvert.

"I feel like throwing up." She rolled down the window after Julie parked the car.

"Don't be nervous. I have a hunch everything's gonna work out fine."

"Where have I heard that before?" She gave her friend a dirty look.

The drone of a helicopter could be heard in the distance. The noise became increasingly louder until the copter came into view and landed.

She suddenly felt faint. "What if he's doing this to be mean?"

"That's ridiculous! He's not a mean guy. I think he just wants to get your attention." Julie gently urged, "Go on. If for some reason you need me, you know I'll hop in the car or on a plane and come."

"Unless something unexpected happens, I'll let you know when we're ready to leave Springfield for the return trip." She leaned over and hugged her friend. I'm scared."

"Don't be. Everything is going to be fine."

Summer's stomach stayed in the sky as the helicopter landed. When she spotted a limousine waiting, her stomach dropped down to her feet before it settled somewhere near its usual resting place. She took off the ear protectors and handed them to the pilot.

As she approached the car, a door opened and Matt stepped out, looking like he'd just posed for the cover of GQ.

Damn him, he seemed perfectly relaxed in his charcoal suit, blinding white shirt and tasteful tie while her knees were almost knocking together.

When he smiled at her, her foolish heart started doing a cha-cha and tears stung her eyes.

"Are you okay?" He frowned as he studied her.

She nodded, banishing the moisture from her eyes.

When they were in the car, Hugh Parker extended his hand. "Good to see you again, Summer."

"I don't know if I can say the same." She sniffed.

Hugh smiled. "We have reservations at a restaurant where we'll be able to speak privately. I hope you're hungry."

Who could eat with nerves like hers?

Conversation was polite and unimportant as they rode to their destination. When they arrived at Rosewood Inn, they entered a very quiet, very posh establishment.

As they were led to a private room, she tried to identify the classical music playing softly but failed. She gazed at the beautifully papered walls as the waiter held out a chair for her.

No prices were printed on the menus, of course. After they'd ordered, the waiter brought a bottle of wine. He poured a small amount in a glass and offered it to her.

She sipped delicately, then nodded her approval. Thank God, she had seen enough movies to know what was expected of her.

She would have preferred a roomful of people to observe instead of all this privacy. Maybe then Matt wouldn't stare at her constantly. Every time their eyes met, she felt her cheeks grow warm.

She turned to Hugh. "Are we going to discuss the reason we're here?"

"After dinner," he smoothly replied before his cell phone rang. He excused himself and stepped out of the room.

"So, how have you been? Are you feeling okay?" Matt asked.

"Fine. I'm fine." She picked up her napkin and placed it carefully on her lap.

"Good. How's everyone? Gyp?"

"Fine. Great." The suspense was killing her, so she had to ask. "Why are you doing this?"

"Doing what? Asking about everyone?"

She shot him an annoyed look.

"Don't you know what breach of promise means?" He calmly picked up his wineglass.

She opened her mouth to reply but Hugh walked into the room.

When their food was brought to the table, she had to admit it looked and smelled tempting but she had no appetite.

The nervousness she'd initially felt had subsided because she'd sipped at her wineglass until it was empty. However, she had no intention drinking more. She wanted a clear head for whatever happened.

It seemed to take forever but finally they all finished eating. She had done little more than pick at her food during all that polite conversation.

"Now can we discuss this lawsuit?" she asked Hugh,

ignoring Matt as he practically licked his dessert plate.

"Summer, no legal action has taken place yet. Remember, this meeting is to avoid a lawsuit. My client is accusing you of breach of promise because you canceled the wedding."

"But I lost the baby."

"I understand and I do offer my condolences. But, nonetheless, you called off the wedding without a sufficient explanation."

"But he forced me to plan the wedding in the first place!"

"If the jeweler were questioned in court, would he say you were forced into selecting a ring?" Hugh asked.

How could he when she'd babbled, *It fits perfectly. It's the most beautiful ring I've seen.* "No, he wouldn't."

"If Tim McAllister, the minister, were subpoenaed, would he testify Matt forced you into meeting with him to plan the wedding?"

She lowered her head and spoke a quiet, "No."

"You see, in court it would be your word against his. One thing my client hopes is that a settlement can be reached and a court case with all the ugly publicity accompanying it can be avoided." The attorney picked up his crystal water goblet.

"I would like to ask a question. If we did go to court, what could Matt possibly sue me for? I mean, he's wealthy and has everything." Nothing was making sense to her.

"The judge would consider the emotional pain of my client and could award him a settlement, which could put a financial hardship on you. Or if your financial situation is limited, your house could be considered."

"My house?" she interrupted. Turning to look at Matt, she cried out, "You'd take my house?"

"Please, don't get upset." Hugh quickly placed his hand on her arm. "As I said before, my client doesn't want that. He wants to avoid going to court, as I'm sure you do."

"Then what does your *client* want?" She narrowed her eyes

suspiciously at Matt, though she'd directed her question at Hugh.

"He wants you to spend one week with him."

Summer's mouth dropped open but no words came out. She'd never expected anything like this.

"And if I don't agree, we go to court?" She felt as though she was the only one in the room confused. What was going on? Had the wine made her fall asleep and miss part of the conversation?

"Yes."

"Is this legal?"

"As soon as the agreement is signed." Hugh patted his suit coat, indicating he had the paperwork already prepared. "All you have to do is to spend time with him."

"When would this week occur?"

"Now."

"Now? I have no other clothes! And you said I didn't need a lawyer!" she heatedly reminded.

"You don't. You're free to sign or refuse. As for clothing and other necessities, my client is willing to purchase anything you want or need."

She looked at Matt and wondered why he was doing this to her. It couldn't be because of love, could it? If he loved her, he wouldn't do this, would he?

"Exactly what does 'spend time with' mean?"

"It means exactly that. You don't have to do anything against your will." he lawyer removed a folded paper from his inside jacket pocket. "Maybe you'll feel better if you read this."

She scanned the document, noting it was written in a clear, straightforward manner. There were no complicated phrases that could be misconstrued, no hidden meanings. It plainly stated she agreed to spend one week in the company of Matt, and clearly explained he could not force her to do anything against her will.

His signature was already scrawled on the appropriate line.

He hadn't spoken one word while she and Hugh had discussed the situation. He just sat there, looking calm.

Did he have a little gleam in his eye?

She blinked.

He did.

Chapter Thirty-Five

Summer remained silent during the ride to the airport, although he knew she was steamed.

"It was nice meeting you, Summer."

She ignored Hugh Parker's extended hand. "I'd rather shake hands with a snake. At least it couldn't hide behind an expensive suit."

"I hope you're as charming as you think you are," Hugh commented, when Matt stepped out of the car to say goodbye.

"So do I." He patted his lawyer on the shoulder. "Don't worry. This has to work because I don't have a Plan B."

As the limo left the airfield, he looked over at the woman he loved. She was sitting as rigid as a statue, no doubt furious. Good thing she didn't carry a gun.

"Summer, can't you relax and have an open mind about this?"

"Just shut up! That agreement says I don't have to do anything I don't want to! Well, I don't want to talk to you. I just want to kill you!"

"Fine. Pout all you want."

"Pout?!" she sputtered.

"How else was I supposed to get your attention?" he demanded.

"Oh, you...!" she stammered and turned her head. After a few moments, she looked at him. "You are a manipulative son-of-a..."

"And you are being ridiculously stubborn and childish," he interrupted, keeping his voice calm.

He decided to wait to tell her the truth. If he told her now, as mad as she was, she'd probably blacken his eyes and knock out a tooth. One of his front ones.

After a significant period of silence, she asked, "Where are we going?"

She didn't yell but her voice was still frosty.

"To Kansas City. Unless you want to stop and get some clothes now?"

"I don't care."

The dark circles under her eyes told him she hadn't been sleeping any better than he had. She leaned her head back against the seat, looking as deflated as a flat tire.

"I just want to sleep. Maybe if I sleep long enough, I'll wake up and discover someone has magically straightened out the mess that's supposed to be my life," she grumbled.

He watched her struggle to stay awake. When she lost the battle, her head wobbled against the seat.

He couldn't wait any longer to touch her. He reached over and pulled her onto his lap. She pushed against him, trying to gain her freedom, but that only made him tighten his embrace.

"I'm bigger and stronger than you. And I'm not letting you go," he warned.

After a few seconds of struggling, she finally gave up.

"You're a bully."

"Only when I have to be."

"I don't want you to touch me." She yawned, then dropped her head on his shoulder. "You've been nothing but trouble since the day your car broke down."

"I know. Just rest. We'll fight some more later." He leaned his head against hers, grateful she was finally in his arms. He'd been dying to get his hands on her since she'd stepped out of the helicopter.

"I have to call Julie," she murmured.

"I already did."

"When?"

"Before we left the restaurant."

"Oh." She let out a long sigh. Within seconds, she fell asleep.

He breathed in the scent of her hair, wallowing in happiness because she was finally with him.

"Sir, we've reached Kansas City. Do you want to go to the hotel?"

The driver's voice on the intercom woke them.

Summer stirred, then slid from his lap onto the seat. Her suit was wrinkled, reminding her she needed clothes.

"Is there a store around here?" she asked.

"There's a fancy mall near the hotel," Matt informed.

"WalMart is fine."

"Do you know where the nearest WalMart is?" He spoke into the intercom.

"Yes, sir."

"We'll go there first." He turned to her. "Who goes shopping in a limo?"

"We do," she primly replied. She suddenly thought of his fame. "Are you afraid you'll be recognized?"

"No. I have sunglasses."

She rolled her eyes. "I suppose no one will notice the limo."

Within minutes, they came to a stop in front of the store. They ignored the curious looks of the other shoppers as they walked inside.

She headed for the casual clothes and browsed until she grabbed some jeans and a couple of tops. In the lingerie section, she ignored all of his suggestions.

While she was in the dressing room, he kept eyeing an ivory nightgown, simple but sexy as hell. He tucked it under his arm.

"Okay, I'm done," she said as she came from the fitting room.

"You forgot shoes. And a jacket."

"Oh, heck."

When they were finally ready to check out, she really didn't expect or want him to pay for everything but he insisted.

"You look really good. Did I tell you that?" he asked after they were back in the car.

"No. Thank you. So do you."

"Sit closer to me."

"No."

"Fine." He slid next to her. "This way, we don't have to yell to hear each other."

She arched an eyebrow and wondered where all her rage against him had gone. Before her nap, she could have killed him with her bare hands. Now, all she wanted was his hands on her.

He had to love her, didn't he? Why else would he go through all this trouble?

"Is there anything else you need before we go back to the hotel?"

"I don't think so." Looking out the window, she pretended to take an interest in the view.

"I've missed you." He leaned on her, resting his cheek against hers. "You've missed me, too."

"I have?"

"Uh-huh." He skimmed his hand under her skirt, up her thigh.

Her heart pounded. She turned her head slightly and...

"The hotel, sir."

That blasted intercom. Summer didn't know if she was thankful for the interruption or not but chose to act as though she was.

She picked up her purse and some of the bags, leaving the others for him to carry. She strolled into the hotel, trying not to think about what was going to happen when they got to the room upstairs because every time she did, she couldn't breathe.

The elegant lobby had a fountain and a wonderful skylight.

As they walked across the marble floor, she didn't want to think about how out of place she felt, while he was used to such glamorous surroundings.

He pushed a button and their ascent to the top was smooth and fast.

"Here we are," he murmured.

They stepped out into a small vestibule. He dropped the shopping bags to unlock the door. Stepping back, he urged, "Go on in."

She walked into the room and, as expected, saw a lavishly decorated, expensive suite but it was the flowers that snagged her attention.

How could anyone ignore all those beautiful red roses?

"Oh!" She let her purse and packages fall to the floor as she counted fifteen bouquets.

"It's been two weeks and a day since you threw me out." He picked up the bags and stepped into the room, pushing the door closed with his foot.

Tears filled her eyes. "I'm sorry. I'm so sorry." She walked over and touched the silky petals. "You got me pink ones before."

"You didn't take pink seriously enough. A desperate man needs red."

"They're beautiful. Thank you." She turned to face him, using her fingertips to wipe away the tears spilling from her eyes.

"I'm in love with you. I have been since the night we danced after the poker game only I was too stupid to realize it."

He tossed the bags onto the sofa, crossed the room and placed his hands on her waist. "I know we need to talk, and we will. Just not now."

"Oh, Matt!" she blubbered, crying harder, pressing her face against his shoulder.

"Shh." He stroked her hair. "I've missed you so much."

"Me, too," she snuffled, lifting her face. "Oh, Matt."

When their lips met, she wondered how she'd survived even fifteen minutes without him. His touch made her forget her anger, her sorrow.

I'm in love with you. His words kept echoing in her head. This time she believed him.

She felt her heart swell with happiness, as though he'd just handed her the moon and a million stars.

"Is it too soon after the miscarriage to do this?" He pulled away from her, gently placing his palm on her cheek.

"Just try stopping now." She hooked an arm around his neck and pulled him close for a kiss.

His fingers were clumsy as he unbuttoned her jacket. Her hands struggled with his tie. Intense need made them stop frequently for heated kisses but finally they stood together, naked.

When he lifted her, she wrapped her arms and legs around him. They barely made it to the bed. Passion made them hurry.

There was no need for words. He told her with his body how much he loved her. She barely noticed the tears of happiness dampening her face again as she rode the waves of pleasure until she was dropped right in the middle of heaven.

"I haven't been with anyone else since I've met you," he said, when he'd gathered enough strength to speak. He lay on his back with her partially draped over him. "You'd better say the same or I'm killing you right now."

"Just half of Haversfield but kiss me some more, anyway."

He obliged, running his fingers slowly through her long curls.

"Sweetheart, why did you cancel the wedding?"

She sighed. "I thought you only wanted to get married

because of the baby. A marriage should take place when two people really love each other."

"When you miscarried, it upset me too. I didn't want to leave you but you were so hysterical, I didn't know what else to do. I wanted to marry you because I love you."

"I didn't believe that." She trailed a finger across his chest.

"What do you believe now?"

"I think you do, but what would it hurt to take things slow? Get to know each other a little more."

"You mean date?"

"I guess."

"Hmm. I'll think about it." He flipped her onto her back.

"I love you." Summer looked up at him, wondering if her heart would always miss a beat every time she looked into his eyes. "Oh, Matt, I really, really love you!"

"In that case, promise you won't get mad if I tell you something?"

"What?" She eyed him suspiciously.

"You have to promise."

"Okay. I promise."

"And no hitting." He nibbled at her lips.

"What? Tell me."

"I lied. I would never have filed a lawsuit against you. Even if you refused to spend time with me." He rubbed his mouth against hers.

"I figured that out already. I guess deep down I knew you weren't doing it to hurt me."

"Hugh's letter was the only way I could think of to get you to see me. Actually, the breach of promise idea was Howard's." He grinned.

"Howard? Well, so much for blood being thicker than water."

"Don't be mad at him. He was only trying to help."

"Right now, I'm not mad at anyone." She smiled. "But I

267

might be later."

Chapter Thirty-Six

"I won't know anyone."

"You'll know me. You'll be sitting backstage on the side. I'll be able to see you." He finished drying off and tossed the towel over the shower rack.

It hurt him that she may not want to go to his concert, but he wouldn't push. At least, he thought he wouldn't.

"That's okay. If you don't want to come with me, I'll understand." He put on his underwear. "Don't wait up."

"I never said I wasn't going." She gently combed through her damp hair. "Besides, I might have to pry all those groupies off you."

When they reached the auditorium, he made sure the final sound checks had been done and all the band members were present. Right before the concert began, he told one of the gofers to find Summer a chair.

He was grateful all his concerts had been sold out. As a matter of fact, he was more than grateful everything in his life seemed to be working out better than he'd ever thought possible.

Although he was tired of traveling, he felt he owed each audience on the tour a great performance and wasn't satisfied unless he walked away feeling he given exactly that.

The show opened with the band performing *When We Gonna Meet*. Every time he sang this song, he was reminded of the first night he was in Haversfield, when she learned his identity due to his foolishness. Looking over at her, he thought she must have been thinking the same because she was smiling.

The crowd responded overwhelmingly to each number. When the concert ended, the fans stamped their feet and cheered until he came back for two encores.

He walked off the stage and led Summer back to the lavish room where they'd spent time before the concert.

"My manager rented out a little pub. Want to go hang out? He said it has pool tables."

"Okay." She hooked her arm through his.

They left by way of a very secret exit to avoid the mob of people waiting outside, hoping for a close encounter.

Shortly after arriving at the pub, Matt knew she felt out of her element, but no one else would ever notice. She spoke easily with everyone and was a good sport when other band members teased her.

He never knew she was such a pool shark. And she wasn't a gracious winner. She crowed and cackled like an old hag.

"Don't be mad. You can still beat Howard." She slid an arm around his waist.

"One more game." His bruised ego demanded a rematch.

"Whatever. Go ahead and rack 'em."

They finally left in the wee hours of the morning. On the way back to the hotel, she asked, "Are you still tired of touring?"

"Yeah. Especially since I've met you. There's only a few more concerts left."

"Won't it be hard to walk away from all that adoration?"

"Not if I'm walking towards you." He nuzzled her neck. "I want us to spend a couple of weeks locked in a bedroom."

She let out a censuring puff of air. "A couple of weeks? Is that all?"

While they flew to Denver the next morning, she did a lot of thinking about the future. She'd been totally intimidated by the vast differences in their lifestyles. She'd thought of all this before but until she'd sat in a huge arena filled with fans shrieking his name, she'd never fully thought about his superstar status and all it entailed.

270

After the kind of life he'd led the past several years, she worried he would grow tired of her. Bored with one woman.

What would she do if that happened?

She was so in love with him, she couldn't see straight. Her life had been so simple, so empty, before him. It was as though she'd been a struggling seedling trying to pretend she was a strong oak tree while craving the sunlight and rain necessary for survival. Then, he had entered her life and provided her with that sunlight and rain.

She never wanted to go back to just existing.

It scared her that he could have practically any woman he wanted but said he only wanted her. She didn't know how that could be possible but she prayed daily he would never change his mind.

She heard him begin to sing *Oh, Suzannah* and smiled. She rose from the bed and walked into the bathroom.

A beard of shaving cream covered half his face. Their eyes met in the mirror as she stood beside him.

"See, you're already singing about some other woman," she accused.

Laughing, he leaned down and rubbed his cheek against her face, causing her to shriek with laughter.

Every day became an adventure, a page from a fairy tale she hoped with all her heart would never end.

A part of her was afraid to believe this happiness would last because she'd been so used to disappointment and heartbreak. It was what she'd cut her teeth on.

Despite her fears, she held nothing back, giving him her heart and trusting him completely.

Two weeks later, they were in Boston, eating breakfast, when Matt suddenly suggested, "Let's fly to Vegas and get married."

Summer placed her fork on the table and looked around

the restaurant, then stared down at her eggs.

"I'm sorry. I obviously said something you don't want to hear." He couldn't keep the hurt out of his voice.

"It's not that. I just think you need to give this a little more thought."

"And I think you're scared." He drained his coffee cup and set it down.

"What's so wrong about wanting to be sure we're doing the right thing?" she asked.

"You aren't sure you love me or aren't sure you want to marry me?" He raised an eyebrow.

"I didn't say that."

"That's what I heard."

"I want *you* to be sure. That's why I'd like us to go slow." She reached over and covered his hand with hers. "I do love you, and you know it. I love you with all my heart."

He knew this was all her damned mother's fault. That selfish woman who'd chosen drugs over her child, probably without a second's thought about the damage she caused.

His parents, of course, were equally as bad. He thought of his inept handling of his emotions when he tried to deny his love for her. His lack of all the right words when he'd discovered she was pregnant. The list of mistakes went on and on. The misconception that, for some ambiguous reason, he didn't deserve to be happy or loved. All because he hadn't learned the right lessons from his parents. Instead, they'd taught him he was unwanted and unlovable.

Thank God he'd finally realized fate had intervened when his car broke down and he'd ended up in Haversfield. He knew deep in his heart he and Summer were meant for each other. He wanted her to realize that too.

Matt could live without performing for crowds. He could survive if he never cut another record. But he wasn't about to live without her. He wouldn't even consider it.

Thank God again for divine intervention! How else would he have ever found her?

"Sweetheart, I'm not going to abandon you. I'm not my parents and you're not your mother. We're two entirely different people with an entirely different life ahead of us." Looking at her, he spoke softly. "But if it makes you feel better, I'll wait. Hell, I've waited my whole life for you so what's a little more time?"

When they returned to the hotel room, there was a message for her to call home.

"I wonder what happened," she murmured as she dialed the phone. Each time they traveled to another city, she'd called Julie to give her a number where she could be reached in case of an emergency.

"Howard's probably just being nosey. He keeps threatening to beat the hell out of me if I screw up," he joked.

"Shh! It's ringing. Ruth? Is that you?"

"Oh, Summer, thank goodness! Julie had to be rushed to the hospital. Turned out her appendix ruptured. She had to have emergency surgery. Anyway, there's a house full of guests and I'm afraid I don't know how to handle things here."

"When did this happen?"

"This morning. Howard's been at the hospital all day and needed someone to come here and watch the house. I hate to interrupt your vacation, but I'm afraid you need to come home."

"I'll be there as soon as possible. Thanks, Ruth."

"What's wrong?" Matt watched her hang up the phone.

"Julie had emergency surgery to remove her appendix. I have to go home and take care of the guests."

"Damn! I can't leave because of the concert tonight."

"I know. Don't worry, I'll be okay."

All her insecurities came rushing back. Would he miss her? When would she see him again?

273

Despite her telling him not to, he arranged for a private plane to take her home.

Realizing she had no suitcase, she said, "I guess I'll leave the rest of my things with you. You said the plane leaves in three hours. That doesn't give us much time."

"I don't want you to go alone." He pulled her into his arms. "You might forget I love you or convince yourself of another stupid reason not to get married.

"Listen very carefully." He placed his palms on her cheeks. "I do love you. Only you. More than anything on earth. Don't ever doubt that." His words were urgent as he looked into her eyes. "I don't want to let you out of my sight."

"Me neither." She started to cry.

By late afternoon, they were separated by hundreds of miles. When she stepped into her house, she felt an immediate rush of loneliness.

It seemed like days, not just hours, since she'd been with Matt.

Gyp whined and barked until she knelt on the floor and hugged him.

Ruth came up the basement stairs carrying a basket of clean towels. "There you are! How was your trip? Aside from being cut short, which I truly hated to do."

"It was great. I really appreciate you helping out." She reached for the basket and placed it on the floor.

"I hate to rush off but the Women's Circle at church is having their fish fry tonight. I'm in charge of everything." Ruth brushed her heavy bangs off her forehead. "I don't know where the guests went or when they'll be back. I'm afraid I've made a mess of things."

"I'm sure everything will be fine. They'll wander back when they need a bed. Thanks again for helping."

After Ruth left, Summer picked up the basket, went upstairs and folded the towels before putting them in the linen

274

closet. She checked the guest rooms, noticing they had already been tidied up.

She went back downstairs and looked up the number to the hospital. She dialed, then waited to be connected with Julie's room.

"Hello?"

"Howard, it's me. How's Julie?"

"She's doing okay. Sleeping off the anesthesia. She's being discharged tomorrow morning. When did you get in?"

"Just a little while ago."

"Everything okay? I mean, between you and Matt?"

"Yeah. Everything's great." Except she missed him so much, she felt sick.

"Good. I'll probably stay until visiting hours are over."

"Okay. If she wakes up, tell her to hurry and get well."

They chatted a few more minutes before ending the conversation.

She wandered into the front room and looked at the registration book. Both couples were expected to check out tomorrow. Another couple and a single were due tomorrow night.

When the phone rang, she rushed to answer, despite knowing at that very minute Matt was performing and could not possibly be on the other end.

"Hello?"

"Summer?"

"Gina! Hi!"

"Our favorite rock star called earlier today. I want you to catch me up on all the details. You know how men are. They leave out all the important stuff."

"Tell me his version first, then I'll tell you the truth."

They both laughed. They talked for over an hour before ending the conversation because Summer's guests arrived back at the house. The couples seemed friendly as she spoke with them before they retired to their rooms.

Restless, she took Gyp for a walk. As she looked up at the night sky, the stars looked too perfect to be real. She wished Matt was with her, looking at the same piece of sky while they held hands.

She and Gyp walked quite a long time before returning home. When she went to bed, the dog jumped next to her and arranged the covers until he was satisfied. He flopped down and sighed contentedly.

"Don't think you're going to make a habit of this," she admonished, leaning over to hug him. She added, "I missed you too."

She thought she'd have a hard time falling asleep without Matt but the next thing she knew, the ring of the telephone woke her.

"Hmm?"

"Sweetheart, it's me."

Smiling, she murmured sleepily, "Hi."

"You didn't think you'd hear from me once you got home, did you?"

"That's not true." She paused. "Maybe the thought crossed my mind for just a second."

"See why I don't want you out of my sight? You're getting senile. You keep forgetting I love you."

"Well, then I guess you'll just have to keep telling me."

"No problem."

Chapter Thirty-Seven

The florist delivered a bright, colorful bouquet for Julie and a dozen red roses for Summer. Both were from Matt.

"Sit down and tell me everything!" Julie insisted, patting the bed beside her. "I was so glad to get home today but I thought Howard would never leave. So, what happened? Don't leave anything out."

While Summer talked about her time with Matt, the two of them squealed and laughed, carrying on like they had back in college.

Julie smirked, "I told you he loves you. Threatening you with a lawsuit was really clever, wasn't it?"

"Yeah, and I hear your boyfriend is the mastermind behind that little plan. I should be mad, but I'm just too happy! I'm so afraid it won't last."

"I think you don't have a thing to worry about. Is he going to be here for Thanksgiving?"

"I'd forgotten about Thanksgiving! That's when? Next week?"

"Yes."

"His last concert is the night before. I don't know if he can make it here in time." She bit her bottom lip, trying not to let her disappointment show.

"Oh, I bet he can."

"I hope he does. I really, really hope he does."

Summer received a dozen roses from Matt daily. He called every morning when he woke up and late at night when he went to bed.

During one of their conversations, she asked if he would be able to come for Thanksgiving.

"Of course," he replied. "By the way, I'm miserable without you. Does that make you happy?"

"Immensely." She added, "I miss you so much. I wish you were here right now."

"What do you have in mind?"

"Well," she made her voice sound low and breathless, "You could help me hang the Christmas lights up outside."

He laughed, but quickly became serious. "Damn it, Summer, don't go climbing up on any ladder! Wait until I get there."

"Don't be silly. I always do it."

"I mean it! Why do you have to be so bullheaded?"

Sensing an argument, she said, "I hear Julie calling me. She still isn't fully recovered. I'd better check on her."

"Summer, I..."

"Gotta go. I love you. Miss you." A sudden, intense longing for him took her breath away. "Oh, Matt, I really do miss you so much!"

"Soon, sweetheart." His voice softened. "We'll see each other soon."

Immediately after the last encore at his concert in Jacksonville, Florida, Matt's driver took him to the airport. His flight took off only ten minutes late but landed in Atlanta right on schedule.

He was relieved he had enough time to make his connecting flight to St. Louis. However, that flight was delayed because of mechanical difficulties.

"Great," he muttered to himself, "Just when I'm deliriously happy with life, I'll probably die in a plane crash."

He asked the ticket attendant what was wrong with the plane and was told one of the bathroom doors kept jamming. An hour later, he was in the air. He fell asleep until a baby seated a few rows back started to cry.

The rest of the flight was turbulent due to storms. When they approached St. Louis, the pilot announced, due to inclement weather in the area, they would have to circle until clearance was received to land.

Matt wished he'd been smart enough to charter a private plane but he'd waited too long. He'd never realized transportation was so difficult to arrange around Thanksgiving. Oh, sure, he'd often spent holidays with Vinny and Gina but he'd never had such an urgent need to reach their house for a holiday.

He was tired, running out of patience, and so anxious to see Summer, he thought he'd go crazy.

God, he missed her. He couldn't wait to get home.

Home.

He didn't know when he began thinking of her house as home.

If she hadn't miscarried, they'd have been married weeks ago. He would have taken her on tour with him. He would have watched her body change as they planned for their child and started a life together.

Maybe things did happen for the best because had that happened, she would always think he married her because he'd felt obligated or trapped. He certainly wished she hadn't lost the baby but now when they married, she would have no doubt it was only because he truly loved her.

Sometimes, just thinking of her made his stomach lurch. He would never before have believed it was possible to love someone so much. He was a believer now.

She owned his heart.

He recalled her words. Date. Go slow. Be sure.

Yeah, right. The woman was crazy if she thought they were sticking to that plan.

He stewed in his thoughts until the pilot informed the passengers to prepare for landing.

By the time he rented a car, it was dawn. An eternity later, after the rain changed to snow and too many hours of bad radio created a pounding headache, he exited the highway and headed for downtown Haversfield.

As he neared her house, he noticed the Christmas lights.

Damn her! She never listened to a thing he said. Well, she was going to have to learn to take his feelings into consideration. What if she had fallen and broken a leg? Or worse? Just the thought made his breath catch.

Gyp barked and danced around the yard when he pulled into the driveway. He opened the gate, greeted the dog and took the back steps two at a time.

Summer stood at the stove, spooning scrambled eggs into a serving dish, when she heard the back door open.

"Hey, Matt, 'bout time," Howard drawled from his seat at the table.

She put the spoon down and turned. Her heart flipped over when she saw him. Their eyes locked. Oh, God, she was so happy!

It took a few seconds to realize he was glaring at her.

"The hell with this dating crap! It sucks!" He walked toward her. "You're being an ass about this!"

His words startled her. She didn't know whether to laugh or start throwing dishes at his head. He'd evidently also startled Gyp, who'd hurried out of the room.

"As her cousin, I have to take offense at that remark," Howard commented. "But as your friend, I agree."

He gave Howard a nod of appreciation but kept his eyes on her. "You think we're going to have a long distance relationship forever? Well, think again!"

"It's only been little more than a week," she quietly reminded. "And stop yelling."

"It's been longer!" He lowered his voice. "You and I are getting married. I'm not listening to any more excuses. You're driving me crazy. I love you. I don't want anyone else. I want to spend the rest of my life with you. Have children, only with you.

"We'll live right here. I'm going to make that building next to the garage a sound studio. That way, I can record right here. I already told you I don't want to do any more tours. We are not going to be apart from each other again. If you don't like that, it's too damn bad."

He pulled her into his arms and kissed her.

She forgot about pounding him over the head with a heavy kitchen appliance, forgot her doubts and insecurities. Forgot everything except how much she'd missed him. How much she loved him.

"That's what you call being romantic?" Howard nudged Julie with his elbow.

"Shut up." Julie sighed.

"Understand?" Matt lifted his head and softly asked.

Since he'd kissed her breath away, Summer could only nod.

"Good. Let's eat. I'm starving." He stepped away from her and sat down at the table.

The men started a conversation about the snow, the football games on television later and what type of materials would be needed to convert the building into a sound studio.

Julie checked the turkey in the oven since Summer, looking as dazed as though she'd just fallen off a spaceship, seemed to have forgotten she'd put the huge thing in there.

"All Ruth needs to do is put the date and time on the invitations. You guys have to reserve the church again. Don't worry, it'll be a piece of cake." Julie patted her on the shoulder.

"She's not worried." Matt winked at her. "Are you, sweetheart?"

"No." She suddenly felt giddy. "I'm not worried about a thing."

"I just checked. They fell asleep." Julie shook her head. "Men. Give them a belly full of food and a game on TV and they'll be snoring their butts off in no time."

"I know," Summer laughed. She finished drying the last plate and put it away. "I think I'll make a fresh pot of coffee."

"That sounds good."

"Are you and Howard still planning on a spring wedding?"

"I think so. I forgot to tell you we have a closing date on the Sullivan house next week. We'll be moving soon. Won't that be great? We'll only be two doors away."

"I'm happy for you but I've gotten used to you guys being here."

"I know but you and Matt need privacy." Julie watched her sit down. "You don't still have any doubts about marrying him, do you?"

"No. Some things you can't slow down. I've been just as afraid of getting hurt as he's been but he's figured things out faster than I have and he's willing to throw years of caution to the wind. I know exactly how he feels. Marrying him feels so right. I finally feel this sense of peace I've never felt before. I was going to tell him as soon as he stepped through the door but I didn't want to spoil his caveman entrance."

Julie laughed. "Funny, isn't it? You and I are best friends, now we're going to be neighbors. Married to men we're crazy about."

"You and Howard are going to be so happy. He really is a great guy. I'm not just saying that because we're related."

"I know. I think he's wonderful but I don't want him to think he's got me wrapped around his finger. One caveman in the neighborhood is enough."

They laughed.

"What's so funny?" Matt shuffled into the kitchen, looking like he could use another few hours of sleep.

"Nothing. Just girl talk," Julie answered. "There's some fresh coffee."

He stretched and yawned. "I think I'll pass."

Summer looked up at him. When he grinned sleepily and put his hand out, she placed her palm in his. Rising, she let him lead her out of the room.

"Talk to you later," she said over her shoulder to Julie.

They held hands as they climbed the stairs. He closed the bedroom door behind them, turned and watched her pull her sweater over her head.

"Wait." He put his arms around her, nibbling at her lips until their kisses became heated and urgent. They tumbled into bed.

"Oh, hurry! It's been so long." Her fingers worked at his shirt buttons.

"Uh-uh. I've decided you're right. We need to slow down."

"No, I'm not right about anything. You should know that by now."

Matt chuckled.

Chapter Thirty-Eight

Summer woke early and couldn't fall back asleep. How could she? It was her wedding day!.

She wasn't nervous about getting married. How could she be when she was marrying her soul mate?

How lucky could a woman get?

Careful not to wake Matt, she gingerly rose from the bed and put on her robe. She went downstairs and started a pot of coffee. Standing at the back door, she watched as the sun eased slightly higher in the sky.

She gave thanks to the God she hadn't always been on the best of terms with for sending someone like Matt into her life and making her so happy. She felt certain the bizarre way their paths had crossed had been no accident.

She sensed his presence before she felt his arms slide around her waist.

"Nervous?"

"No."

"Still scared I'll get bored with you?" he teased.

"No," she chuckled.

"When one of us dies, I'll beg God for just one more day with you."

"Don't you dare get me all worked up with those words that sound like a song." She felt a lump form in her throat.

"Hey, that *would* be a good line for a song, wouldn't it?" He rested his chin on top of her head. "Are you worried not many people will come?"

"No. I told you not to get carried away and invite everyone in town. All that's important to me is that my true friends will be there. I don't care if no one else shows up."

"I'm glad we didn't run off to Vegas. I want to see you walk down that church aisle, holding your head high with pride. You have nothing to be ashamed of. You're a good person. In case you haven't noticed, I kind of like you." He kissed her cheek.

"We're not supposed to see each other before the wedding. It's bad luck."

"Bull. We've had enough bad luck already. There's nothing but clear sailing ahead."

"You're absolutely beautiful!" Julie's eyes misted as they were dressing for the wedding. "This is so wonderful! You deserve to be happy!"

Her great-grandmother's dress fit perfectly, as though it had been made especially for her. The elegant lace veil, anchored to her head by the small cap, floated over her hair like a cloud.

"Yes, she does," Gina agreed, reaching out to straighten a wayward tendril of Summer's hair.

"You two aren't so bad yourselves. You look like you just stepped off the cover of a magazine." She glanced at the mirror, seeing the reflection of the three of them.

She knew her friends would look gorgeous in the forest green, tea length, soft velvet dresses the moment she'd seen them last week at the mall. She'd been right.

"Enough of this mutual admiration. We need to get to the church. In case you forgot, there's a wedding scheduled to take place in just a half hour." Julie glanced at her watch.

They went downstairs, slipped into their coats and headed to the car.

Summer felt warm enough in the black velvet, full length coat Julie insisted she borrow. The morning clouds had vanished, revealing a breathtaking blue sky but the cold wind definitely came from the north. Still, she thought it was a perfect day for a wedding.

When they neared the church, she was surprised to see the parking lot was filled. Cars were also parked up and down the street.

She really hadn't expected so many people. She wondered how many came out of curiosity or just because of the groom. Everyone probably knew his real identity by now. Especially since that confrontation with his mother on national television.

"I'm parking right here in this reserved space." Julie looked in the rearview mirror at the bride. "Ready?"

"Yes."

They entered the church through the side door and continued down the hall until reaching the room designated as the women's dressing area.

Ruth, who'd stepped in and helped organize everything, was waiting. She helped Summer out of her coat before handing her a bouquet made of white, pink and red roses. Julie and Gina were handed bouquets consisting of small rosebuds in the same colors.

The notes to *Ave Maria*, played gently on a harp, drifted sweetly from inside the church.

"It's time," Ruth said. "Let's go out into the lobby. The men should already be standing in place."

The women left the room.

"You're first." Julie patted Gina's arm.

Gina stepped through the double doors and started down the aisle. Julie soon followed.

After a few seconds, Summer walked to the doorway. She saw the pews filled with people and felt only slightly nervous.

Bob, Howard and Ernie had each offered to walk her down the aisle. She was touched by their thoughtfulness but gently declined. She would need no one, other than the spirits of her grandparents, which she firmly believed would walk with her.

Bob and Ernie, serving as ushers, each gave her a quick pat on the shoulder before she started down the aisle.

Her step was steady, her eyes dry as she remembered to do what Matt had told her. Lift her head proudly and not be ashamed of anything.

When she glanced at the people, friendly smiles greeted her.

As she neared the altar, her eyes met Matt's. When he smiled and winked, she smiled and winked back. Happiness made her want to skip like a child the rest of the way.

He was the most gorgeous man she'd ever met. Of course, she admitted, her opinion could easily be backed up by millions of female fans.

Howard and Vinny, looking terrific in those black tuxes they'd sworn they weren't going to wear, stood beside him.

Matt linked his arm with hers, whispering, "Hi, sweetheart."

"Hi." She grinned.

The sermon was old fashioned yet just as warm and meaningful as anyone could want. By the time they were pronounced man and wife, there were few dry eyes in the church. Matt would later swear he saw Howard and Ernie wiping their eyes.

When the bride and groom kissed, a collective sigh drifted from the guests.

As the new wife walked up the aisle with her husband, she wondered how he'd gotten so smart that he knew to invite everyone in town. Whether he did it out of love for her or because they would be living in Haversfield and raising their children here, she didn't know but for the first time, she felt a warmer, kinder attitude from the people. She would give them back no less.

Church bells rang as the bridal party stepped outside into the sunshine. They posed for countless pictures taken by friends and town residents.

Clifford Humes, a friend of Summer's grandparents and owner of Haversfield Portrait Studio, was the official wedding photographer. The only media person in attendance was

Harriet Farley, social reporter for the *Haversfield Times.* Kayla Thomas of the Fox News Network has been invited but couldn't rearrange her schedule, though she'd tried.

Town residents congratulated the couple, genuinely wishing them happiness as they slowly streamed out of the church. Most people walked the short distance but some drove to the reception held at Maisie's, of course.

The storybook romance had captured the attention of the entire town, softening some of the hardest hearts. When people started talking at the reception, the general opinion was no one could ever remember Summer doing anything wild or naughty. She'd always been well-behaved and respectable, unlike her mother.

Didn't the girl deserve some happiness after all she'd been through?

Well, they'd certainly never seen a more beautiful bride, that's for sure. She looked just like a princess and her groom won the hearts of all the ladies in the Women's Circle when he danced with every one of them. He certainly was handsome enough to be a prince. They didn't pay much attention to all that talk about him being a big rock star. Besides, nobody's perfect and that was old news, anyway.

What did amaze them was the couple could afford to live anywhere in the world and they were going to settle smack in the middle of Haversfield, right where Summer's family had lived for generations.

The celebration lasted well into the night. No one could say for sure when the bride and groom left. With all that laughter and carrying on, who could keep track of them?

It wasn't every day the town had such a happy ending to celebrate.

Epilogue

Matt stepped up to the microphone and looked out at the crowd. He smiled at his wife, sitting with Julie and Howard on one side, Ruth and Bob on the other. Ernie was there, too.

Matt had performed all over the world but he'd never been happier than right where he was - sitting in, as he often did, with Six Easy Guys, the group that had become the regular band at Maisie's.

"I'd like to do a song I wrote last summer for my wife. Well, she wasn't my wife then but you all know what I mean. It's called *Turn This Plane Around.*"

After an upbeat intro, he began to sing.

> *"I howled out my troubles to the man in the moon,*
> *but he don't want conversation.*
> *I told my story to the stars in the sky,*
> *but they just twinkled in frustration.*
> *I used to be a ladies man,*
> *free and happy as can be,*
> *Until that mean, heartless woman*
> *got a hold on me.*
> *Turn this plane around,*
> *I can't leave her, though I know it's sad.*
> *Like I been sayin', can't you tell?*
> *I got the blues real bad.*
> *She clipped my wings and now my roving eye*
> *ain't even lookin'.*
> *I'm too busy in the kitchen,*
> *Doin' all the cookin'.*
> *That woman put a ring through my nose*
> *but don't want one on her finger.*
> *She says I'm too wild, I'll always be*

just a women-crazy singer.
If she don't come to her senses
and take my last name soon,
you'll find me in the fields at night,
just howlin' at the moon.
Turn this plane around,
I can't leave her, though I know it's sad.
Like I told you, can't you tell?
I got the blues real bad. "

Summer laughed along with everyone else while her husband performed. Although they'd been married for over a year, her heart still bumped around in her chest whenever she looked at him.

When he finished, the crowd cheered and clapped their approval while they watched him leave the stage and join his wife.

"You okay?" He gave her a quick kiss before sitting next to her.

"I'm fine. Quit worrying. Women have babies every day."

When they first learned she was pregnant, he had discussed with the doctor, at length, her chances of miscarrying again. Despite the doctor's assurances the baby was fine, the mother was doing great and the father should relax, Matt had hovered over her like a mother hen for months. But he was even worse now that her due date had come and gone.

He picked up the glass of ice water the waitress placed on the table and drank thirstily. A cold beer would have really hit the spot but he needed to be alert in case she went into labor.

"You're my wife. I love you. I'll worry if I want."

She rolled her eyes. "You're crazy. If you don't start behaving, I'm never getting pregnant again."

"Don't be ridiculous. We can't have an only child. They turn out all screwed up."

"Is that so?"

He nodded. "Just look at Howard."

She laughed.

Two days later, Summer gazed down at her son as he nursed. The labor pains already fading from memory, she lightly traced her finger over his forehead.

William Tyler Zeller looked just like his father, right down to the same birthmark - the small, half of a heart on his upper back.

"The nurse said you guys can come home." Matt walked in and sat on the edge of the bed. He leaned over and kissed her before placing a soft kiss on the baby's cheek.

"How are we going to take all these flowers?" she asked.

He looked around the room. Every available space was filled with either plants or blossoms. But this was nothing compared to what awaited her back at the house. He wondered if there was anyone left in town who hadn't sent anything.

"Ernie and Bob should be here any minute with their vans." His attention focused back on his son, who had drifted off to sleep. "I think every woman in the county has baked something and brought it over. If there was enough freezer space, we wouldn't have to cook for a year."

She leaned her head back on the pillow. "Everyone's been wonderful." Tears gathered quickly and flowed from her eyes. Oh, Matt, I'm so happy."

"Me, too, sweetheart." He brushed her tears away with his fingertips. He then very carefully picked up his son. "You get dressed so we can take Will home. Gyp's anxious to meet him."

She laughed.

*

*